THE BLIND CHASE

Also by Cap Daniels

THE
BLIND CHASE

CHASE FULTON NOVEL #15

CAP DANIELS

ANCHOR WATCH
PUBLISHING
** USA **

The Blind Chase
Chase Fulton Novel #15
Cap Daniels

This is a work of fiction. Names, characters, places, historical events, and inci-
dents are the product of the author's imagination or have been used fictitiously.
Although many locations such as marinas, airports, hotels, restaurants, etc. used
in this work actually exist, they are used fictitiously and may have been relo-
cated, exaggerated, or otherwise modified by creative license for the purpose of
this work. Although many characters are based on personalities, physical at-
tributes, skills, or intellect of actual individuals, all of the characters in this work
are products of the author's imagination.

Published by:

ANCHOR WATCH
PUBLISHING
** USA **

13 Digit ISBN: 978-1-951021-26-9
Library of Congress Control Number: 2021946883

Cover Design: German Creative

Printed in the United States of America

The Blind Chase

CAP DANIELS

Chapter 1
Take the Shot

Summer 2004

I closed one eye—I seem to remember it being my left—and brought my target into perfect focus and alignment. My target that evening was impossible to ignore. In fact, every eye within miles of my position was focused on nothing else. That target was moving, or at least appeared to be moving faster by the second, and would, in mere minutes, be completely out of sight. My next opportunity to bring it into crystal-clear focus was more than nine hours away, and only God knew where I'd be in nine hours. I couldn't hesitate. Too many people depended on me to take the shot at precisely the right instant, and letting them down would never be an option. Their lives meant more to me than did my own, and the thought of disappointing them sickened me beyond words. So, before the fleeting moment and precious opportunity slipped away, I made the decision. The shot had to be taken, and waiting another minute would make it forever too late.

With my target unquestionably identified and solidly acquired, I raised my glass. "Here's to you, Sol, our closest star. May you sink into the sea once again in peace, leaving us the long night to celebrate your passing. And may you rise again over yonder horizon when morning comes, reminding us all—except Singer, of course—that we should've stopped after the first four bottles."

And I took the shot . . . The shot of some of the best rum that had ever been distilled on any island anywhere in the world.

My brothers, albeit brothers-in-arms and not blood, raised their glasses alongside mine, and we toasted another perfect sunset on another perfect beach under another perfect Caribbean sky.

Singer, our Southern Baptist sniper, held up his tea glass. "Why can't every day end like this?"

I touched the rim of my glass to his. "Every day does end like this somewhere, my friend. We're just rarely in those somewheres."

Singer was a man of enormous extremes. His faith in the god he loved was stronger than any passion I'd ever seen anyone exhibit. When we weren't in some long-forgotten corner of the world that most people would describe as being godforsaken, Singer led the choir at a beautiful old church in Saint Marys, Georgia. When he wasn't making a joyful noise, he spent a great deal of time with the Trappist monks at a monastery in South Carolina, where his brother had been since they were children.

"Yeah," he said, "we all know we'll be back in some cold, dark hole soon enough, but I could get used to life like this."

I stared out over the waves gently lapping at the beach and absorbed the sound of the Caribbean breeze blowing through the palms. "It's almost enough to make a man think about retiring, isn't it?"

The greatest sniper I'd ever known raised both hands as if pointing his rifle straight at me. "Retirement ain't what men like us do, Chase Fulton. You know that."

I gave him a halfhearted smile. "Yeah, but we can still think about it, can't we?"

"Sure we can, as long as we don't let those thoughts turn into action. Where are we, anyway?"

I shrugged and scanned the open-air, seaside restaurant my team and I had essentially commandeered. "I don't know. I think we're somewhere on Eleuthera or maybe Harbor Island. But does it really matter?"

Singer's tea glass made its way back into the air in salute. "No, my friend, it does not."

Clark Johnson, my first partner turned handler, gave my bare foot a nudge with his. "I've got to hand it to you, College Boy. You sure know how to vacation."

"This isn't a vacation," I said. "It's recuperation. After getting blown to hell back in Montana, we all needed some time to let our wounds heal. And there's no better place on Earth for letting the sun cure what ails you than a Caribbean island with an endless supply of rum and clear blue skies."

"You're not wrong about that," he said as his world-renowned chef wife slid her dainty hand across his shoulder. "Mind if I join you boys? I mean, if you're not talking about any of that secret squirrel stuff . . ."

Clark laid his hand on top of hers. "Not at all. We were just discussing the difference between vacationing and recuperating."

Maebelle pulled up a cane-bottom chair as close to Clark as possible and nestled herself in. "Yeah, now that you mention it, Chase, I've been meaning to talk to you about that. I've had enough of you dragging my man all over the world and bringing him back all beat up. That's gonna have to stop."

I opened my mouth to defend myself and fill her in on the fact that I had no control over Clark. He always came on every mission of his own free will, but he slid his arm around Maebelle's shoulder and cut me off. "Those days are behind me now."

I lowered an eyebrow. "What do you mean, those days are behind you? You know better than me that missions are stacking up for us as soon as we're back to full strength. You can't quit on us now."

"It's not quitting, College Boy. I'm acknowledging two of life's undeniable truths. First, I'm too old for that shoot-'em-up stuff, and second, you've proved that you're exactly the leader this ragtag gang of misfits needs and deserves. You don't need me out there anymore. I'm officially retired from gunslinging. I'm just your handler now, and I have every faith you're more capable of leading this team than I ever could've been."

Maebelle grinned as if her every wish had just come true.

I said, "That means more to me than you'll ever know. A lot of things on the Montana mission really opened my eyes. I think I was blind to the reality of what I've become."

Clark shook his head. "No, it's not what you've become. It's what you've always been. You just needed a little nudge to make you believe what everyone around you already knew."

Penny Thomas Fulton, my wild-haired, North Texas wife, stepped behind my chair, pulled off my UGA hat, and wrangled her hair into an almost-obedient ponytail that tucked perfectly through the hole in the back of the baseball cap. "Nice hat, cutie. Are you some kind of ballplayer or something?"

I pulled her hand to my lips and kissed every knuckle. "I used to be, but now, I'm just a boring old sailor."

She leaned down and kissed my forehead. "I bet your butt would still look pretty hot in those baseball pants."

Clark slid a chair toward Penny. "Join us. Maebelle and I were just kicking our baby bird out of the nest. It's time to watch him fly on his own and feed himself for a change."

Penny squeezed my hand. "I've seen him fly, and it's pretty impressive, but I think he'll still need me to feed him from time to time."

I returned the squeeze. "I wouldn't have it any other way. Now that you're learning to play analyst, you're not just another pretty face. We're putting you to work."

She held up a finger. "I've already got a job. I'm a soon-to-be-famous screenwriter, remember?"

"Of course I remember," I said. "When's the screening?"

Penny had written a screenplay that had been sold to a Hollywood producer by a Nashville agent. The fact that my team and I recovered the agent's granddaughter from a pair of ransom-hungry kidnappers may have played a role in initially opening the door, but it was Penny's talent as a writer that scored her the movie deal.

"I'm still not sure. They tell me it's still in editing. I don't know how long that takes, but it feels like it's been going on forever."

"Whenever it is, we'll be there," I said.

Tony, our favorite bartender on the island, no matter which island, peered through the crowd and caught my attention. He held his thumb and pinky finger to his ear and mouth as if to say, "Phone call for you at the bar."

I pushed off my seat, and Penny protested. "Where are you going?"

"I've got a phone call at the bar. It's probably Disco. He's going to take Clark and Maebelle back to South Beach in the Citation."

Maebelle Huntsinger, in addition to being my only living blood relative, was South Beach's hottest chef, and her restaurant, El Juez, made the cover of a different foodie magazine every month. Her flair for the creation of Cuban- and Caribbean-inspired dishes mixed with true American Southern cooking kept the reservation book filled to overflowing and her fame climbing the charts. Nobody cooked like Maebelle, and South Beach could only survive so many days without her, so the time had come for her and Clark to wing their way back to Miami and return to the real world.

"I'll be right back, and I'll send over another round of drinks while I'm at the bar."

I twisted and slid my way through the throngs of dancers, drunks, vacationers, and ex-pats until I finally made it to Tony and he handed me the receiver across the bamboo bar. I took it from him and covered the mouthpiece. "Is it Disco? I've been expecting to hear from him."

Tony shook his head. "No, it's not Disco. I'd recognize his voice. It's some serious-sounding guy."

I peered across the bar. "What does the caller ID say?"

Tony tossed a wet rag at me, rolled his eyes, and held up the fifty-year-old phone base. "Does this thing look like it has caller ID?"

I stifled the chuckle and stuck the receiver to my ear. "Hello."

Just as Tony had described, the voice booming through the phone was commanding, confident, and undeniably military. "Is this Chase Fulton?"

I searched my memory, desperately trying to identify that voice, but it wouldn't come. "Who's asking?"

"Mr. Fulton, my name is Alvin Brown. You killed my entire team in Montana. You and I need to talk."

Chapter 2
Cubans

I squeezed the telephone receiver until I feared it may crumble in my hand. What was I supposed to say to the former leader of a treasonous band of traitors, especially when my team had killed every one of them?

"Mr. Brown, I can't say I was expecting to hear from you, and especially not here. How'd you find me?"

The voice continued in its no-nonsense tone. "How I found you is not the kind of question men like us answer, Mr. Fulton. For what you did in Montana, the free world and I owe you a debt of gratitude."

He left the line hanging in the air like a storm cloud looming overhead.

I said, "I'm not sure I'd go that far. It was just another mission, and we did it. Men like you and me don't do what we do for gratitude. We do it because it's the right thing to do, Mr. Brown."

"Call me Al," he said. "And nevertheless, what you did deserves more than just a paycheck. But I'm afraid there's still a lot of work to be done, and I can't do it alone. As I said earlier, you and I need to talk, but not on the phone. I'm still recovering from the kidney transplant—that's another thing I need to thank you for—but we can talk about that face-to-face. When will you be back in the States?"

"I'm not on a schedule. We got pretty banged up tussling with your former team, so we're taking a little time off to put ourselves back together."

"I think our meeting should happen sooner rather than later," he said. "I'm still moving pretty slow, but I can come to you if you're going to be on Eleuthera for a few more days."

I took in the environment around me and couldn't hold back the smile. "Yeah, I think we'll be here awhile. If you want to talk with us that badly, come on down."

We ended the conversation, and I returned the ancient receiver back to its ten-pound base. "Thanks, Tony. This behemoth is all yours again."

The bartender gave me a wave as he poured what was likely his one millionth daiquiri.

Back with my team on the deck overlooking the sea, I gave Clark's elbow a squeeze. "We need to talk."

Without a word, he stood from his chair, placed his drink on the table, and led me toward the railing outside the range of curious ears. "What's up?"

I checked the area to ensure no one was close enough to eavesdrop. "That was Al Brown, the leader of the Montana team."

Clark's eyebrows arched in disbelief. "Really? What did he have to say?"

"He wants to come down and have a face-to-face sit-down."

Clark pointed to the deck. "Here?"

"Yep, right here. He says he'll be here in a couple of days, so I told him we'd wait for him."

Clark frowned. "What does he want?"

"I get the feeling he wants to clean up the mess his team made over the past few months, and he needs our help to do it."

"Is that what he said?"

"No, not in so many words, but that's the feeling I get."

He stared out over the ever-darkening water and scratched his chin through the beard that was beginning to show the first indications of gray. His wheels were undeniably turning behind eyes that had seen more evil in more parts of the planet than most people would see in a thousand lifetimes. There was little doubt he was trying to come up with an excuse Maebelle would buy so he could stay on the island and give Al Brown the audience he wanted. To my surprise, though, he said, "Okay, hear him out. Ask good questions, get good answers, and tell me what you need. I'll be in Miami and only a phone call away."

I found Clark's faith in me both flattering and sobering. I'd no longer have him to turn to when I didn't know what to do. The decisions would be mine, and so would their weighty consequences.

I said, "If I'm right, and he does want us to clean up the messes his team made, is that a mission the Board will sanction, or will we be on our own?"

He patted his pockets and withdrew a small, plastic humidor from the pocket of his cargo shorts. From inside the humidor, he pulled out a pair of Cuban Cohibas. We punched one end and toasted the other before drawing the smoke of some of the world's finest tobacco onto our tongues and watching the night's first smattering of stars dot the eastern sky.

He took a long draw and exhaled the white plume of smoke into the air above our heads. "Does it really matter?"

I inspected my cigar and considered his question. "Yeah, I think it does matter this time. Of course, I'm willing to try to right the wrongs his team committed, but I'm not willing to put the lives of those men on the line just to let Al Brown sleep better at night. He's a good man. I have no doubt about that. But some bad stuff happened on his watch, and it's only right that he has to eat some of it."

Clark pointed the butt of his cigar at me. "Now you're thinking like a leader. Hear the man out, and feel him out. If it doesn't smell right, walk away. But if you think he's acting in the best interest of the country and not just his conscience, I think I can sell it to the Board."

I took another draw. "We may be worrying about something that's never going to happen. I could be wrong about what Brown wants, but I don't think I am."

"You've got the instincts of a falcon, Chase. I trust you. All you have to do is ring my phone, and you'll have whatever you need. Now, get back over there and listen to your men tell semi-true war stories."

"Thanks for the Cuban," I said. "And for the confidence."

Stone W. Hunter, former Air Force combat controller and my current partner, led Tina Ramirez off the dance floor with sweat dripping from his face. He downed a glass of water and then reached for his daiquiri.

"You look like you've been wrestling a bear in a sauna. Are you all right?"

He wiped the sweat from his brow and shot a thumb toward Tina. "She's no bear, but trying to keep up with her on the dance floor is almost as challenging as tangling with a Kodiak."

Tina had been a federal parole officer in Texas before Hunter and I uncovered a plot she'd hatched to cover for a federal parolee who just happened to be my mother-in-law. The revelation cost Tina her job, but it had been the genesis of a potential relationship with Hunter.

I said, "I'm glad you decided to come with us, Tina. It's nice for Hunter to have someone to dance with other than me."

She squeezed my partner's arm. "Thanks, Chase. It feels a little weird to be able to tag along. Usually when you guys run off, I never know where you're going and when or if you're coming home."

Stone put a daiquiri in Tina's hand. "Don't get used to this. It's not like we have an annual company picnic with horseshoes and grilled hamburgers."

Tina grinned. "Something tells me your company picnic games would more than likely involve high-powered rifles and hand grenades, but I'll take any time I can get. Thanks for letting me join you."

"I don't want to break up the party with work," I said, "but I do need to talk with you for a minute. Have you seen Mongo?"

Marvin "Mongo" Malloy was our own private giant. Like most of the team, he was a study in contrasts. His massive physical size garnered more than a little fear from the people who dared square off with him, but his intellect was even larger than his shoulders. Capable of learning and retaining any academic information after one reading, he constantly amazed the team and me with his knowledge of some of the most bizarre subjects imaginable. I don't know how many languages he spoke, but he'd displayed Latin, Spanish, French, Russian, and Arabic in the short time I'd known him.

Hunter scanned the bar. "I saw him answer a phone call about half an hour ago, but I've not seen him since."

"Who would be calling Mongo? We're all here."

He shrugged. "How should I know? Maybe it's Anya."

Anya Burinkova was a former Russian assassin who defected to the U.S. after an ill-advised *affaire de coeur* with me. Naturally, our affair had been powerful but short-lived, and Penny Thomas's left ring finger is where my gold band found a home. Anya was undeniably beautiful, in true Eastern European style, but I'd always believed she wanted the world to look past her exterior and find a reason to value her for something other than her looks. I believed Mongo was the one man on Earth capable of doing exactly that, but no matter how hard he fell for her, she couldn't return his affection. She broke his heart on a telephone call while she was working with the U.S. Justice Department on an undercover case.

"Maybe so," I said, "but I think the big man has put her astern."

Hunter looked over the crowd once again. "That girl has a way of getting under a man's skin. You of all people know that."

"Yeah, but Mongo isn't just any normal man. He's . . . well, Mongo."

"*That* he is. I'll see if I can find him and meet you back here."

Hunter disappeared into the crowd just as our chief pilot stepped onto the deck.

"Hey, Disco!" I said. "Where've you been? We've been drinking without you."

The former Air Force A-10 Warthog pilot threw on a grin. "Some of us still have to work for a living. I'm just here to pick up Maebelle and Clark and head back to Miami."

"They're hanging out by that mango tree over there, but I'm glad you're here. We need to have a little business meeting before you get gone."

Hunter returned with our giant in tow, and the five of us strolled down the weathered steps to the beach below the deck of the bar.

"All right," I began. "The gang's all here. I need to brief you on something, and then I'll let you get back to enjoying your time off. Al Brown, the former leader of the Montana team, is coming here tomorrow or the next day. He says he wants to talk with me face-to-face."

Hunter grimaced. "Is that a good thing or a bad thing?"

"I don't know yet," I admitted, "but I think he'll probably ask for our help in cleaning up the train wreck his team caused over the past several months."

"Are we going to do it?" Mongo asked.

"Maybe, but it's too soon to make a decision. And there's an outside chance that I'm wrong. He may be coming to talk about something else entirely, but we'll only know after he arrives."

Disco asked, "Does that mean you're staying here for a few more days?"

"That's exactly what it means," I said. "And I'd like for you to be here with us when Brown shows up. You're part of the team now, so your input is always welcome and always expected."

"Am I still taking them to Miami?" Disco asked.

"Yes, but I want you back on the island tomorrow."

"You got it," he said.

"Okay, that's all I have. I just want everyone to know what's going on, and I'll fill you in when I know more."

The briefing broke up, and everyone turned back for the steps leading up to the bar.

I caught Mongo by the arm. "Stick around a minute."

He nodded and stepped aside.

When everyone else was gone, I said, "Is everything okay? Hunter said he saw you answer a call and walk off. I'm not checking up on you. I just want to make sure you're all right."

A broad smile found its way to his lips. "Yeah, everything is just fine. But there *is* something I need to talk with you about."

"Let's hear it."

He looked away as if ashamed. "You know the woman and little girl Anya moved into the house in Athens?"

"Sure," I said. "Irina and little Anya Volkovna."

"Yeah, that's them. I think maybe they're feeling a little homesick and lonely there in Athens not knowing anybody yet, and I thought maybe it might be okay with you if they came out here with us for a couple of days."

I forced myself to hide the smile. "Irina hasn't been vetted yet, so we have to be careful what we say around her, but I think it'll be fine for them to come spend some time in the sun. In fact, Disco can bring them back tomorrow."

The giant glanced up the steps and back at me. "Maybe I should go with him. You know, since Irina and little Anya don't know him yet. They might feel better if I was there."

"That's a great idea, but you'd better hurry before he gets away."

Without another word, the big man trotted up the stairs, three at a time, with a bounce in his step like I hadn't seen since the Russian broke his heart.

Chapter 3
Don't Worry, Be Happy

As I lay in bed aboard *Aegis*, our fifty-foot, custom-built sailing catamaran, I replayed the activities of the day on my mind's movie screen. I wondered if most people did the same or if sleep came quickly and easily to those not bearing the responsibility of a team of tier-one operators who were hungry for action and another opportunity to prove their mettle.

Beside me lay the angel sent from Heaven above—via North Texas—who represented the counterbalance to my chaotic world. Fascinated by everything, Penny represented the innocence and joy the world wanted, while my team and I were the epitome of the ferocity the world demanded.

She rolled toward me, leaving the view of the night sky through the portlight she'd been admiring. "What's on your mind? I can see it in your eyes when the wheels are turning."

"I'm thinking about Al Brown and what he might have to say when he gets here."

"Why are you worried about that?" she asked. "There's nothing you can do to change whatever he's going to say, so wasting time and energy worrying about it is ludicrous."

I laced my arm beneath her neck and pulled her close to me. "What would I do without you? I love how you perceive the world, and I envy that ability."

"It's not an ability. It's a choice. Most of the things we worry about can't be changed, so I choose not to let them pull me down. I can understand you thinking about what Brown has to say and how you'll react, but there's something else burning behind those eyes of yours. What is it?"

I pulled her even tighter than before. "I'm not sure I love the fact that you always know when something's happening in my crazy head."

"It's all part of loving you, big boy, so get used to it."

"I'm thinking about Mongo."

"Mongo? Why?"

"I think he's developed a taste for Eastern European women. He pulled me aside tonight and asked if it was okay if he invited Irina and Anya Volkovna to come spend time with us."

Penny pulled away and propped up on an elbow. "Oh, really? That's the woman and daughter who big Anya got out of Russia and installed in the house in Athens, right?"

"Yes. Apparently, Viktor Volkov, the Russian mafia kingpin she busted in New York, was the brother of Irina's dead husband. It's a long, convoluted story, but it seems to have come to a happy ending for everyone except Viktor."

She raised an eyebrow. "And what did you tell him?"

"I told him it's perfectly fine, but we'll have to watch what we say around them since they haven't been vetted yet."

"Do you think there's something going on between Mongo and Irina?"

I stared past her at the two dozen twinkling stars through the portlight. "I don't know. Maybe. I know it messed him up pretty badly when big Anya dumped him."

"Is he living in the house in Athens with them?"

"No," I said. "He bought a place on Hilton Head, but apparently, he's been moving his stuff from Athens, little by little, and I'm sure they've spent some time together."

"Interesting," she whispered. "Have you met them?"

I shook my head. "No, not yet, but we'll all meet them tomorrow when Disco gets back. He's flying them back out here after he drops off Clark and Maebelle."

"That's going to be a little weird for them, don't you think?"

"What is?"

"Getting on an airplane with some American they don't know."

"Mongo went with Disco, so he'll be there."

She folded her elbow beneath her and laid her head back on my shoulder. "This is definitely going to be interesting to watch."

I gave her a squeeze. "Yes, it sure is."

After accepting Penny's philosophy of not worrying about things I can't change, I drifted off to sleep, worrying about nothing.

* * *

Singer, Hunter, and Tina showed up at the dock with a bag of croissants, pineapple, mango, and papaya the next morning, shortly after the sun reclaimed the Caribbean sky.

They climbed the ladder to *Aegis*'s upper deck. Hunter and Tina bounded up the ladder like kids on a playground, but Singer hobbled, using the handrails as crutches.

"We brought breakfast," Hunter announced as he turned back to watch Singer limp over the top step. "And we brought Hop Along with us."

Singer had broken his ankle on the side of a mountain in Montana during our latest mission and was still a few weeks away from being back at full strength.

Singer showed Hunter a fist. "Go ahead and make fun, Air Force. We'll get out the rifles and see which one of us is crippled when it comes to hitting a golf ball a mile away."

Hunter held up the bag. "Yeah, but I brought croissants."

Penny snatched the bag from his hand. "Be nice to Singer. He's hurt."

"Yeah, be nice to me," Singer echoed.

Hunter threw an arm around the sniper's shoulders. "You know I love you, Singer. If I didn't pick on you, you'd think something was wrong."

The wind instrument reported fourteen knots out of the southeast.

"I've got an idea," I said. "Let's go for a sail."

Penny dropped the bag of croissants onto the table. "Breakfast can wait. I have the helm."

I turned to Hunter and Singer. "I guess that makes me the deckhand . . . again."

Penny wasted no time firing up the diesels while I tossed off the dock lines. Soon, we had an acre of brilliant white sail in the air, and *Aegis* was cutting through the water like a dolphin. When properly rigged, our boat didn't require a lot of attention. She managed the wind and waves with grace and style. With a little fine-tuning of the rigging, she could dance like a racehorse. But for a breakfast sail, gentleness is the order of the day.

We ate, enjoyed orange juice and coffee, and drank in the salt air of The Bahamas.

Hunter wiped his mouth. "Hey, did you know Mongo went with Disco last night?"

Penny beat me to the punch. "Yeah, we know. He went to pick up his new girlfriend."

"New girlfriend?" Hunter said. "What new girlfriend?"

She said, "You remember Irina and little Anya? I think Mongo's got the hots for the momma."

Tina lit up. "I think that's sweet. He's such a sweetheart, and he needs somebody to love."

Hunter rolled his eyes. "I guess one Russian wasn't enough to make him swear off Slavic women, huh?"

"I guess not," I said. "Just remember . . . when either Irina or Anya is around, watch what you say about work. Neither of them has a clearance."

Hunter cocked his head. "You don't think they're . . ."

"No, I don't think they're spies, but we can't be too careful until we get to know them. And if Mongo cares about them, I'm sure I speak for the whole team when I say we care about them, too."

Tina grinned. "That's so cool. I've never seen a group of people more like family than you guys. It's amazing."

"Friends are the family we get to choose," I said. "There's no question that every one of us would take a bullet for the others."

Singer piped up. "Yeah, that's true, but we'd rather make the bad guys take the bullets."

I raised a glass of orange juice. "Spoken like a true sniper."

We finished breakfast and sailed for a couple of hours. Hunter gave sailing lessons to Tina while the rest of us soaked up the morning sun.

My phone chirped around eleven thirty, and I saw Disco's number on the tiny screen. "Good morning. Are you leaving the mainland soon?"

Disco said, "We left the mainland thirty minutes ago. We're on deck at the airport now. The RHIB is still docked at Harvey's, so we'll catch a lift over there and meet you at the marina in half an hour."

"There's no need to cram everyone into the RHIB. We're out on the boat now. We'll pull into Harvey's and pick you up."

"Great," he said. "We'll see you there in a few minutes. Oh, and Chase . . . there's something I need to tell you."

Don't waste time worrying about things you can't change.

Penny's words echoed in my head, but Disco's tone restarted my churning mind. "What is it?"

"It's probably nothing," he said. "I know I'm not a tier-one guy like the rest of you, but I've noticed the same guy four times. I wrote it off as a coincidence until now when I just saw him again."

"Okay, tell me about the guy."

"He seems to be trying to blend in with the tourists. Right now, he's wearing a bright shirt with cocktails all over it and a Cuban hat. He has the look of a tourist, but he doesn't move like one."

"What do you mean?"

"He moves like you and Hunter move. I know that doesn't make any sense, and I'm probably overthinking—"

"No, you're not overthinking anything. Is he at the airport now?"

"He was a few seconds ago, but I've lost him now."

"Where were the other places you saw him?"

"He was at the bar, but only for a few minutes. Before that, I saw him at the marina. I know it's a small place, but I just thought you should know."

"You did the right thing, Disco. We'll be there to pick you up in about thirty minutes. Do you have Irina and little Anya with you?"

"Yes, they're here. We just went through Customs and Immigration. Did you know they both have American passports?"

"No, I didn't know that, but I find it interesting."

"I thought so, too," he said.

"Have a drink at Harvey's, and we'll be there soon. You can fill me in on the guy who keeps popping up."

"Will do."

I tucked the phone back into my pocket and found Singer and Hunter staring.

Hunter said, "What was that all about? It sounded serious."

"It may be serious, but most likely, it's Disco overthinking. He saw the same guy three or four times yesterday and today. He says the guy is trying to play tourist, but he moves like us."

Singer said, "It could be a retired military ex-pat who hasn't adjusted to island life yet."

"Could be," I said, "but I think it's worth checking out, especially if Disco sees him again."

"Are they back on the island?" Hunter asked.

"They just made it through customs, and we're picking them up at Harvey's."

Hunter gave the Windex a look. "Do you think we can sail through the cut at Coral Crest?"

"We can try," I said. "Take us in as far south as draft will allow, and stay on the wind. Get the engines idling just in case we get a wind shift in the cut. We don't want to be behind the power curve in that shallow water."

Hunter briefed Tina on the plan and held up his hands in an effort to demonstrate the condition of the sails they'd need to create to make it through the cut. I believed we could make it, but it never hurts to have a second form of propulsion available if the first one fails.

Not wanting to feel *Aegis* stick to the bottom, I parked myself behind Hunter and Tina in the cockpit.

Everything was going perfectly until the shallow water alarm beeped, sending Tina into a reactionary convulsion. She jerked the wheel to the left and stuck the boat in irons with the wind trailing directly over the bow and the sails luffing like sheets on a clothesline. The maneuver halted any forward motion we had but presented little danger. With the wind out of the southwest, doing nothing would simply allow the boat to drift backward into deeper water.

Hunter turned, wide-eyed. "What do we do?"

"I don't know, but you should probably do something. Otherwise, we'll get blown to the English Channel."

Tina gave up and retreated from the helm while Hunter went to work. He studied the Windex, sails, chart plotter, and sonar. With the sails luffing, he took advantage of the opportunity to trim them even closer as we were blown backward out of the cut. With the wheel hard over to port, *Aegis*'s stern made a slow turn to the left, bringing the bow off the wind and the sails back to life. Hunter's patience paid off, and the boat accelerated back into the cut without the use of the twin diesels below deck that were anxious to join the fight.

He turned and reached for Tina. "Come on. Get back up here. You have to finish what you started. This time, though, let's not make any abrupt turns . . . especially not to port."

Tina took the wheel, and on the second attempt, we sailed through the cut like an America's Cup crew.

With a little help from Hunter, Tina laid us alongside the dock at Harvey's, where Mongo, Irina, and little Anya stood with smiles almost as wide as Tina's.

I gave them a wave. "Hey, guys. Welcome to The Bahamas. Throw me your gear and climb aboard."

Little Anya turned to her mother and repeated my instructions in Russian. Three small pieces of luggage came aboard, followed by Irina and Anya Volkovna."

I took Irina's hand. "*Dobro pozhalovat' na bort.*"

She scowled. "*Spasibo, ma* do not do this. Marvin says to me I must learn English."

I whispered in Russian, "You're on vacation. You can learn English when you're not relaxing on an island."

She smiled. "*Spasibo*, Chase."

Mongo picked up little Anya as if she were light as a balloon and tossed her aboard. The dancer landed with the grace of a cat, giggling all the way.

"Where's Disco?" I asked.

Mongo motioned toward the dinghy dock. "He's bringing the RHIB around."

Almost before he could finish, Disco appeared with the small boat's engine at full RPM. He roared past us with barely an inch of the hull touching the water. Little Anya watched in wide-eyed amazement. Disco made a narrow turn and plowed into the wake he'd created from the opposite direction. The hull of the RHIB left the water, jumping the wake and splashing back down a few feet astern. Anya was mesmerized.

I motioned toward the small boat. "Do you want to try it?"

Her already-saucer-sized eyes widened even more as she jerked her gaze to her mother. "*Mozhno, Mama?*"

Irina brushed her daughter's hair back. "English, Tatiana. You may, but careful, yes?"

The girl kicked off her shoes, pulled an elastic ponytail holder from her wrist, and tamed her windblown hair. Disco shut down the engine of the RHIB as the tubes kissed *Aegis*'s hull, and little Anya—who was apparently Tatiana to her mother—leapt from the deck and into the RHIB.

Disco looked up at me in utter confusion. I wanted to leave him dangling on the line for comedic value, but Penny saved him. "Get out of there, Disco. The girls are going for a ride."

Penny stepped aboard the RHIB as Disco climbed onto *Aegis*. Seconds later, she and Tatiana were cutting wakes and jumping the overpowered little boat like a steeplechase horse. Tatiana's giggling and squealing were louder than the engine, and Irina's fear-consumed eyes never left her daughter.

Mongo laced an arm around her and leaned down. "She'll be fine. Penny is the best boat handler I've ever seen. There's no need to worry."

Irina's eyes floated skyward as she tried to piece together Mongo's English. When it finally came to her, she laid her head against his chest and smiled. Her Slavic features gave her a simplistic beauty most women would kill to possess. I watched her and Mongo for a moment and then gave him a nod and wink. He offered back an almost imperceptible copy.

Chapter 4

Rendezvous with Destiny

Disco tossed off the lines, and I motored away from Harvey's dock.

Irina shot panicked glances between me and the RHIB. "*Ma Tatiana!*"

Mongo patted her leg. "It's okay. We're just going across the bay to the resort. Penny and Tatiana will meet us there."

She appeared at least a little relieved, but she couldn't look away from her daughter.

As we motored across the shallow harbor, Penny brought the RHIB directly in front of us and slowed to just above idle speed. She put her arm around Tatiana and lowered her head beneath the windshield.

Irina's nervousness returned, but once again, Mongo comforted her. "It's okay. We do this all the time."

As the RHIB disappeared beneath *Aegis*'s bow, Irina gasped, but Mongo pointed toward the stern. "Just watch and wait."

Seconds later, the bow of the RHIB poked its way from beneath *Aegis*'s deck and between her pontoons. Tatiana waved to her mother as she smiled with delight."

Irina timidly waved back and turned to Mongo. "This is how to vacation for Americans?"

Mongo laughed and answered in Russian. "No, this is how *we* vacation, but *we're* not most Americans."

Back ashore at the resort, Penny and I hoisted the RHIB back onto the davits while Tatiana regaled us with excited stories of her grand adventure. Most of it was in passable English, but occasionally, a little Russian snuck in for her mother's benefit.

Penny secured the RHIB and leaned toward me. "I actually like *this* Anya. It's okay with me if she sticks around."

I chuckled. "It's nice to know you don't hate *all* Russians."

"It's not hate. It's more like . . . well, something slightly less than hate. And only for one particular Russian."

Tatiana stared up at my wife with wonder-filled eyes. "Thank you, Mrs. Penny! We can do this again, yes?"

At six feet tall, Penny towered over the ballerina, so she planted herself on the settee. "We can definitely do it again and again. I love it just as much as you, but you have to stop calling me Mrs. Penny. It's just Penny. I'm not really that much older than you."

Tatiana threw her arms around Penny. "Then I will call you Pennechka. You know what this means, yes?"

"Actually, yes, I do know what that means, and I'm flattered. Do you prefer that I call you Tatiana or Anya?"

"I am Tatiana. When I was dancer for Bolshoi, my name was Anya, but this is only because my uncle paid for my school, and this is the name he liked."

Penny smiled. "Good. I prefer Tatiana."

"Do you know the Anya who was my uncle's friend?"

Penny glanced at me and back at the girl. "Yes, I know her."

"She was very nice to me, and she brought my mother to America."

At a rare loss for words, Penny said, "Yeah, she can be nice sometimes."

Obviously detecting both Penny's glance toward me and her unease with the situation, Tatiana said, "Uh oh. I think Mr. Chase likes Anya more than you do."

Penny gathered her wits. "No, not anymore he doesn't."

Even Tatiana understood that particular topic was closed.

With *Aegis* secured against the dock, we stepped from the boat onto the boardwalk. Mongo took a gentle step, still in a little pain from the ordeal in Montana. His hesitance sent Tatiana running toward him, and she grabbed his enormous hand in hers. "How is your ankle? I can wrap for you again, yes? Every dancer knows how to wrap ankles."

Perhaps the big man thought no one would hear him, or at least wouldn't understand him if they did hear. In flawless Russian, he said, "I would really like that."

I've seen Mongo nearly blown apart by a flashbang grenade on an oil-drilling rig two hundred miles offshore. I've plucked him off an Afghani mountainside with a leg broken almost beyond repair. But I've never once seen him admit being injured. Tatiana's hands may have disappeared inside his, but there was no question the giant was firmly wrapped around the dancer's little finger.

He sat on the starboard side pontoon, dangling his legs toward the dock, and pulled off his boot and sock. His ankle was swollen and still discolored, but I had a feeling his submission to the girl's care had little, if anything, to do with pain. Although his size fetched fear in every corner of the world, he was little more than putty in her hands. She wrapped his ankle with the precision of an orthopedic surgeon and carefully slid his sock and boot back on.

He slid from the boat back to the boardwalk and gave Tatiana a thankful smile. "Look at that. It's better already. Thank you."

She giggled and leapt en pointe, with nothing more than her tortured toes touching the dock. "Soon, you will be able to do this."

Mongo said, "I think I'll leave the ballet to you."

"I think this is best, but you can maybe dance with Mama sometimes. She is wonderful dancer."

Irina pressed her index finger to her lips and scolded her daughter in harsh Russian. "Stop this, Tatiana. You are embarrassing me."

The girl leaned near her mother. "But he likes you, Mama."

Instead of a response, Irina blushed.

Although the soap opera that was Mongo's recent life was fascinating, I needed some quality time with Disco, so I laid a hand on his shoulder. "Let's go have a chat."

He followed me to a quiet corner of the dockside bar. "I guess you want to talk about the man I saw, huh?"

"Yep, I do. Can you describe him?"

Disco cast his eyes to the sky. "Maybe mid-forties, short dark hair, almost a crewcut, but not quite. Clean-shaven, about my height, fit, big through the shoulders, chest, and arms. Twice I've seen him wear a white Panama hat, and once he was wearing a baseball cap."

"What team?"

Disco scowled. "What?"

"The cap. You said he was wearing a baseball cap. What team logo was on it?"

"The Marlins, I think."

"Was the hat dirty or worn?"

He frowned. "I don't know. I don't remember. But I don't think so."

I checked our environment for hungry ears. "These are important details. If the hat is new, he probably bought it as part of a disguise. If it's worn or dirty, he likely wears it often. If he wears a Florida Marlins hat regularly, he's most likely from Florida. If it looks new, he's probably not."

He closed his eyes for several moments. "Okay, the Panama hat was dirty, but it was also too big for him. That might mean he stole it. Why would someone buy a hat that was too big?"

"Now you're thinking like a spy," I said. "What about the Marlins hat?"

He continued clenching his eyelids tightly shut. "It was definitely newer, but the bill was bent really round. You know, the way Clark wears his."

When he opened his eyes, I shoved a finger toward his face. "Hey! Don't hate on the redneck roll. That's how hats should be worn. It also likely means he wanted the hat to look well-worn."

"I wasn't hating on it. I was just pointing it out. But I don't know what all of this has to do with the guy."

"This is what we do, Disco. We pay attention to things other people ignore. It's what keeps us alive. I think you're right about the Panama hat. If it's too big, it wasn't his, and it was most likely stolen. Hats are easy to steal, and they make great concealment. That, coupled with the new Marlins cap bent out of shape, likely means this guy is trying to make other people think he's something he isn't. It also lends credence to your suspicion that he's watching us . . . or you."

He said, "I'm not sure I'll ever learn this stuff."

"You will. It just takes time. Now, I need you to think carefully. Have you done or said anything in the last few weeks that would make anyone want to pull surveillance on you?"

Disco recoiled. "Like what?"

"Anything. Have you talked with anyone about the work you're doing with us? Have you told anyone about where you've been or what you've been doing?"

His frown continued. "No, nobody. Well, I mean, except my sister. I told her I'm flying for a company in Georgia, and I told her

I'd been to Montana. She's always wanted to go out west, but her husband is a homebody. He never wants to go anywhere."

"What do your sister and her husband do for a living?"

"She works at a bank. She's a head teller, and he manages an auto parts store. They live in Raleigh. Why does that matter?"

"It matters because those are normal jobs for normal people—the kind of people who wouldn't spark any curiosity from somebody in our line of work. Are you sure you've not talked with anyone else about what we do?"

"Yeah, I'm sure. Just my sister."

"Okay, that means he's not watching you. He's watching us. I'm surprised we haven't picked him out of the crowd."

He raised a finger. "There's one more thing."

"Let's hear it."

"I know this is going to sound strange, but I think I may have seen him before. Something about him looks familiar, but I'm sure I don't know him. Does that make sense?"

I waved him off. "That's likely the result of your brain trying to make sense of seeing him so often in so many unlikely places. Our brains often create false memories to make things appear logical. If you see a guy four times, your brain begins to build memories of him, and sometimes it shoves those memories into the past, making us believe we've seen something or someone before. It's crazy what our brains do."

"That could be it," he said, "but the thing that stands out most about the guy is his bearing. He walks without bobbing up and down like most people. Like I said, he moves like you and Clark—not like a normal person."

"Oh? So, Clark and I aren't normal?"

He huffed. "No, not remotely."

"Okay, let's piece it together. Based on his physique, haircut, and movement, this guy is likely former or retired military. He's at least had some paramilitary training. He's trying to hide beneath deceptive headgear, and he tends to pop up where we are."

Disco nodded. "All of that sounds right."

"I've got one more question, and it's important. Does he move like he's sore or injured?"

Closed went his eyes again. "Now that you mention it, he takes short strides and doesn't pivot at the waist very much."

I snapped my fingers. "Got it! Now, close your eyes and keep them closed."

He did as I asked. "I want you to picture the guy, but get him out of the hat and let his hair grow. Put a beard on him. Drop a cowboy hat on his head, and picture him walking with normal strides. Can you see him?"

He grimaced behind closed eyes. "I'm trying, but it's not coming to me."

"That's okay," I said. "It came to me. Here's what I want you to do. When you see him again, I want you to take off your glasses and inspect them as if a bug has just crashed into your lens. Then I want you to fold one stem of your glasses closed and point the other stem toward the guy. Do it subtly, and try not to look like you're pointing him out. It's time for a little cloak-and-dagger. Can you handle it?"

He shrugged. "Sure, I can do that. But what was the beard and cowboy hat all about?"

I turned back for the rest of our group. "Don't worry. It'll come to you. Just remember the glasses thing."

"Whatever you say. You're the boss."

When we found the rest of our team, it was obvious that Mongo had taken little Anya's—Tatiana's—advice and asked Irina to dance. The Russian was five foot six or maybe seven, but she was nearly invisible dancing with Mongo's three hundred pounds of muscle.

Hunter and Singer leaned in when I curled my finger and spoke barely loud enough for them to hear. "Disco spotted a tail. He's average height, mid-forties, wearing a hat that doesn't make sense, works out, former military, a little sore in the hips. If he sees him again, he's going to point him out with his . . ." I turned to see our chief pilot yank his glasses from his face, fold down one stem, and point the other to his three o'clock position. "Well, speak of the devil," I said. "Dirty Panama hat, blue T-shirt over khaki shorts, and gray Merrells. I'm moving to the beach with Disco. You two pin him down as soon as he's out of sight of the crowd. I think I'd like to have a chat with him."

"What about Mongo?" Hunter asked.

I peeked across his shoulder to see the big man trying to teach a Russian woman the Texas two-step to an old Jimmy Buffett song. "Let's leave him. He's do-si-doing to "Cheeseburger in Paradise." I don't want to break that up. We can handle this one without him."

Disco and I gave our companions a wave, lit a pair of cigars, and turned for the beach. Hunter and Singer turned as if heading for the marina parking lot. Our watcher would have to make a de-cision. With our team split into three elements, who would he choose to follow? If I was right about who he was, I was betting he'd follow Disco and me.

"Don't look back," I whispered. "If he follows us, I don't want to spook him."

Disco took a long draw from his cigar and kept walking. We de-scended the sand-covered stairs to the beach and moved toward the waterline. The water of the bay was dead calm with the excep-tion of the occasional boat wake, and we were far enough from the restaurant and bar for the air to be relatively quiet.

About a hundred feet into our leisurely stroll, a voice came from the twisted mangroves. "Okay, okay. Easy, guys. I'm not go-ing to resist."

"That's our cue," I said, and we turned on our heels, heading for the tree line.

When we found our teammates, the Panama-hat-clad surveillance man was kneeling in the sand with Hunter twisting one of his arms tightly behind his back. The man's prosthetic leg didn't share the results of time spent in the sun like his one remaining human leg showed.

I stepped within inches of the man and pointed down at him. "Is this the guy?"

Disco nodded, so I pulled the oversized hat from the man's head and tossed it onto the sand. "Maybe next time, you should steal a hat that fits."

I took a knee, positioning myself eye to eye with our watcher. "Hello, Alvin J. Brown. I'm Chase Fulton. Fancy meeting you here."

Chapter 5
Turnabout Is Fair Play

"Okay, you've made your point," Brown grunted. "Let me up so we can either talk—or fight—like men."

I gave Hunter a nod, and he released the arm he'd been wrenching. Al Brown immediately reached for the ground in front of him, but I caught his left shoulder in my palm. "No, no, no. Keep your hands out of the sand while we're still deciding if we're talkers or fighters."

The last thing I wanted was a face full of sand with an elite warrior only inches in front of me, even if my team would have had him back on the ground in seconds.

"Call me Al," he said as he made his way to his feet and stuck out his hand. "And I'm not interested in fighting. We do have a lot to discuss, though."

I put my hand in his, and we shook like gentlemen. "Let's take a walk. I know a great spot for conversation."

I led the way with Brown to my left and my team trailing only a few feet and well within reach should the man change his mind about his intentions. We dusted off the sand from our shoes and shins and climbed aboard *Aegis*.

"You guys seem to do all right for yourselves . . . Airplanes, boats, and extended vacations in the islands."

I slid open the door to the main salon and motioned inside. "The airplanes and boats we earned by doing the things most other people can't. As for the vacation, it's more of a recuperation. We earned that by tussling with your former team. They put up one hell of a fight."

Brown turned and lifted his shirttail. "See that scar? I earned that doing exactly the same. They thought they'd killed me, but thanks to the livestock agents who found me in the barn, and to you for delivering Copeland's kidney, I came out barely worse for the wear."

I took a seat and eyed Brown. "Why were you watching us, and what was that phone call about last night?"

He swallowed hard. "The call was to put you at ease by making you believe I wouldn't be on the island for thirty-six hours, but I see that didn't work so well. It would appear you guys are pretty good at countersurveillance."

I motioned toward Disco. "Al, I've read your file, and everything behind the page stamped 'Top Secret' is nothing short of impressive. But our pilot, of all people, spotted you no fewer than five times."

Disco huffed. "No offense taken."

I chuckled. "None intended."

Disco pointed at Brown's prosthetic. "I did have a leg up, so to speak. I had a sneak peek up in Montana, but you were rocking the Grizzly Adams beard back then."

Brown snapped his fingers and pointed toward our pilot. "And that's the answer to your second question. I was watching your team because you watched mine. After all, turnabout is fair play, right?"

"All right, so we've covered the phone call and the stalking—"

"It was ISR, not stalking," Brown said.

I sighed. "Okay, we've covered the phone call, the intelligence, surveillance, and reconnaissance. Let's get down to the talk you came all this way to have. What's on your mind?"

He examined the main salon. "I've noticed you don't drink cheap whiskey. Do you think I might . . ."

Before he could finish, Hunter slid a tumbler across the table. "I thought this might be a bourbon kind of talk."

Brown raised the glass. "Here's to terrible surveillance."

I accepted a glass from Hunter and joined the toast. "And to countersurveillance even a retired Air Force pilot can pull off."

"Here, here!"

We drank, and everyone relaxed enough to make Brown believe we weren't on the verge of pulling our sidearms.

"Where do I start?" he said. "I had my doubts about a couple of my former teammates for some time, but I let myself believe it was just the paranoia of an old war dog. I guess my gut wasn't wrong, but sometimes it really sucks to be right."

"Yes, it does," I agreed. "I'm sorry it had to come to a showdown."

Brown shook his head and stared between his feet. "There was no other way." He let the line hang in the air as he savored a second sip of some of the finest water, corn, barley, wheat, and yeast Kentucky ever produced. "What are we drinking?"

"It's Pappy Van Winkle from Buffalo Trace," I said.

"Oh, I know who makes it, but this is the first time I've actually tasted it. How old is it?"

I turned to Hunter, and he produced the bottle. "It's twenty-three-year."

"You boys sure know how to live."

"More importantly than that," I said, "we know how to not die. And you seem to share that particular skill, even if your stalking skills are weak."

"Touché."

"All right. Enough small talk. Let's hear it."

Brown cleared his throat. "I'm sure you know I'm done. They'll never give me another team, and they'll never let me do so much as guarding a school crossing. I'm done. That makes me a FAG—a former action guy." Brown continued after another sip. "If you're lucky, you guys will get old one day, and all of this will make sense, but suffice it to say, even though I'm officially washed up, I'm not finished."

I'd spent the previous half hour of my life giving Brown what I believed to be my full attention, but that statement somehow drew me closer. "What do you mean you're not finished?"

"I mean, I still have work to do, and I can't do it alone. Between having only half the legs I was born with, now I've got a dead traitor's kidney in my back. I'm not the man I used to be when I wore that funny little green hat."

"There's nothing funny about a Green Beret," I said. "My team is full of them, and I'd take a hundred more if I could find them."

"I understand that feeling well," he said. "There's a lot to be said for men who grin when they get hit in the face."

I gave Singer a nod, and he put on the goofy grin of the kind of man Brown described.

"So, what is it you want to do, and what do you want from my team?"

Brown rattled the cubes in his tumbler, and Hunter poured.

"Thank you, Mr. Hunter."

That left my partner with raised eyebrows. "You've done your homework."

"You did yours," Brown said. "And we already determined what turnabout is."

"Let's get down to business," I said without a hint of pleasantry in my tone.

"I want to clean up the mess my former team left in their wake, and I want you to help me do it."

I leaned in. "*Help* you do it? Or you want us to *do it* at your direction?"

"That remains to be seen. I'll brief you on the missions that went to hell, and you'll tell me whether or not you're willing to help. Something tells me there's way too much patriotism floating around in this team to turn your backs on an opportunity to undo the work of treasonous lowlifes."

"That's a nice sales pitch, but you're wasting it on the wrong target," I said.

He cocked his head and lowered his chin. "Are you saying you and your team aren't interested in cleaning up the mess my team made?"

I shrugged. "It doesn't matter whether I'm interested or not. I don't know how you ran your team, Al, but I don't have the liberty to strike out on a mission just because I think it's the right thing to do. I've got some of the best operators on Earth who'd willingly jump into any fight I picked, but that's not how it works here. I report to a handler who reports to the Board. They approve and sanction every mission, or we don't do it."

"Is that so? Does that include your mission to break a former Russian SVR officer out of the Black Dolphin Prison? And does it hold true for the mission of finding the arsonist who burned your house to the ground? Oh, I almost forgot. Did you run it up the chain when you decided to avenge the attack on your friend and the sinking of her boat in St. Augustine?"

I leaned back in my chair, swirled my bourbon, and tried not to appear surprised. "Somebody's pretty good at homework."

He raised his glass. "I never said I was pretty, but when it comes to research, I'm tough to beat."

Mongo would step in front of a freight train to protect me, but when it came to verbal jabs, nobody on Earth could hold a candle to Stone W. Hunter. "Maybe you should've researched your team a little more before they started drawing their paychecks from the wrong cash drawer."

Brown frowned. "Perhaps I should've."

I placed my tumbler on the table. "You're wasting your breath if you only brief the men in this room. I'll get my handler and analyst on the phone, and we'll listen to your proposal. I can't promise we'll swallow what you're trying to feed us, but we will listen. I'm a pretty good judge of character, and I think you're a man of honor who's been kicked around lately. I've been there, and it sucks. If we're capable of helping, and my handler and Board approve it, I'll consider it. As I said earlier, I don't know how you ran your team, but we're not your typical follow orders kind of crew. We make decisions together. If anyone is uncomfortable, he can take a knee and bow out of any operation he doesn't like. I don't blindly follow orders, and I'll never expect my team to do so. Those are our initial terms. If you still want to play, we'll listen. If not, we'll pour you another fifty-dollar glass of whiskey and tell old war stories."

"How 'bout we do both?" he said.

"I can live with that. Hunter, would you mind getting Clark and Skipper on the horn? I've got a feeling things are about to get interesting."

Hunter dialed the numbers and handed the satellite phone to me. I covered the mouthpiece with my palm. "I'm going to step outside for a minute."

Once beyond the sliding glass door and nestled onto a cockpit settee, I pressed the phone to my ear. "Good afternoon, guys. I was right. Al Brown is here, and he wants our help. I told him I wouldn't listen to his proposal without the two of you listening in. He wants us to help him clean up the train wreck his former team left behind."

Clark said, "He wants our help, or does he want us to do it for him?"

I chuckled. "People like me tickle me. That's exactly what I asked him."

"And what was his answer?"

"He didn't have one, but I get the impression he's not the kind of man who shies away from getting his hands dirty."

Skipper chimed in. "I thought he wasn't going to be on the island until tomorrow."

"That's what he led me to believe, but it was a ploy. He's been here for at least a couple of days. We pulled a little game of spy on the spy who's spying on the spies, and we put him on his knees. Well, more correctly, on his knee. He's got a prosthetic leg that didn't come from the VA. It's a nice one."

Clark said, "You're still on the island, right, Skipper?"

"Yeah, I'm still here."

Clark clicked his tongue against his teeth. "Do you have any of those little dog collars I like so much?"

Skipper huffed. "I never leave home without them."

He said, "I thought so. Hook up with Chase, and put eyes on Al Brown. Come up with a reason to get close to him and strap him up. Once you're done, kick him out."

"Kick him out?" I said. "What are you talking about?"

Skipper scolded. "Calm down, Chase. Clark and I know what we're doing. Go on with what you were saying before Chase so rudely interrupted."

Clark cleared his throat. "As I was saying, kick him out. We'll watch where he goes, and I'll be back on the island in two hours. Wherever he goes, we'll round him up and listen to his spiel. Who knows? What he's proposing might be fun."

As if she'd been waiting a few steps away, Skipper showed up and climbed aboard. "Okay, let's go have some fun. Follow my lead."

I didn't like the sound of that, but she didn't give me time to protest. After stepping inside the main salon, she stood as if in awe of the old warrior. She examined him up and down without saying a word.

He rose from the settee and stuck out a hand. "I'm Alvin Brown, but please call me Al. You must be the analyst."

Skipper stared down at his offered hand and finally back into his eyes. "I'm a hugger, not a shaker, and if you're as badass as your file makes you sound, you definitely deserve a hug." She stepped around the table and folded herself into his arms.

The disbelief on his face turned to acceptance when the beautiful young woman pressed herself against him.

"Thank you for all you've done for this—well, not *this* country —but our country. You're a hero, Mr. Brown. It's an honor to finally meet you."

Apparently taken aback, he stuttered. "Uh, I guess . . . thank you."

She stepped back from the man, and her flirtatious demeanor turned cold. "Okay, this is when you get out so we can talk about you."

Skipper's performance and the surprise on Brown's face amused me, so I motioned for him to walk away.

He hesitantly stepped through the open door. "Well, thank you for listening to me. I take it your handler will make the next move."

"Probably so," Skipper said. She patted him on the back. "It's time for you to go now."

He nodded with acceptance and unbuttoned his shirt. We watched in disbelief as he tossed the shirt over *Aegis*'s steering wheel and dived from the stern into the bay.

Skipper groaned and plucked the tracking device from the collar of Brown's abandoned shirt.

"Ouch," I said. "I guess he's smarter than we gave him credit. I'm impressed."

Skipper laughed. "Don't be impressed with him. Be impressed with me. This one's a dummy anyway. I intentionally let him feel me place it. The real one—which is waterproof, by the way—is tucked neatly inside the waistband of his pants."

Chapter 6
Upgrade . . . Upgrade

In typical fashion, Clark made his appearance ahead of schedule.

"How did you get here so fast?" I asked.

He checked his watch. "It wasn't all that fast. I told you to expect a couple of hours."

"It's been an hour forty since we hung up."

"Okay, you got me," he said. "I've got a surprise for you."

"You know I'm not a fan of surprises."

"You'll like this one. I guarantee it."

I turned to Skipper. "Do you still have Brown?"

She rolled her eyes. "What do *you* think? Yes, I've still got him, and I'm going with you to pick him up. He's at the Sand Dollar and probably on his fourth or fifth cocktail by now."

"I'm not sure a guy with a brand-new kidney should ever be on his fourth or fifth cocktail again."

Hunter lifted Brown's tumbler from the table. "That new kidney didn't slow him down when he was drinking your Pappy Twenty-Three."

Skipper stood from her computer. "Maybe the guy thinks he's bulletproof since he's cheated death this long."

"Come on," I said. "Let's go pick him up before he changes clothes."

Skipper, Hunter, and I hopped into our rented Toyota four-door pickup for the three-minute ride to the Sand Dollar Inn.

I shoved a pair of folded bills into the valet's hand. "Keep it running, and leave it right here. Got it?"

The young man fanned the bills between his thumb and forefinger and gave them a glance. "Yes, sir. She'll be right here when you get back."

We strolled through the open-air reception area of the Sand Dollar resort.

Hunter took in the surroundings. "Man, this place is a dump."

I surveyed the crumbling tile and mold where the ceiling met the walls. "It used to be beautiful. My parents brought me here when I was ten or so. I remember thinking this place must've been a palace. It could certainly use a facelift now, though."

Skipper snapped her fingers. "Focus, boys. We're here to find Brown, not see the sights."

Hunter spotted him first. "There he is, leaning against the end of the bar and checking his watch."

I said, "He's probably trying to decide how long to let us scour the island for him before he shows up back at the marina."

Skipper held up an arm like a mother playing seatbelt for a kid in the passenger seat. "Wait here, boys. I've got this one."

Hunter gave me a look to ensure I was okay with Skipper's plan . . . whatever it was.

I nodded toward the far corner of the bar area, and my partner silently moved into position. There were only two reasonable ways out of the bar, and we had both covered. The option of exiting through the shrubs and trees still existed, but I didn't think a one-legged, one-kidneyed guy in his forties would put up much of a race.

Skipper quietly slipped up behind Brown and draped his abandoned shirt across his bare shoulders. "You left this on the boat, and I thought you might want it back. It's a nice shirt."

Brown jumped and immediately scanned the area. His eyes paused barely perceptibly when he found Hunter and me. Cornered, treed, and bagged, Brown slid his hands into the shirt and held out an arm for Skipper. She took it and led him toward the front of the resort. Hunter fell in behind them about ten feet, and I joined him in locked step.

The jacketed valet held open the door of the Toyota for us, and Brown slid onto the back seat. As we pulled through what remained of the once-ornate wrought iron gate, I met Brown's eyes in the mirror.

"Hello . . . again."

He sighed in disbelieving acceptance. "How?"

Skipper said, "I was impressed when you shed the shirt, but the tracker on your collar was just a diversion. If I were going to plant a real tracker on you, you'd never feel me do it."

He slid his hands inside the waistband of his almost-dry shorts and let his fingers explore the elastic cloth. When his fingertips ran across the button-sized device, he plucked it from the material and laid it in Skipper's waiting palm. "Well, aren't you the grown-up spy?"

"When were you coming back?" I asked.

He shrugged. "I don't know. I thought I'd make you sweat a little and then find my way back to that boat of yours after your handler had plenty of time to make it back to the island. What time do you expect him?"

"He's waiting for us back at the boat," I said.

He scoffed. "Back at the boat? How did he get back out here so fast?"

I let my eyes trace the lines on his face and wondered if the old trick of estimating a tree's age by counting the rings worked on old operators. The gray in his hair and age in his eyes put him closer to fifty than forty, but perhaps life in Big Sky Country weighs heavily on a man's face, or more likely, his former team had given him most of those lines. I was starting to like the old operator, even if he was easy to find.

"We have resources others don't," I said. "We rarely struggle finding a ride."

The short drive back to the marina produced nothing valuable and left the Toyota's seat a little damp from Brown's shorts.

"Home again, home again, jiggidy-jog. I hope you've got your speech memorized," I said. "We're a tough audience."

When we climbed back aboard *Aegis*, Clark looked Brown up and down and stuck out his hand. "Hello again, Mr. Brown. You look a little different without the beard, but it's good to see you again. I'm Clark Johnson. You can think of me as the chaperone for this little dance we're about to have. Come in and have a seat."

Brown gripped Clark's hand. "You don't remember me, do you?"

"Sure I do. I watched you for almost an hour cleaning out the stalls in your barn out in Montana."

Brown gave an exaggeratedly slow shake of his head. "First Battalion, First Special Warfare Training Group Airborne, Fort Bragg, North Carolina."

Clark froze in his tracks and studied the man's face. "SERE School."

Brown nodded. "Yep. That's survival, evasion, resistance, escape training for the civilians at the party." He gave Skipper and me a long look.

Clark scowled. "You were a real S-O-B back then."

Brown grinned with one corner of his mouth. "And you were too stupid to know when to tap out."

"The bad guys don't let us tap out, so we tap them out in the real world."

Brown finished the grin. "*De Oppresso Liber*, Sergeant Major Johnson."

It was Clark's turn to shake his head. "No, I never made sergeant major. I got plucked out of Delta Force selection and traded in my BDUs for blue jeans. It pays better, and there aren't so many S-O-Bs to deal with."

"Fair enough," Brown said. "I guess we can stroll down memory lane later. I get the feeling there's a few folks here who'd like to hear what I have to say."

Clark motioned toward the sliding glass door. "Come on inside where the air conditioner makes it a little more comfortable."

We settled into seats in the main salon, and Brown took the floor. "May I assume everyone here has a clearance, need-to-know, and an NDA?"

Without looking up, Clark said, "You can assume that everyone here has a higher clearance than you, so let's hear it."

"It's pretty simple," he began. "I let a den of vipers move in on my watch, and they opened up a lot of wounds that aren't so easy to stitch up. The first is a team of Chinese spies from the Ministry of State Security. I don't know if you've ever danced with those guys, but they're like ants. When they find a juicy morsel, they line up and march in time until everyone one of them has eaten his fill."

I said, "We had a run-in with them in Panama a couple years ago. We put a water devil onboard a spy ship dressed up like a cargo boat. The Chi-coms sank their own boat in the Miraflores Locks at the southern end of the canal."

Brown surveyed my posture. "That was you?"

"It was."

He tipped an imaginary cap. "In that case, you know all too well how determined and relentless they are."

"We do," I said.

"My team was tasked with the enviable assignment of infiltrating a facility run by a nest of Chinese spies in a place called Red Deer, about halfway between Calgary and Edmonton, Alberta. We were supposed to grab anything capable of storing information: notebooks, hard drives, memory sticks, SD cards, everything. Then we were supposed to torch the place and reduce it to ashes. The problem was, those bastards knew we were coming. Instead of gathering up all their toys and running back home to the motherland or whatever they call it, they brought in enough reinforcements to start a war, and that's almost what they did. It was the worst gunfight I've ever seen. Fortunately, for us—well, fortunately for me—the Royal Canadian Mounties showed up and shut it down. We got out in the melee and headed for the hills. Even though they were traitors and you boys gave them exactly what they deserved, that team of mine was full of mountain men like none I'd ever seen. They could survive off black dirt and twigs at twenty below and gain weight doing it. We let it blow over while we holed up in the hills on the Alberta British Columbia border."

"Did you get the hard drives?" I asked.

"No. We didn't get nothing, and that's not the half of it. The Chinese filed for protection under some crazy Canadian law, and the prime minister gave it to them. They got a multi-layered security system and a compound that makes Fort Knox look like Candy Land."

Skipper was typing as fast as her fingers could hit the keys, and Clark said, "What was on the hard drives and memory sticks?"

"How should I know?" Brown said. "I told you we didn't get nothing, but we left a few thousand bullet holes in the building they used to have."

Skipper spun around in her chair. "I'll tell you what was on those hard drives. Every missile launch code America has."

My heart felt like it was going to explode. "Missile codes? You can't be serious. How?"

Skipper stared between Brown and me for several seconds before finally saying, "I don't think he has the clearance for this."

I locked eyes with Brown and focused on his pupils for any sign of dishonesty. "Do you know why or how the Chinese would have our missile codes?"

He took a deep breath. "I know why they'd want them, but your analyst is right. I don't have the clearance to know how they got them. I'll step outside while she briefs you, and I promise not to jump overboard again if you promise I can have another glass of that Pappy Twenty-Three when I come back inside."

Clark held up a hand. "Wait just a minute. Without revealing anything classified above us, break it down for us, Skipper."

She scratched just behind her ear and pulled off her glasses. "It's a matter of geography, topography, astronomy, and geosynchronous orbit."

"That's what I thought," Clark said. "Let me guess. Directly over Red Deer is the perfect spot to see Cheyenne Mountain and the Aleutian Islands."

"Bingo!" Skipper said.

Clark turned back to Brown. "Before we split up this little show-and-tell session, I want to know what you're asking us to do."

Brown said, "I thought you would've figured it out by now. The Board wanted what the Chinese had in that Red Deer facility. My team didn't get it, though that doesn't suddenly mean the Board forgot all about it. They still want it, but with the increased security

provided by the Canadians. And not physical security, but legal security. It's all but impossible for us to get back inside, and all but
impossible seems to be what you guys do best. I want to go back in
there, melt the place down, and run out with a wheelbarrow full of
intel—just like we should've done the first time, if my so-called team
hadn't tipped off the Chinese that we were coming."

Clark pulled his satellite phone from his pocket. "That's what I
thought. Excuse me for a minute."

He descended the stairs into *Aegis*'s portside hull, closed two
doors behind him, and turned on the shower.

All eyes looked to me.

I said, "He's getting a permission slip to upgrade Brown's security clearance."

Chapter 7
We Know

Skipper's sat-phone vibrated beside her laptop, and she flipped it over. She recoiled and furrowed her brow before holding the phone toward me. "It's Clark. Why would . . ."

"Just answer it," I said. "I'm sure it's not a butt-dial."

She stuck the phone to her ear. "Yeah?"

After a few seconds, she raised her shoulder to hold the phone in place while her fingers danced across the keyboard. "Okay, sure . . . Yeah, I've got it."

The phone landed facedown in the same spot it had been before the call, and Skipper leaned over the computer to retrieve a two-page document from the printer. After skimming over the pages, she slid them across the table to Brown. "Sign and date both pages. Chase, you witness the signatures."

Al Brown signed the two pages without taking the time to read them. He slid them toward me and handed over his pen. It took only a cursory glance to recognize the document as a standard Intelligence Community non-disclosure agreement, so I added my signature beneath Brown's and handed the pages back to Skipper. She slid them into the scanner and set her fingers to work, once again, on the well-worn keyboard.

"I think it's time for a new computer," I said. "You've worn the letters off the keyboard of that one."

She shot me a look as if I'd suggested sailing to the moon. "I built this one, and it's fine. I don't need letters on the keys. I know where everything is. I don't tell you when you need a new pistol, Operator, so your analyst doesn't need you telling her when she needs a new computer."

I threw up my hands. "I meant no offense."

She gave me a wink. "None taken, but the tritium in your night sights is looking pretty weak, so maybe it is time for a new pistol."

I pulled my Glock from its holster. "I built this pistol, and I know exactly where the sights are, so mind your own business, Analyst."

Brown stared back and forth between Skipper and me with confusion on his face. "Is this how you run your team?"

I re-holstered. "Oh, no. We're usually far less formal."

Before I could disappoint Brown any further, Skipper pounded the heel of her foot on the cabin sole and yelled, "Okay, Clark. It's done."

I motioned toward her with my chin. "And that's our official classified intercom system."

Brown stood and ambled toward the bar. "I'll pour my own drink."

He returned with only one cocktail and reclaimed his spot on the settee.

Moments later, Clark emerged wearing his all-business face. He took the drink from Brown's hand and placed it on the table. "Raise your right hand, and repeat after me. I, state your name, acknowledge and willingly accept . . ."

Brown frowned again but played along. "I, Alvin J. Brown, acknowledge and willingly accept . . ."

Clark continued. "That if I turn out to be a dirtbag, Master Sergeant Clark Johnson, retired, will shoot me in the face until I am graveyard dead, and then shoot me some more."

Brown shook his head and picked up his glass. "You guys are a bunch of idiots."

In his unmistakable baritone, our typically demure, quiet sniper said, "We may be idiots, but we'll never be traitors."

Brown sank into the settee as if he wished he were invisible.

Clark turned to our analyst. "Skipper, you have the floor."

She held up one finger as she focused on a stream of data scrolling on her screen. When she'd devoured the information, she turned to face the team. "Do you know what geosynchronous orbit means?"

To no one's surprise, Mongo spoke up. "Sure, everybody knows geosynchronous orbit means a satellite orbiting the Earth just over twenty-two thousand miles high, whose orbital period matches Earth's rotation on its axis of twenty-three hours, fifty-six minutes, and four seconds, or one sidereal day. If you stood on Earth and looked straight up at a satellite in geosynchronous orbit, it would appear to never move." He paused in thought for a moment. "Well, it may appear to move a little, but if it did, it would likely appear to move in a figure-eight aligned with the Earth's rotational axis. And, of course, the farther from the equator, generally, the more the orbiting body appears to move."

Hunter said, "Duh! Of course everybody knows that." He shot a look at me and mouthed, "Did you know that?"

I shook my head in tiny motions, hoping only Hunter would notice.

Skipper said, "Yeah, that, exactly. Now, imagine standing on a spot at fifty-two degrees, twenty-eight point one minutes north by one hundred thirteen degrees, seventy-nine point nine minutes west. From that point, you could look straight up and see SunStar

Two-Six-One-One. That's a classified military satellite in geosynchronous orbit directly over Red Deer, Alberta, Canada."

Mongo said, "Hey, two-six-one-one is Ronald Reagan's birthday—February sixth, nineteen eleven."

Clark palmed his forehead. "Why? Why would you know that?"

Mongo stared back as if to say, "Doesn't everybody know that?"

Skipper reclaimed the floor. "Okay, I didn't know that, but it's an interesting tidbit, even though it has no relevance to what we're talking about here. What we're talking about is the reason the Chinese chose to build their Tàitóu Observatory in Red Deer. There's no better place on the planet to intercept every piece of data SunStar Two-Six-One-One processes. Doing so would've given them an almost up-to-the-second report of the status of every U.S. intercontinental ballistic missile in every silo all over the world."

Al Brown tapped the rim of his tumbler with a thumbnail. "And the Board told us it was a supposed weather observatory."

Mongo said, "That's what the Chinese released as the official function of the observatory. If you'll excuse my terrible Mandarin, we all know that's an absolute crock of *fèihuà.*"

Clark rolled a napkin into a ball and threw it at our giant. "Even I know what that means."

Mongo rolled his eyes.

Skipper snapped her fingers. "Focus! This is important. Please tell me everyone knows what NORAD is."

Everyone nodded, and Skipper said, "Just in case any of you are nodding yes because you're ashamed to admit you don't know, NORAD is the North American Aerospace Defense Command, and they live inside Cheyenne Mountain in Colorado Springs. If you want me to brief you on that compound, I will, but essentially, all you need to know is that it's a top-secret installation built inside a mountain of granite . . . and it's huge. There are thirteen three-story buildings and two two-story buildings built on a bed of thirteen hundred springs. That makes them capable of absorbing the energy of an earthquake or a nuclear weapon detonation. This is all gee-whiz information for the most part. The important thing to remember is that there's a compound built inside a mountain, and it doesn't belong to the United States."

In sync, a round of "What?" came.

I'm not talking about the Cheyenne Mountain complex. Of course, that one belongs to us, but there's another one—a much smaller one—tucked neatly into the very same mountains Brown and his team of—whatever they were—ran to for cover after the debacle in Red Deer. That subterranean hidey-hole belongs to the Chinese Ministry of State Security. We think the Chinese knew their real mission would be discovered in Red Deer, so they were excavating their scaled-down version of Cheyenne Mountain in the Canadian Rockies near a place called White Goat Park."

Singer stuck a finger in the air. "How far is that from Red Deer?"

"About a hundred and thirty miles," Skipper said. "But the distance isn't the important thing. What's meaningful is that their new, mostly hidden observatory is on the same line of latitude as the former Red Deer facility. That means they can still accomplish the same mission as they did in their previous facility simply by adding a basic calculation to their observations."

Mongo spoke up again. "Yeah, of course. All they would have to do is factor in the—"

Clark interrupted. "So help me, Mongo. If you keep talking, I'm going to shoot you in the kneecaps."

The big man covered his knees with his island-sized hands and shut up.

Brown took the floor. "I'm not saying you're wrong, but . . . well, okay. I am saying you're wrong. Once the Canadian government gave the Chinese permission and protection in Red Deer, they opened back up and continued their day-to-day as usual."

Skipper smiled. "That's exactly what they *want* you to believe. A skeleton crew of make-believe Chinese weather observers shows up every day at the Red Deer facility, but they go inside and play Risk or whatever fake Chinese weather observers play. I assure you they're doing nothing meaningful in that building."

Brown argued. "But it's a high-security facility with around-the-clock, heavily armed guards, dogs, and extremely high-tech anti-invasion fencing and barriers. They're definitely guarding something behind those walls."

Skipper nodded. "Yes, they're guarding a secret, and that secret is . . . there's nothing there to guard. The real work is being done over a hundred miles west from a long way beneath the mountains."

Clark slid to the edge of his seat. "Thank you, Skipper. I think that's enough for now. Let's get back to the initial reason we're all here. Mr. Brown, go ahead and tell us exactly what you wanted us to do when you came here to find us."

Brown stuck the tip of his index finger to the top of the ice cube in his glass and gave it a twirl. "The truth is, what I wanted you to do would've resulted in exactly the same thing as my first attempt. We likely would've gotten ourselves into one hell of a gunfight and left with nothing to show for it."

"Yep, that's right," Clark said. "So, maybe it's time for you to change your opinion of my—I mean Chase's—team. We're not quite the idiots you recently believed us to be. You wanted us to raid a nearly empty building with a handful of fake weathermen inside, and probably get shot up doing it. Now that we know the truth about what's going on in Alberta, do you have a new mission in mind?"

Brown nodded slowly. "Same mission, different longitude."

"I thought so," Clark said. "And how many more of these little cleanup jobs do you have in mind?"

Brown sighed. "Just this one. The rest are lost causes, and it's too late to do anything about them."

Clark bit the corner of his upper lip. "Somehow, I don't think that's the whole truth, but I'll let you get away with it for now. Here's what's going to happen next. Chase is going to discuss the potential mission with his team. If they decide the potential gain is worth the risk, they'll ask me to send it up the chain. If I agree, the Board will review the potential action and either authorize the mission or shoot it down. If they shoot it down, we're done. There's no appeal, and there's no chance of us going rogue on an unauthorized mission. If they approve it, we move quickly and decisively. We'll conduct the mission with only slightly higher-than-necessary force and restore your good name with the Board, and maybe, just maybe, give you a few nights of better sleep with one of your dangling demons vanquished. Any questions?"

Brown stared down through the golden whiskey in his tumbler, pulled it to his lips, and swallowed the remaining ounce. "When you make your decision, you can find me at the Sand Dollar, room three thirty-one."

In unison, six voices said, "We know."

Chapter 8
Skills and Scars

"I guess it's time to huddle up," I said. "Let's start with Skipper. She knows more about our target than the rest of us combined."

In a show of rare disconnection from technology, Skipper closed her laptop and turned to face the team. "It's stupid."

"What's stupid?" I asked.

"The whole idea of invading a Chinese installation inside a sovereign country. There's no chance the Board would authorize it in the first place. If they did, there's no way we can do it without getting busted."

Hunter said, "I'm not quivering in fear at the thought of getting caught by the fierce Canadians."

"That's not the point," Skipper said. "It's not a matter of them catching, capturing, and imprisoning us. It's a matter of conducting an armed raid in somebody else's country on a facility that's been promised protection from the host nation. We're butting heads against a status of forces agreement. That's international law —not a speeding ticket from the Mounties."

I turned to my handler. "Clark, what do you think?"

"I think Skipper's right. It's not *if* we get caught. It's *when* we get caught. Who's going to clean up the mess we make while cleaning up the mess the last guys made?"

I crushed a piece of ice between my molars. "Are you certain this can't be done without getting caught?"

"Certain? No," Skipper said. "But the probability of getting busted is well into the ninetieth percentile."

I shot looks between Hunter, Singer, and Mongo. All three of them were putting on grins that said, "I like those odds."

I joined my teammates in their glee. "I'll take ten percent odds any day of the week, and twice on a day in Canada."

Skipper shook her head. "No, Chase. It's not a ninety percent chance of getting caught. I said it in the high ninetieth percentile, like ninety-eight percent."

"So, you're saying there's a two-percent chance of success?"

"Definitely not," she said. "There's a one hundred percent certainty you guys will get in and back out with the intel. The ninety-eight percent comes into play when you try to get out of there."

A quick glance at Clark revealed an almost imperceptible nod, so I asked, "Who says we have to leave right away? Why can't we stay for a shift change or two and maybe make some friends?"

One by one, my team each raised a hand, and even Disco, the new guy, caught on. Instead of a protest to our obvious insanity, our chief pilot and newly minted gunfighter chuckled and sent his hand into the air with everyone else's.

Skipper declared, "You guys are insane."

Clark pulled his phone from his cargo pocket. "I'll make the call."

Skipper turned back to her laptop and disappeared into the keyboard. The rest of us sat in silence, our eyes cast toward Clark as he detailed the mission. I'd never been privy to one of his upward briefings, but nothing about his phrasing or tone implied a request.

"I'm deploying Chase and his team to Alberta to complete the mission the Montana team dropped the ball on. The initial budget is three million with thirty-percent reserve. Expect no more than ten days lead, ten action, and ten recovery. Any questions?"

I found myself wishing I could hear the voices from the other end of the line, but Clark sat in silence wearing a look of utter boredom. When the questions had apparently ended, my handler said, "There's one additional element. I'm briefing in Al Brown. He'll be an advisor and analyst on the mission, but he won't be on the ground."

Thirty seconds of something came from the other end, and Clark pocketed his phone. "They're still talking, but when they figure out I hung up, they'll approve the mission."

"Is that really how it works?" I asked. "You call them up, tell them what we're going to do, and then you hang up?"

He cocked his head. "That's how my dad did it, so if it worked for him, why reinvent the mousetrap?"

I palmed my forehead. "I'm going to make a list of common sayings for you to study. You're the world's worst at clichés."

He snapped and pointed. "And that's where the rubber meets the immovable object."

I shook off his verbal incompetence. "I guess it's time to go have a cocktail with our new friend, huh?"

Penny had been waiting on the trampoline at *Aegis*'s bow. As badly as I wanted her to be involved in every aspect of my life, there would always be information she simply couldn't know. I left the main salon and climbed from the cockpit onto the starboard hull. The lines were secured in a fashion that would make a career Navy man proud. Penny lay on her back with her eyes closed and rolling her head in time with the reggae beat wafting through the marina. I tucked my arms, spun on a heel, and fell onto the trampoline beside her.

Without opening her eyes, she laid her hand in mine. "Is the secret squirrel meeting finally over?"

"It is," I sighed.

She whispered, "When?"

"A week or so. Do you want to hear about it?"

She rolled over and nuzzled her chin into my shoulder. "Can you tell me?"

"I can tell you most of it."

She let out a soft sound as if savoring the last bite of something delicious, and I took that to mean she wanted to hear my story. I explained what had happened in Canada with Al Brown's team and how somebody had to clean up the scraps.

"Does it have to be you?"

"It does," I said. "We're the best-equipped team to pull it off without casualties."

She groaned. "Call it what it is, Chase. *Casualty* is just another word for somebody going in but never coming back out."

I explained the operation, what was at stake, and how we planned to pull it off.

"How much does it pay?" she asked.

I pulled her tightly against me. "I don't know. Probably nothing. We're not doing it for the money. We're doing it because American missile defense data is being funneled to the Chinese from Canadian soil."

"Have you ever done it for the money?"

I let her question roll around in my head. "No, I guess I haven't. I'm sure guys who've been day-wage contractors like Singer and Mongo may have done it because it's the only work they could find. There's not a lot of ads for combat-hardened warriors in the Sunday paper. Guys like that developed skills and scars under Uncle Sam's flag, and for some of them, it's all they know how to do."

"That's just one of the gazillion reasons I love you, Chase Fulton. Who goes gallivanting off into Canada to break into a Chinese spy facility just because it's the right thing to do?"

"And that's just one of the infinite number of reasons I love you. You accept what I am and love me in spite of it."

"No. I'd never love you *in spite of* what you are, but I love you to pieces *because* of what you are."

I pulled her even closer and let my body sway with hers as the sound of the music continued its dance on the Bahamian breeze.

After two or three more songs, she said, "Sometimes I wish I were Anya."

I pushed her away, leaned back, and stared at the woman I loved more than anyone else on the planet. "What?"

"I mean it," she said. "She's been through the training, and no matter what I dislike about her, she's a real badass. I'm kinda envious of that. If I were like her, and I'd been through the training, I could go with you on these missions that scare the crap out of me. They scare me because I don't know what's happening when you're in the field. And not knowing is the worst part. I dream up all sorts of terrible thoughts while you're gone."

"You got to listen in to the Montana mission from the ops center with Skipper, so now you have a better understanding of what it's like when we go to work."

She chuckled. "Is that supposed to make me feel better? Every member of the team—except for Disco—got shot up, beat up, blown up, and every other bad 'up' I can think of. If anything, that peek behind the curtain only made me worry more."

"We've had this talk before," I said. "Do you want me to quit?"

She took my hand and pulled herself back into my arms. "No, silly. I'd never ask that of you. I just want you to know what I'm feeling. That's all. I'm one hundred percent on board, and I'm proud to be the wife of a man like you. I don't want you to think

I'd ever want anyone else. Besides, anyone else would bore me to death. Life with you is never dull. That's for sure."

I kissed her forehead. "I'm glad you're not like Anya. Although . . ." I cast my eyes into the endless blue sky as if searching for my next line.

Penny slapped my chest a lot harder than I deserved. "Chase Fulton, don't you dare finish that sentence. I may not be a trained assassin, but that doesn't mean I won't gut you like pig in your sleep."

I pulled her body across mine and tossed her across the trampoline. She landed gently, rolled to her feet, and assumed her best fighting stance.

I waved her off. "Ooh, now I'm really scared."

She jumped up and down on the netting. "You'd better be, Secret Agent Man. I could be your worst nightmare."

I hopped to my feet. "Oh, you spend plenty of times in my dreams, but never my nightmares. Come on . . . Let's motor over to the Sand Dollar. We've got a former action guy to brief."

We cast off the bowline and spring line on our way to the cockpit, and she had the engines warming up in no time. As *Aegis*'s de facto captain, she gave one prolonged blast on the horn followed by three short blasts—the international signal for leaving the dock and operating in reverse propulsion.

I tossed the stern line ashore and reported, "All lines clear!"

Penny backed us from our rented slip and brought the boat through one hundred eighty degrees as if her twenty tons were a child's toy in a bathtub. There was something about her ease at the helm that I loved to watch.

A few minutes later, Penny laid *Aegis* alongside the dock at the Sand Dollar resort where Al Brown leaned against a piling as if waiting for his date for the prom.

Brown stepped from his perch and lifted a line from the dock. "Are you tying up or picking me up?"

"Hop aboard," I said over the sound of the engines.

He let the line fall back to the dock and held out his prosthetic leg. "*Hop* aboard? Is that some kind of amputee humor?"

I ignored his jab and offered a hand. He slapped it away and leapt from the dock, landing like a cat on *Aegis*'s sugar scoop boarding stairs.

"I suppose there's only two ways this is going to go," he said. "One, you've called me aboard to tell me the good news that the Board approved the mission and we're ready to start the mission planning. Or, two, you're taking me somewhere deep and knocking me over the head to eliminate the only surviving witness to the debacle in Canada."

"Actually," I said, "it's option three."

"Hmm . . . I'm not sure I'm smart enough to come up with a third option. Care to share it with an old, worn-out warrior?"

Clark, Singer, and Mongo emerged from the main salon, and the sniper put a tumbler in Brown's hand.

"We've come to celebrate," I said. "We'll plan tomorrow, but tonight, we finish off a good bottle of Pappy and tell a few semi-true war stories."

Chapter 9
The Tears of a Warrior

Al Brown, former Green Beret, civilian covert operative, recipient of multiple Purple Hearts and one Distinguished Service Medal, stood in the cockpit of my beloved catamaran and pressed his eyes closed in what could have only been a wasted effort to dam up the flow of tears welling up inside.

A warrior's tears are almost invisible, but they come. They come when no one is listening, when no one can hear, and when no one can call them weakness. Behind the tortured, scarred, battered armor the warrior wears as his skin, lies the endless beating heart of freedom surrounded by the sinewy muscle of a body that's been asked to do the things men should never have to do. Warriors don't tear the hearts from the chests of their enemies because of the bloodlust of hatred for their foe. The warrior presses the trigger and plunges the blade because the enemy before him has vowed to destroy the family, the home, or the country the warrior loves more than he loves the very breath within his own chest. The warrior kills not out of hatred of his enemy, but out of boundless love for those who cannot stand and fight for themselves. He fights and kills and continues to fight even as the pain he's forced to suppress claws at his eternal soul with talons like razors that would destroy a lesser man. When the warrior fights, he fights with his brothers at his side and a fire within that neither fear nor pain can quench. But when a warrior cries, he cries alone.

My priest, shaman, spiritual guide, and sniper laid an arm around the warrior standing before us, and every member of my team followed suit.

Singer whispered, "You're not alone, my brother. You didn't fail. You simply took the wrong team into a battle they wouldn't win." The sniper pressed his palm against Brown's chest. "I watched my former team leader, Rodney "Snake" Blanchard, devour himself when he believed he'd failed. Snake didn't fail the team. The team failed Snake. When we should've carried him, he fell beneath the weight of trying to carry all of us. The men you see surrounding you will never let that happen to one of our brothers again."

Brown stared skyward and swallowed the lump in his throat. "I was going with or without you."

"Yeah, we know," Singer said. "But that's the thing about men like us. We don't have to lean into the driving rain and incoming fire by ourselves. That's what brothers are for."

The unmistakable sound of crystal tumblers touching rims lightened the mood and changed the tone.

I settled into a cushion on the starboard side. "Tell us about what happened to your leg."

Brown held out his prosthetic and gave it a tap with the base of his glass. "There's nothing much to tell, but I like to say that it got blown off by an IUD and then see how many people let me get away with calling a roadside bomb a 'birth control device.'"

"That's cute," I said. "But what really happened?"

He gave his tumbler a swirl and savored another sip as the memory of the incident apparently washed over him. "It was just one more bad day in a long string of bad days. We were trying to teach some goat herders how to act like soldiers in the mountains of Afghanistan, northeast of Kandahar. Some friendly neighborhood Taliban thought it would be fun to interrupt our class. My goat herders turned gunmen gave them a bellyful of fight they weren't expecting, and they turned to run. Running from Green Berets rarely ends well. My A-team jumped into the only vehicles we had—four hoopties they called trucks—and took off after them. There were a couple of platoons of Marines conveniently located near a mudhole called Abe Istada. Our commo sergeant gave them a call and invited them to come out and play with us and the Taliban. Being the nice, friendly Marines they were, they accepted our invitation."

Everyone leaned in, smitten with Brown's story.

He continued. "What we weren't expecting was Taliban reinforcements. They had some old Soviet artillery pieces welded to the backs of trucks. They weren't very good shots, but with artillery, precision isn't always required. It turned into a little more than a scrimmage. When we discovered we'd stolen more gold bars than we could swim with, our combat controller called in a few of his friends to rain down hell from above, but they weren't as quick to join the fight as the Marines were. It took them fifteen minutes to get overhead, but it felt like hours. We got a bunch of Marines hurt and killed that day and lost a good medic from our team. I lost the leg and turned in my green active-duty ID card for a blue retired one. And just like Forrest Gump, that's all I've got to say about that."

Clark chewed on his bottom lip and bowed his head.

I asked, "Are you okay?"

He nodded. "Yeah, I'm all right. The medic who died that day was a kid I recruited into SF. I knew him pretty well."

Brown gave Clark a nod. "You can't carry them with you, brother. They get too heavy."

Clark took a long breath and blew it into the evening air. "You're right, but it's never easy. I thought tonight was supposed to be cocktails and lies, not group therapy."

I raised my glass. "To the fallen . . . and to those still standing."

We drank, and the mood shifted almost audibly.

"You're not seriously thinking of going outside the wire with us on this one, are you, Brown?"

He gazed around the cockpit at the faces of my team, obviously assessing as he went. "I'm an old man with one borrowed kidney. As much as I want to put my boots on the ground, I'd only slow you down."

Clark said, "I know the feeling. I broke my back on the Khyber Pass, and Chase had to pull my butt off the mountain. Just when I thought I was healing up, some kind of infection set in, and they had to cut me open and scrape out my spine. My ego thinks I'm still twenty-two and bulletproof, but my body says otherwise."

"That was you?" Brown asked.

Clark nodded. "That was all of us. We blew a raid on an ammo train and lost a helo pilot. Singer broke his leg, and Chase hauled us off the mountain in a borrowed Russian Hip with a Tajiki pilot and a Defense Intelligence operator."

Brown said, "Those DIA guys are tougher than they look."

I chuckled. "This one certainly was. *She* looked like a beauty queen but fought like a honey badger."

Brown raised his eyebrows. "Oh, really? A female operator."

"Yep. I'd take her down range with me any day. She's a crack shot and completely fearless."

"I've never worked with female operators," he said.

To my surprise, Penny spoke up. "If you think Bimini the DIA chick was something, you should meet Anya, our Russian."

Brown turned to me with inquisition in his eyes. "*Your* Russian?"

I glanced between him and Penny, uncertain how much praise I should pour out on *our* Russian. Discretion being the better part of valor, I played it safe. "She's not technically *our* Russian. She's a former SVR officer who defected to the U.S."

"A sparrow?" Brown asked.

"Not exactly," I said. "She's been through Sparrow School, but first and foremost, she's a bladed weapons assassin."

He smiled. "Interesting. I think I'd like to meet her."

Penny said, "Oh, you'd definitely like to meet her, just like every other man on Earth, but you don't want to get tangled up with her."

"That's for sure," I said. "I'd take one Bimini over a thousand Anyas."

Brown waved a finger back and forth between Penny and me. "I get the feeling there's more to the story of Anya than either of you are admitting."

I opened my mouth to speak, but Penny held up her left hand and waggled her wedding band. "Oh, there's a lot more to the story, but Chase picked me, so I win."

Desperate to change the subject, I stepped to the helm. "I've got an idea. Let's get out of this shallow water. I want to show you something."

I took the helm and motored out from the protected water behind the islands. The Bahama Bank is essentially a mountaintop in the enormous valley that is the North Atlantic. On the outside, the banks slope off into thousands of feet of water in just a few miles. The deep-water ocean is an entirely different animal than the shallow waters of The Bahamas.

Penny took the opportunity to show off her nautical prowess a little. "Hey, Clark. Do you know the three elements that create a wave?"

Clark said, "Uh, water, wind . . . and something else."

He got a hearty chuckle from the peanut gallery before Penny said, "You're not entirely wrong. Wave height is determined by three things . . . Wind speed and direction, duration, and fetch."

"Fetch?" said Clark.

"Yes, fetch. That's the distance the wave has spent in its creation. Out here in the Atlantic, waves sometimes form off the coast of western Africa and have thousands of miles of fetch to build height and energy."

Clark turned to Mongo. "Did you know that?"

The big man nodded. "Yes, Clark. Everybody knows that."

Clark tapped at his temple. "No, Mongo. Nobody knows stuff like that, and nobody *needs* to know stuff like that. I leave room in my brain for useful stuff and throw away the meaningless garbage."

Mongo pulled a piece of ice from his tumbler and tossed it at Clark. "I agree that there's a lot of empty space in that head of yours."

Clark swatted the ice cube from the air. "And now you know why."

I pointed *Aegis*'s bow at the North Pole and pulled the throttles to idle. After a few minutes of fine-tuning, I checked my watch and pointed toward the western horizon. "If my timing is right, this is going to be something you'll never forget."

Penny looked up at me. "What are you doing, Chase?"

I smiled and pointed westward again. "You'll see. Just watch."

She narrowed her eyes and lingered a moment before turning to the west like everyone else.

The orange orb of the sun kissed the blue Atlantic and sank across the horizon with breathtaking oranges, browns, and blues filling the sky. A round of satisfied oohs and ahs rose from my passengers.

"That's only half of the show," I said. "Now look over the starboard rail."

Everyone turned to face the east as the full moon broke the horizon. The moon and sun moved in concordance and opposition. As our closest star kissed the world good night, our lunar lantern cast her yellow-white light across the waves.

Penny stood and wrapped her arms around me. "Thank you for choosing me."

I smiled and pointed toward the sky. "I didn't choose you. You were a gift from the heavens, and only a fool would turn down such a gift."

She rose to her tiptoes and gave me a gentle kiss. "Maybe you should be the writer, and I should be the spy."

Everyone on the boat roared, "We're not spies."

Chapter 10
Displaced Land Mammals

Penny reclaimed the helm after we dropped Al Brown off at the Sand Dollar and motored back to our resort to break the bad news to the rest of our caravan. I'd never known anyone who handled a heavy boat with more finesse than my wife, but when she laid us alongside the dock, it felt as if a drunken monkey was at the helm.

I shot a look into the cockpit to make sure someone was actually at the wheel and saw Penny wrestling with the controls.

"Is everything all right?"

"No! Everything is *not* all right," she said as she forced the two engine cutoffs into position.

The diesels hummed to a stop, but there was still plenty of work to do getting *Aegis* centered in her slip and tied down. Clark, Mongo, and I won the battle and soon had the boat firmly attached to the dock.

I leapt into the cockpit to find Penny donning a mask, fins, and snorkel.

"What happened?" I said.

She pulled her hair into a quick ponytail, tucked it beneath her mast strap, and flipped on the underwater lights. "I don't know, but something's not right. I'm going in to check the props. Check the engine rooms for water. I don't know how bad this is yet."

Mongo leaned into the cockpit. "What's going on, Chase?"

"It's something mechanical," I said. "We may've picked up some debris with the props or rudders. Check the portside engine room. I'm going starboard."

Tatiana's youthful, Russian-accented tone brought an innocence to the anxiety hanging in the air. "Hey! You're back. Where have you been?"

Mongo turned to the girl. "Hey, *milyy*. Stay on the dock for right now. Something's wrong with the boat. I'll be back in a minute."

The playful name, *milyy*, Russian for *darling*, caught my ear, and I spun to face the biggest man I knew. "She's really got you wrapped around her finger, doesn't she?"

Mongo smiled and shrugged. "She's a sweet kid, and she's had a rough go of things."

I looked past him to see Irina trotting down the dock toward her daughter.

"What about her mom? Is she a sweet kid, too, or is she your *Irinechka*?"

He didn't offer an answer, but the look on his reddening face said I'd hit the nail on the head.

I scampered into the starboard engine room to find everything perfectly dry and exactly where it should be. The heat from the engine made the cramped space uncomfortable, but there was no sign of any failure. I sealed the engine room and opened the square plexiglass hatch designed to be used as a means of escape from the boat if she were to ever find herself upside down.

The murky water of the marina gave the underwater lighting a ghostlike appearance but made it impossible to see beyond the surface. A few of Penny's exhaled bubbles broke the calm surface a few feet away, and I paused to wait for her to come up.

After a minute or so, I closed the hatch and climbed the steps back to the main salon just as Mongo emerged from the port side.

"How's it look down there?" I asked.

"Looks fine. Everything is shipshape."

We turned for the cockpit just as Penny rose from the water astern. Under normal circumstances, there are few things I enjoy more than watching my beautiful wife climb the boarding stairs with salt water cascading from her hair, but the look on her face was like nothing I'd ever seen.

"What is it?" I demanded.

She spat the snorkel from her lips and took in several gasping breaths. "Chase . . . You've got to see . . ."

Without giving her time to explain further, I pulled the dive mask from her hand, plucked my wallet from my pocket, threw it on the deck, and stepped off the boat into the shallow water. Without fins, I was reduced to a clumsy land mammal in the sea, barely able to propel myself through the water with my clunky boots. The visibility below the surface was barely better than from above, but I grabbed the portside rudder and pulled myself toward the propellers.

Remembering the mortified look on Penny's face, I tried to prepare myself for what I was about to encounter. I tried to imagine what Penny might have seen. The worst thing I could predict was a dolphin trapped in a piece of fishing net and pulled into one of the props. I didn't look forward to the gruesome task of removing the net and remains, but the anxiety I'd felt at the prospect of my boat being damaged below the waterline waned as I pulled myself farther beneath my floating home.

The shadowy form of the portside propeller and shaft came into blurry view, and I ran my hand across its surface. There was no damage to the shaft or prop and no sign of netting or victims of the spinning blades. My lungs gave me a jab, reminding me of my vulnerable status as an air-breathing mammal beneath a boat. I raised a hand and followed the elegant curve of the portside hull until I surfaced beneath the cockpit.

I rewarded myself with several long, fresh breaths before descending along the smooth surface of the starboard hull. The deeper I dove, the less benefit the hull-mounted, underwater lights provided. I wasn't looking forward to plunging my hand into an unknown clump of animal carcass, so I blinked rapidly in hopes of improving my night vision. No shredded net or filet-o-fish came into view as I reached the propeller. Instead, a mass of twisted rope appeared, completely fouling the shaft and propeller. The rope led from its winding in two directions: one angled downward and toward the bow, and the other straight down toward the bottom only a few feet away.

I gripped the rope heading straight for the bottom and gave it a tug. Whatever was attached to the other end didn't offer to make an ascent toward me; instead, the force propelled me downward about three feet. Making a mental inventory of my situation, I found my lungs well oxygenated, my vision poor but better than blind, and my orientation beneath the boat perfectly safe. I gave the rope another tug and produced the same results. The object at the end of the rope remained relatively stationary, and I descended another few feet. Another assessment revealed nothing had changed except my vision. I was now in total darkness, pulling on a rope that was holding an unknown weighty object.

My lungs weren't burning, so I gave one final pull and extended my right hand down the rope until I discovered something hard, rectangular, and rough. Feeling a common object in pitch-black water half a dozen feet beneath the surface plays bizarre tricks on the mind, and my mind was not exempt from that phenomenon. Calling on what little sanity I possessed, I lunged both hands toward the unknown object and discovered there were three objects. They all felt identical with sharp edges and coarse surfaces. I let my hands play across them like an octopus exploring a rock she'd never seen before, and then it hit me. The objects weren't rocks to be explored by some eight-legged sea creature. They were common concrete blocks tied together to form a crude anchor.

Relieved, I reached over my head, gripped the rope, and pulled myself back toward the surface. My lungs insisted on a refill. I carefully avoided the sharp blades of the prop and let myself surface. A few deep breaths satisfied my lungs' demands, and I pushed myself back beneath the starboard hull.

Back at the prop shaft, I felt for the rope and found it quickly. Knowing exactly what one end held, I was determined to solve the mystery of what waited at the other end of the line. A tug on the rope resulted in dramatically dissimilar results than pulling on the cinder block end had given. Instead of resisting my pull and sending me deeper into the water, the object at the other end of the rope moved slowly toward me. It didn't appear particularly heavy, but it apparently had enough surface area to produce some resistance as it slid through the water.

I shot a look overhead and identified two lights in the hull. I knew where I was, and I had plenty of air in my lungs to continue my investigation. Instead of pulling in long, singular lunges, I pulled the object toward me with hand-over-hand motions on the rope. As the object drew ever closer, I watched the form slowly take shape. It was a long object, bulbous in the middle and tapering to narrow ends. The rope I was pulling was clearly attached to one of the ends of the object, leaving the other end to waggle through the water like a six-foot-long fishing lure. Perhaps I was seeing Penny's now-deceased dolphin.

Whatever it was, the object drifted with ease toward me and the hull lights. I surrendered the rope with my right hand and pulled my knife from the right pocket of my cargo shorts. A press of the

button set the switchblade in motion. Once I had positively identified the object tied to the collection of blocks, I would begin the
long task of cutting it free from my prop shaft. But as the bound
object came into focus only inches from my mask, the terrified
look on Penny's face suddenly made sense.

In an instinctual reaction, I shoved both hands toward the
slowly rising form of a decaying human body. The open, razor-
sharp blade of my knife easily pierced the softened flesh and sent
particles in every direction, making the already murky environment even more unwelcoming.

Regaining my composure, I rolled toward the surface and extended my hand. Driving my head into the hull of my boat would
likely result in a pair of corpses in the water, and that was not an
outcome I was interested in experiencing.

My hand collided with the hull much harder than I'd planned,
and I braced for the impact, but thankfully, it didn't come. When
I surfaced between the hulls, my lungs convulsed, and I sucked in
air in short, choppy bursts until I finally got my breathing under
control and swam to *Aegis*'s stern. I pulled myself onto the bottom
boarding step and looked up to find Mongo's enormous hand
reaching toward me.

I pushed him away. "Get Tatiana out of here, and call the authorities!"

Chapter 11

A Proper Mess

Marvin "Mongo" Malloy scooped Tatiana into his massive arms and hit the dock in a run. Clark pressed a series of buttons and stuck his satellite phone to his ear.

Penny stepped toward me with a towel and a terrified expression still lingering on her otherwise flawless face. "I assume you saw it."

I pulled the towel from her hand and dried my face and hair. "Yeah, I saw it."

She squinted against her own disgust at what she'd discovered. "So, it was a body . . . right?"

I pulled off my shirt and wrapped the towel around my shoulders. "It is a body, but I don't know any more than that. We'll have to wait for the police. Do you know anything about Bahamian law?"

"I know we're not allowed to have guns in our possession, but I've never needed to know the details of having a dead body dragging beneath our boat."

I pulled her close to me. "It's okay. Whoever that is down there, we had nothing to do with him, so we have nothing to worry about from the police."

She looked up at me, her hair still dripping wet. "So, it's a man?"

I shrugged. "I don't know for sure. I didn't examine the body."

She groaned. "You said *him*, so I thought you might have . . ."

"No, I misspoke. I should've said *them* instead of *him*, but we'll know soon enough. Here comes the first wave of uniforms."

A pair of Royal Bahamian Police officers dressed in the formal black dress uniform with leather belts strapped diagonally across their chests led the procession with Mongo and two other men dressed in street clothes.

The first of the officers came to a halt two strides from *Aegis*'s starboard side. "Excuse me, sir. We received notification of an incident hereabouts. May we come aboard?"

Penny's reminder of the prohibition against firearms on the islands flashed through my head, so I said, "The incident isn't aboard my boat. It's beneath it."

Confusion overtook both officers, and the older of the two said, "What do you mean, sir?"

Before I could answer, a sweat-covered man stepped from the dock onto my boarding stairs. "I am Chief Inspector Barton. Are you Mister Fulton?"

I turned to face the man. "I didn't give you permission to come aboard, Chief Inspector. As I was telling—"

He cut me off. "I do not need your permission to board your boat on my island, Mister Fulton. You are not inside the United States of America anymore. You are in The Bahamas, and thereby, bound by Bahamian law."

I turned to Penny and whispered, "Find us a lawyer."

She disappeared into the interior, and the inspector watched her like a hawk. "Where is she going?"

He took a step toward the main salon, and I put a hand in the center of his chest.

He stared down at my hand at the same instant the two uniformed officers leapt aboard and flanked me, twisting both of my arms behind my back.

I shot a look at Clark to call him off. The last thing we needed was him throwing two Bahamian cops into the ocean with a dead body. He read the look in my eyes but stayed close just in case the local cops wanted to turn it into something a little rougher.

I didn't put up a fight. "Chief Inspector, I'm no threat. If you'll have your men unhand me, I'll tell you what's going on."

Barton gave both officers a barely visible nod, and they released me. They did, however, stay close by my side—I assumed so they could control me if I got handsy with their boss again.

"Inspector Barton," I said, "I've discovered what I believe to be a dead body beneath my boat. It's bound by a length of rope to at least three cinder blocks. The rope fouled my prop shaft, so I went in the water to check it out."

Barton turned to the older of the two uniformed officers and issued instructions in Bahamian patois that could've been Greek as far as I was concerned. The officer pulled a radio from his belt and keyed the mic. His broadcast sounded equally meaningless, but what came back through the radio's speaker rendered the prior gibberish meaningless.

"Da divahs be comin' ri'tway, mon."

As if I were the team's interpreter, I turned and said, "They're sending divers."

Clark rolled his eyes. "Thank God we've got you, Lieutenant Obvious. We'd have never figured that one out."

I threw my dripping shirt at him. "Thanks for the demotion."

Chief Inspector Barton cleared his throat and pulled a notepad from his pocket. "I have some questions, Mr. Fulton."

I motioned toward the stern settee. "Of course. Have a seat."

He made eye contact with the two officers and cast his eyes up the marina dock. Without a word, he set a pair of guards and secured the landside perimeter. I was impressed, but the water offered a bit more of a conundrum when it came to preventing nosey boaters from drifting by. Or so I thought . . .

By the time my butt hit the cushion, a pair of Bahamian Royal Police patrol boats roared into the marina, and their pilots positioned them fifty feet off each of my stern quarters. Inspector Barton wasn't riding in his first rodeo.

"Mr. Fulton," he began. "Give to me your full name, date of birth, country of citizenship, and make sure you have a passport to support your answer."

Penny came through the sliding door from the main salon before I could answer Barton's opening volley. "Chase, wait!"

Barton and I looked up simultaneously.

The inspector said, "I will need your information as well, madam."

Instead of an answer, Penny extended a hand, offering a pair of passports and a black leather wallet to Barton.

He took the offered items, laid them on the seat beside him, and poised his pen, once again, above his waiting pad. With raised eyebrows, he turned back to me and waited for my answers.

"My name is Chase Daniel Fulton, and I was born—"

Penny laid a hand on my shoulder. "Chase, wait."

She turned her attention to Barton. "Sir, we are represented by counsel."

Barton looked up. "American barristers may not practice law in da Bahamas, madam?"

"We have Bahamian counsel, sir, and he is on his way."

"And who would dis Bahamian counsel of yours be?"

"Sir Edwin Castlebury of Castlebury Chambers, and he has advised us to provide documentary evidence of our identity but nothing further until he arrives."

Barton lowered an eyebrow and glared at Penny. "Madam, I'm afraid Sir Edwin Castlebury da costliest solicitor on da islands, and he does not accept new clients over da telephone at dis hour."

Penny smiled the smile that means she knows something no one else knows, then she pointed toward our passports.

Barton huffed and lifted my passport, propped it open with the heel of his hand, and scratched several lines on his pad. He repeated the process with Penny's passport, and then handed them back. When he lifted the black wallet with the embossed seal of the United States Secret Service on the exterior, he closed his eyes and let out a barely audible chuckle. He opened the cred-pack and closed his notepad. "Why didn't you lead with dis, Supervisory Special Agent Fulton?"

"Because I'm here on vacation with my friends and family."

He tossed the credentials to me and stared into the sky for a long moment. "In dis case, you definitely do not need Sir Edwin Castlebury. You and I can talk now as colleagues, don't you see?"

A flurry of activity on the dock caught Barton's attention, so I followed his gaze to a group of men jogging down the dock, rolling a cart behind them. The missing bulbs from every other overhead light on the dock made it impossible to see the contents of the cart, but Barton didn't appear concerned.

As the wagon train continued ever closer, the inspector said, "Before da divahs go into da water, did you disturb da body in any way before you phoned da police?"

"No," I said in haste, but then paused. "Well, I suppose we disturbed it by having the rope fouled around our prop shaft."

He took on a stern, authoritative look. "Did you or da misses mutilate da body in any way?"

"Mutilate?" I recoiled. "No, we didn't mutilate the body. What kind of question is that?"

He said, "What da divahs find, then, it will be da body undisturbed and unmutilated other den the condition it be in before you discovered it, yes?"

"Yeah, it'll be just like we found it."

"Thank you, Special Agent Fulton. I need for you to stay here to witness da body coming from da water."

By the time Barton and I finished our conversation, the men on the dock had emptied the cart, set up half a dozen bright lights, and two divers were geared up and ready to hit the water. The inspector stepped from the boarding stairs and onto the waiting dock. He gave instructions to the divers in the dialect I'd never understand and pressed a cell phone to his ear. The two divers powered up their underwater torches, checked their consoles, and stepped from the dock.

I left the subsurface lights on, hoping what little light they provided might be enough to help the divers recover the remains in relatively good condition. I played the scene over in my head until I could either remember what I saw in detail, or my brain had time to make something up that convinced me I remembered the details.

The body was definitely a man. He was too big to be a female. I examined the cadre of black faces staring into the water and remembered that the body had been white . . . or at least appeared to be.

Why would a body be tied to three cinder blocks, in the Eleutheras, beneath my boat?

As I pondered that and a thousand other questions, the tell-tale sound of divers surfacing pulled me from my stupor.

One of the men spat his regulator from his mouth and pulled off his mask. "We have her, sir, but we can't pull her from da water without da board. She'll come apart, for sure."

Another man pulled a plastic backboard from the cart and slid it across the edge of the floating dock. The diver pulled his mask back in place and stuck his regulator into his mouth just as he and his partner disappeared again into the inky water.

It must have been only minutes, but it felt like days before the divers reemerged. Between them, they cradled the backboard with the bloated, disfigured body of a white female with long dark hair spread like the snakes of Medusa around her head. My stomach churned, and Penny turned away in disgust.

Four of the men from the dock stepped off the wooden platform and plunged into the water. They relieved the divers of the board and body and swam toward the nearby rocky embankment.

"Hand down anudder board, mon. Dere's anudder one down dere."

Someone slid a second backboard into the water, and soon, the pair of divers were making their way toward the rocks with the body of a man strapped to the board.

"This is just too weird," Clark said. "How do we get into stuff like this?"

"I don't know," I said, "but it's definitely weird. I can't believe I only saw one of the bodies down there. How could I have missed the second one?"

Clark said, "What kind of sick mind keeps searching for bodies after he finds one?"

"You've got a point."

He motioned toward the dock. "Here they come. Why are they bringing them out on the dock?"

Penny said, "They'll probably haul them away on one of those patrol boats. That's the only way out of here without causing a bigger scene than they already have."

The men carefully laid the bodies on the dock beneath the lights, and I couldn't resist taking a closer look. I stepped from the boat and stared down at the gruesome scene before me.

Chief Inspector Barton knelt between the bodies and examined both of them carefully. When he came to the upper body of the male victim, he paused and held out a hand toward one of the uniformed officers. "Give me your light."

The officer slapped a long, heavy flashlight into the inspector's hand. He pressed the button and leaned in close to the dead man's chest. Next, he stuck the light beneath his chin and retrieved a pair of rubber gloves from his back pocket. He carefully probed at the corpse until he slowly withdrew a long narrow object from the man's flesh. He held the object up to the light, and my heart sank.

Barton carefully turned the object in his hands, examining every inch of the black plastic handle and polished steel blade of the Benchmade switchblade I'd carried all over the world for the past several years.

Without hesitation, I said, "That's mine."

Barton spun on one knee and held the knife between us. "Dis is your knife?"

I nodded. "Yes, it's mine. I took it underwater with me to cut the rope from the prop shaft, and I must have—"

Chief Inspector Barton held up a finger, so I paused. He dropped the still-open knife into a plastic evidence bag and wiped the sweat from his brow. "Vacationing Special Agent Chase Fulton, I tink perhaps you need da services of Sir Edwin Castlebury after all." He turned to the pair of officers who'd escorted him onto the dock half an hour before. "Take Mr. Fulton into custody, and impound da boat."

Chapter 12
Who Are You?

I didn't resist when the two officers cautiously placed me in the crude restraints that apparently qualified as handcuffs on Eleuthera. While remaining relaxed, I surrendered to their temporary authority over me and turned to meet Clark's eyes.

I expected to see concern there, but instead, I found amusement and his patented crooked grin. He pressed an index finger to his lips in the universal signal to remain silent, regardless of possibly not having that right in the custody of the Bahamian Police.

I gave him an obedient nod, and he returned the waggling thumb and pinkie finger telling me to hang loose. That garnered a chuckle. Hanging loose in the custody of the Royal Bahamian Police Force wasn't how I'd planned to spend my evening . . . or next several days.

Just as the two officers flanked me and began to encourage me to join them on their evening walk, a white-haired, besuited, Bahamian man of perhaps seventy stepped directly in front of me and looked up as if inspecting me for some defect. "Sir, are you Chase Daniel Fulton?" His British accent made him sound as if he'd been sent over from central casting to play the role of some leftover servant of the Queen.

I shot a look back at Clark, and he returned his finger to his lips while he held his phone against his face.

The gentleman before me grunted in frustration. "I am Sir Edwin Castlebury, and if you are this Chase Daniel Fulton, I am your barrister. Have you been officially informed of the reason for your arrest?"

"No, sir," I said, still uncertain if Clark wanted me to remain silent, even with my own attorney.

Sir Edwin locked eyes with the younger of the police officers and demanded. "Are you the arresting officer of this citizen of the United States of America?"

"No, sir."

He then turned to face the older of the two. "And you, sir . . . Are *you* the arresting officer?"

"No, sir," came the officer's bored reply.

"Then I demand that the arresting officer be delivered this instant."

Barton stepped around my escorts and me and stood toe-to-toe with my attorney. "I'm Chief Inspector Barton, and I am the arresting officer, Sir Edwin."

Sir Edwin slid his wire-rimmed glasses up his hawklike nose. "I see. Perhaps in your unduly hasty rise to chief inspector, you were tardy on the day you were to have learned that every arrestee must be advised of the reason for his arrest in a timely fashion. Allow me to educate you, Chief Inspector, on the finer points of Bahamian law, since you are clearly ignorant of the most basic of human rights on these islands."

Barton scowled. "He's not been officially charged yet."

"So, am I to understand it has become the practice of the Royal Bahamian Police Force to shackle, chain, and escort foreign citizens to detention without official charges? If this is the case, perhaps I am the one who should be educated on the law. Is this your intention, Chief Inspector, to educate *me* on the law?"

Barton said, "It is my intention, Sir Edwin—"

The attorney cut him off. "I thought not. So, I demand he be unshackled at once, and he will receive your deepest apology for your ignorance of the law."

Barton rolled his eyes and turned to me. "Mr. . . . ."

I raised my chin. "That's Supervisory Special Agent Fulton."

"So you contend," Barton said. "Regardless, Chase Daniel Fulton, you are under arrest for the crime of desecration of a corpse."

The inspector turned back to Sir Edwin and placed a hand on his upper arm. "If you will kindly step aside, sir, I will be on my way with my prisoner."

Sir Edwin spread his feet against Barton's urging. "I will do no such thing. We are far from finished here. I shall have the name of the individual within the U.S. Consular Section who took your official notification of the arrest of an American citizen. Certainly, you made the required notification without delay, as the law demands."

"We've not officially taken Mr.—"

I cleared my throat in interruption, and Barton sighed. "We've not officially taken Special Agent Fulton into custody yet. He has not been processed into the . . ."

Sir Edwin made a sound that could've come from a bulldog. "My good man, shall I quote to you the definition of *custody* according to Bahamian law?"

Barton set his jaw in determination. "Step aside, Sir Edwin. You can speak to your client at the station."

Unfazed, Sir Edwin pulled his telephone from his leather satchel and dialed a number before handing the phone to Barton. "When the U.S ambassador answers, you will, as the law requires, inform him of the arrest of an American citizen with federal law enforcement credentials."

Instead of waiting for an answer, Barton thumbed the end button on the phone and tossed it back to Sir Edwin.

My attorney then pulled a micro-cassette recorder from his pouch and spoke into the microphone. "Chief Inspector Barton refused to notify the United States Embassy Consular Section of the arrest of an American Supervisory Special Agent of the Secret Service beneath the U.S. Department of Treasury. Further, Chief Inspector Barton demonstrated further contempt for the laws of The Bahamas and the rights of my client, Supervisory Special Agent Chase Daniel Fulton, by binding him in chains and relocating him against his will under the escort of two uniformed officers of the Royal Bahamian Police Force without proper notification of charges, and further demonstrated gross negligence of the lawful definition of custody during his outrageous overstepping of his supposed authority."

He thumbed the recorder's buttons and slid the device back into his pouch.

Barton ignored Sir Edwin and turned to a second pair of uniformed officers standing by at the edge of the dock. "Seize da boat into impound at once."

Sir Edwin leaned toward me and whispered, "How many people slept aboard your boat last night?"

"Four," I answered, unsure why that mattered.

"Were you one of the four?"

"No, sir."

The barrister stepped back and readdressed Barton. "Under whose authority are you seizing the home of at least four American citizens who are charged with no crime and are under no suspicion of any crime, Chief Inspector?"

Barton began to speak, but Sir Edwin raised a finger. "Speak with caution, Chief Inspector. One wrong answer here will likely leave you with the rank of reserve deputy constable when the sun rises in the morning."

Sweat beaded on the inspector's forehead. "Da boat is being impounded due to its use in the charged crime. Dis falls well within my authority, Edwin."

My attorney raised his eyebrows. "That is *Sir* Edwin to you, Constable. And do tell, soon-to-be-former Chief Inspector. I find myself hanging on your every word in your grand experiment of fiction this evening. We cannot wait to hear just how the home of at least four innocent Americans was used to desecrate a corpse."

Barton stuck a finger into my chest. "Your client jumped from dat boat and climbed back onto dat boat before and after desecrating da corpse."

Sir Edwin threw his hands into the air in a flourish. "Oh, by all that is holy, Chief Inspector, you must then impound this dock, and the sand of the beach, and the waters of the bay."

The inspector leaned into the barrister. "You'll forgive me, sir, but if you wish to continue this drama, you'll have to follow us to the station."

Reeling from the light brush from Chief Inspector Barton, Sir Edwin Castlebury staggered backward several steps, tossed his satchel to the dock, and fell backward into the water.

The two uniforms who'd been hanging onto my elbows as if their lives depended on their grip, released me and ran to the edge of the dock, kneeling with outstretched arms for the senior attorney.

Their concern for the barrister waned when compared to that of my partner, Stone W. Hunter. Hunter left *Aegis*'s bow in a perfect dive and disappeared beneath the black water. As everyone on the dock waited for Sir Edwin to surface, I relaxed knowing Hunter would soon emerge with the man in his arms.

I was not disappointed. The water parted, and Sir Edwin's head rose a foot above its surface. Seconds later, Hunter's face rose from the water. He drew a long breath, took an appraising look at his rescued victim, and confidently stroked toward the beach. Hunter helped the soaked man to his feet on the sandy slope and walked in locked step with him toward the wooden stairs back to the deck. A pair of younger men, each dressed similarly to Sir Edwin, waited at the top of the stairs, and I found the scene impossible to ignore.

Sir Edwin looked to the younger of the two men and asked, "Did you get that, son?"

The young man held up a small camera and smiled. "Yes, father. I captured every minute of it."

Sir Edwin motioned with a flourish toward the policemen gathered on the dock. "In that case, do your worst, my boy. I would have it no other way."

The man with the camera strode toward me and the officers while the other man accompanied Sir Edwin toward the bar. He held up the camera and gave it a shake. "Justice here in the islands isn't quite as blind as it is in the American courts, and this video will likely keep you well clear of any Bahamian courtroom. I'm Edwin Castlebury the Fourth, and it's splendid to meet you, Mr. Fulton."

His accent wasn't as purely British as his father's, but I had no doubt there was an Oxford diploma hanging on his wall.

"Thank you, Mr. Castlebury. I hope you're right about that video keeping me out of court."

He said, "Oh, I'm quite right. I assure you. This is what we do, and you are in very fine hands, sir. My father and a few friends will meet you at the police station, and we'll have this ugly mess sorted out in two shakes. Have no doubt." With that, he turned on a heel and strode away with the confidence of a man doing God's work.

For my sake, I hoped his confidence was well-founded and not merely Oxford arrogance.

From somewhere behind me, I heard the sigh of a defeated man. Without giving the officers any reason to pounce, I slowly looked across my shoulder to see Chief Inspector Barton shaking his bowed head. I'll never know what warped sadism made me do it, but I couldn't resist. "Are you still planning to impound my boat, Inspector?"

Through gritted teeth, he growled, "Get him out of here!"

In an unexpected move, Clark stepped between Barton and me. I assumed he was on the verge of giving the cop an earful, but he instead slipped a small, cone-shaped plastic bottle in my cuffed hand. Without ceremony, I curled my fingers around the bottle and let myself be led from the scene.

The two uniforms took charge of my arms again, but this time, they were far more gentle than before. Perhaps I was receiving the courtesy owed to an innocent man, or perhaps the officers weren't so sure they wanted to be in Chief Inspector Barton's corner when the bloody clubs of the Bahamian legal system came to bear on him. Either way, I was looking forward to the next few hours of my life, but I didn't have time to play pawn in an island-pissing match between Sir Edwin and the Royal Bahamian Police Force. I had a mission that demanded my full attention in part of the world where the environmental climate was much colder and the stakes were immeasurably higher.

The police car wasn't a car at all. It was, in fact, a four-door pickup truck with the unmistakable markings of the RBPF and an impressive light bar on top. The officers cautiously placed me on the back seat and pulled the seatbelt around me. I offered no resistance and behaved like the model prisoner . . . as far as they knew. What they didn't know was just how badly the remainder of their night was about to go.

I twisted the cap from Clark's bottle of anti-fingerprint solution—commonly known the world over as superglue. As we made our progress toward the station, I meticulously worked the glue into the swirls and ridges of each of my fingers and thumbs until I'd emptied the bottle.

"What is that smell?" the driver demanded.

I lowered my head and repositioned myself in the seat. "I'm sorry, guys, but this kind of stuff really upsets my stomach. I can't control it."

Both men simultaneously pressed their buttons to lower their windows. The driver thumbed the buttons for the rear seat, as well. My plan was working like a charm.

Just as Castlebury the Fourth had promised, his father was dry, redressed, and in excellent company before I'd made it through the booking process. In fact, I was still being fingerprinted by a young officer who was growing more frustrated with every attempt. No matter how many times he scrubbed my fingers and reapplied the ink, the smudges on the card never changed.

Sir Edwin walked by the fingerprint tech and me, and the lawyer gave me a wink. Trailing my attorney were three other men in suits who looked far more important than I ever wanted to be.

Frustrated beyond his ability and desire to continue the ill-fated fingerprinting task, the young officer slid the half dozen smudged, meaningless cards toward the edge of his desk and rose from his well-worn chair.

"Come on, mon. You be goin' to lockup. I'm done wit dis, and you ain' got no fingerprints no way."

I stood to allow the officer to apply the handcuffs again, but Sir Edwin stepped a few inches in front of me. "Have a seat, Mr. Fulton. I think the chief inspector has a few words he'd like to say, but before that, I would like to introduce some friends of ours."

One of the men from behind Castlebury stepped to my side and stuck out a hand. "I'm Ambassador Woodford of the U.S. State Department, and I'd like to thank you for your service to our country, Mr. Fulton."

I stood again and shook the ambassador's hand. "It's a pleasure to meet you, sir. I'm sorry to have brought you down here for all of this trouble tonight."

"It's no trouble at all. It would appear you and I have some mutual friends in high places. Thank you again for your service, and I'm glad to have been of assistance tonight."

The two remaining men introduced themselves as the chief consulate and the public affairs officer from the U.S. Embassy.

The consulate shook my hand and gave my shoulder a solid slap. "There will be an Embassy car waiting for you out front. All of this is taken care of."

Still uncertain why I'd drawn such a crowd, I said, "Thank you, sir. And again, I'm sorry to have been so much trouble."

"It's no trouble at all, Mr. Fulton. Just keep doing what you're doing, and we'll remain at your beck and call."

Chief Inspector Barton eyed the fingerprint technician and stuck out his palm. "Give me the print card."

The young officer scooped up the stack of worthless ink blotches and stammered. "I wasn't able . . . I mean, I could not . . ."

"Just give me the cards. It doesn't matter."

He handed over the stack, and Barton tore them to shreds and deposited most of the pieces into an overflowing garbage can.

Barton locked eyes with me. "I don't know who or what you are, but it would be in both of our best interests if you left the island on the morning's high tide, and we never met again. You are free to go."

I should've kept my mouth shut and simply walked away, but I couldn't do it before twisting the screws a little tighter for the inspector. "Thanks for the advice, but I think I'll hang out on the island until I find my knife. I think someone may have stolen it. Perhaps I should file a police report. What do you think, Inspector?"

I couldn't see the steam escaping his ears, but I'm confident it was there. He tore a hole into the clear plastic evidence bag, pulled my knife from inside, and stuck the tip into the cluttered surface of the young officer's desk.

I motioned to my still-vibrating knife. "Ah, there it is. Imagine that."

With exaggerated effort, I pulled the knife from the desk, closed it, and slid it back into my pocket. "I think you've made your point, so to speak. I think I will take advantage of that high tide tomorrow morning."

He drove a finger through the air and toward the door. "Get out!"

I leaned close and whispered, "Good luck catching the real killer. And for the record, I didn't do it."

Chapter 13

Tradecraft, Baby

By the time the Embassy driver dropped me off back at the resort, there was no evidence of a pair of decomposing bodies ever lying on the dock. More importantly, there was no crime-scene tape, and there was no empty marina slip. *Aegis* was still tied just as she had been when I was arrested.

Clark met me on the dock. "Well, look who's home. Did you make any new friends in prison?"

"I wasn't in prison, smart-ass. I was never even in a holding cell. Their local Barney Fife spent thirty minutes trying to take my fingerprints, which were, thanks to you, completely undetectable beneath the superglue."

"Tradecraft, baby. Tradecraft."

"That's you," I said. "Double-Oh-Seven. Now, where's my wife? I have some questions."

"Questions?" he said.

"Well, really just one question."

He shot me with his finger pistol. "I'll bet it's the same question I've been asking for half an hour, but she won't answer me."

Before I could take that line of questioning any further, my bride appeared in the cockpit. "Hey! You're home. That was quick. Are you okay? What happened at the station? Is everything all right? Is Sir Edwin okay? What happens next?"

I shook my head in reaction to her flurry of questions. "I'll try to answer those in order. Here goes. Yes, I'm okay. They let me go. Yes, everything is all right. Yes, he's fine. And we go home. Did I get them all?"

She giggled. "Yeah, I think you covered them. I wasn't really worried."

I cocked my head. "Your husband gets arrested in a foreign country because his knife was found stuck in a dead man's chest, and you weren't worried?"

"Nope, I knew it was all under control."

"Okay, now I have a question for you. Who did you call when I told you to get us a lawyer?"

She shot nervous glances between Clark and me until she finally whispered, "I'll tell you when we're alone."

I was suddenly more intrigued than ever. "Then, now is a great time for us to be alone. Let's go for a walk on the beach."

Never one to turn down an offer for a moonlight stroll on the beach anywhere in the world, Penny leapt from the cockpit onto the dock and grabbed my hand. Immediately upon lacing her fingers through mine, she yanked her hand away. "Oh, gross! What is that?"

"Tradecraft, baby. Tradecraft."

"Whatever that means, it's still gross."

"Don't worry. It'll wear off in time."

She made a gagging noise. "Yeah, well, until it does, don't touch me with those things."

"How about these things?" I pressed my lips to hers.

She sighed. "Yeah, those things are welcome anywhere you want to put them. Just not those fingers."

I chuckled and kissed her again. "Spill it. Who did you call to get me the U.S. ambassador and the best defense lawyer on the island?"

She glanced back toward our boat. "I'll tell you, but you can never tell Clark. Deal?"

I stuck out my hand. "We can shake on it if you'd like."

She screwed up her face and withdrew both hands. "Uh, no! I'll just take your word that you'll never tell."

"I'll never tell. I promise."

"A promise from a spy . . . Ha! What's that worth?" she said.

"I'm not a spy, and I've never broken a promise to you."

"Fair enough," she said. "I called Dominic."

Dominic Fontana had been my first handler. He was a brilliant field operative for decades before the years caught up with him and relegated him to running operators like me instead of being one himself. He'd spent a lifetime in the covert operations business, but more important than that, he was Clark Johnson's father.

"Ooh," I said. "Now I understand why you didn't want to mention that in front of Clark. You didn't want to hurt the poor guy's feelings. Aren't you sweet . . . and sneaky?"

"Yes to both questions," she said. "I figured if Clark had any answers, he would've jumped into the middle of things, but he seemed just as lost as the rest of us, so I took the bull by the horns."

I held up both hands as if surrendering. "It's superglue so they couldn't fingerprint me."

She grabbed my left hand and pulled it to her face. The full moon overhead provided enough light for a thorough examination.

"That's cool! Where do you learn stuff like that?"

"I learned it from Clark, but now you know, too."

She tapped at her temple. "I'm making mental notes. All of this is going to make a great movie someday."

I quivered. "That's the last thing the world needs—a movie about my life."

She stuck her hands on her hips. "Hey! I think you've got a pretty great life, and even though you'll never admit it, you're a spy, and everybody loves stories about spies."

"I'm not a—"

It was her turn to press her lips to mine, and we spent the next hour watching nearly transparent crabs scamper along the beach. At some point, she even let me hold her hand.

Back aboard the boat, the whole gang had assembled for a family reunion. Mongo sat on the cockpit deck playing jacks with Tatiana while Irina sat in the helm chair smiling down on the pair.

I motioned toward the largest human I'd ever seen playing jacks. "Hey, Tatiana. Mongo is terrible at fivesies, so my money's on you."

The girl giggled. "No, he's not."

"Okay, maybe not, but I still think you're going to kick his butt."

She said, "Hey, did you know that jacks make great burglar alarms?"

I gave Mongo a nudge with my toe. "Have you been teaching her tradecraft?"

Mongo huffed. "Check this out." He spread two handfuls of jacks across the deck and pointed at Tatiana. "Go ahead. Show him."

She hopped up with the agility of a gymnast and placed her left bare foot on top of at least a dozen jacks. She landed her right foot on another pile and hopped up and down several times.

I couldn't believe my eyes. "How do you do that?"

"I'm a ballerina. My feet are tougher than anything, so I guess that means jacks are terrible burglar alarms if the thief is a ballerina like me."

"I guess so," I said as I headed for the main salon.

The rest of the family was hanging out and talking about everything except our coming mission. It was nice to see them relax.

I shot a thumb toward the cockpit. "Did you guys know Mongo is playing jacks?"

Hunter said, "That girl has our giant wrapped around her little finger. He's obviously goo-goo over Irina, but he'd beat somebody to death if they tried to hurt Tatiana."

I joined the revelry for half an hour before saying, "I hate to be the bearer of bad news, but our vacation has to come to an end. I made a deal with the authorities we'd be off the island tomorrow, so we'll sail out on the morning tide. Besides, we've got a mission to plan and execute."

Clark spoke up. "I didn't get to show you the surprise."

"What surprise?" I asked.

He sighed. "Telling you isn't the same as showing you, but I guess it'll have to do. The guys out in Kansas finished installing the new carbon-fiber floats on the Caravan. That's how I got out here so fast. Your second-favorite airplane is at the airport."

I immediately turned to Penny, and she smiled. "Yes, of course I'll take the boat back across the Gulf Stream so you can fly your second-favorite airplane."

"How do you know the Caravan is my second favorite?" I asked.

She shook her head. "It's simple. The Mustang is clearly your favorite, and every other airplane on Earth is tied for second."

* * *

Morning broke with a few patchy clouds floating across the Atlantic and my excitement to get back in the cockpit of the Caravan boiling over.

Talking eight people into abandoning vacation to return to work should be a daunting task for any manager, but my team beat me to the punch. By the time I crawled from my luxurious king bed in my resort suite, I was alone. I poured a cup of coffee down my throat and headed for the marina.

Penny, *Aegis*'s de facto captain, had Mongo and Tatiana hard at work lashing everything movable to the decks for the always-rocky crossing of the Gulf Stream.

When I stepped aboard, our favorite ballerina grinned from ear to ear. In perfect Russian, she said, "Mr. Chase, Ms. Penny said I could sail back with her if Mama agrees. Will you tell her that she agrees?"

Cautious to ensure my Russian was clean, I said, "I think I can do that."

Tatiana squeaked out, "*Spasibo,*" and dove back into her work on deck.

Irina came through the sliding door from the main salon as I slipped off my boots. She looked up with a knowing smile and practiced her English. "Tatiana is to ride on boat, yes?"

I took some of the stress off the concerned mother and continued in Russian. "Penny is an excellent captain, and Tatiana is absolutely welcome to sail back to the States if you're comfortable with that."

Relieved for the language barrier to come crashing down, she said, "If you say it is safe, she can do it."

"It's probably the safest way to get home," I said. "And you're welcome to return on the boat with her or aboard either airplane."

She glanced toward Mongo and her daughter going about their tasks. "I need to ask you something, but I do not know if it is appropriate."

I motioned for her to follow me. "Let's take a walk. I'm pretty sure I know what you want to discuss."

She looked back at her daughter, and I said, "She's fine. Don't worry."

We stepped from the boat and down the stairs to the nearly empty beach.

It was obvious she didn't know how to start the conversation, so I opened the door. "This is about Mongo, isn't it?"

"I say his name Marvin, ma da."

"Russian is fine," I said. "I think I can keep up."

We continued in her native tongue. "I do not call him Mongo. I call him Marvin because this is what he said his name was. He is a very sweet man and so kind to Tatiana."

"He's one of the most sincerely kind people I've ever known," I said.

"I need to know if he is nice to my daughter only because he wants to be my husband."

I stifled the laughter that so desperately wanted to come. "I assure you that Marvin is exactly what he appears to be. The English word is *genuine*, and he is the epitome of genuine."

"This is *podlinnyy* in Russian," she said.

"Yes, it is, and there's no better example than Marvin. But I'm not sure he's ready to be anyone's husband."

Irina blushed. "I did not mean to imply this."

I chuckled. "It's fine. I know what you mean. Let me set your mind at ease. Mongo clearly adores your daughter, and I think the feeling is quite mutual. That won't change if you don't go out with him. If you're interested in him romantically, I'm sure he would be the best boyfriend, and eventually, the best husband any man could be."

"You are his friend," she said. "Please do not be offended, but you would naturally say these things about your friend."

"You're right, of course, but I would say the same about him if he weren't my friend. In fact, the woman who brought you to America would tell you the same."

She looked through narrowed eyes. "Anya would say these things about Marvin?"

I turned to face her. "Anya is a complex and complicated woman. She's nothing like you. First, she's not a mother, so she could never understand the depths of your love for Tatiana. Second, her lifestyle isn't supportive of a romantic relationship. I'm sure you know she and Marvin had a brief relationship, but it couldn't work."

Irina bowed her head. "Yes, I know this, and I do not want to be *otskok* for him."

I pored through every Russian word my brain knew, but it wouldn't come. "I'm sorry, Irina, but I don't know what that means."

"I do not know English word. Is meaning to be first person after breaking up."

"Ah! Rebound," I said. "I don't think you have to worry about that, but it's perfectly fine to have that conversation with Mongo."

We walked on in silence for several minutes as Irina's wheels obviously churned inside her head.

Finally, she reached for my hand. "Thank you, Chase. I think I will go on boat with Penny and Tatiana, and I think I will love Marvin."

Chapter 14
The Crossing

Within minutes of my arrival on the boat, the whole team, including Al Brown, had assembled. I pulled a pan from the locker and struck it with a metal spoon until I had everyone's attention.

"All right, guys. Listen up. We have three ways to get everyone back to the States. We've got the boat. She'll make the trip in thirty to thirty-five hours, depending on the wind, if we sail nonstop. It'll take three days if we sleep in a harbor somewhere for two nights."

Penny jumped in. "I declare a girl's cruise. You guys can get back anyway you want, but Irina, Tatiana, Skipper, Tina, and I are taking the boat. And no boys allowed."

I shrugged. "I guess that settles that. The Citation can carry six, and the Caravan can carry twelve."

Hunter stuck a finger in the air. "Dibs on the driver's seat in the Caravan."

I snorted. "Not hardly. I'll be taking the wheel for this one."

"We'll see about that," he said.

Disco and Clark gave each other a knowing nod, and my handler said, "Disco and I will take the Citation."

"Sounds good to me," I said. "The rest of us will take the Caravan."

Al Brown spoke up. "I think I'd prefer the plush leather seats of the Citation, so I'll join Disco and Clark."

That left Mongo, Singer, Hunter, and me in the newly shod Caravan.

Penny and I spent a few minutes alone, as did Hunter and Tina and Mongo and the two Volkovnas. We were only going to be apart for three days, but men like us had grown to understand the value of every second with the people we care about.

Our lives too often hung in the balance when we left our daily lives to butt heads with the bad guys that never seemed to stop coming. As long as those guys kept crawling out of the woodwork, my team and men like us would rise to meet the challenge and fight until there wasn't a drop of blood left inside us so that the people who were blind to our existence could sleep peacefully behind doors without locks.

* * *

Just as I'd suspected, Hunter beat me to the left front seat of the Caravan. His passion for flying machines was at least equal to mine. Although I enjoyed ribbing him about it, I enjoyed flying in the right seat beside my partner. He was safe, competent, and confident without being cocky at the controls. Although he'd been at the helm when the Caravan tried to beat herself to death on an icy river in the wilds of Montana, I didn't blame him for the damage. In fact, I gave him all the credit for saving the lives of everyone on board, as well as the airplane itself.

"We need to get you a multi-engine ticket sometime soon," I said. "It would be nice to have another pilot with the Citation type rating."

"Just tell me when," he said. "Put me in any airplane you want, and I'll fly it 'til the wings fall off."

"Or maybe the floats."

He gave me a look across his sunglasses. "Words hurt."

"Not as bad as airplane crashes."

"Hey! It wasn't a crash. It was a touch-and-go . . . really hard. I can't help it the airplane doesn't like it rough."

"Over a quarter of a million dollars in damage, and you say it wasn't a crash?"

He pushed his glasses up his nose. "I flew it away from the river, didn't I?"

"Yes, you did," I admitted.

"That means it wasn't a crash. Airplanes are unflyable after crashing, and this old girl got us all the way back home without complaining a bit."

I motioned toward his kneeboard. "Just run the checklist. We'll argue semantics later."

With everyone aboard, checklists complete, and the turbine whistling its siren song, Hunter eased the throttle forward, and my second-favorite airplane began her takeoff roll.

Hunter kept his eyes trained down the runway, and I monitored the panel and made the calls.

"Airspeed alive and building . . . Cross-checked . . . Sixty . . . Seventy . . . Eighty knots . . . Rotate."

Hunter pulled the nosewheel off the ground and stuck the prop spinner just above the horizon. We watched the runway disappear beneath our nose, and he said, "No runway left . . . gear up."

I responded. "Gear coming up. Through one hundred knots."

Rigged for climb, Hunter set the autopilot, leaving the idyllic island life behind with a real-world mission before us that promised to be one of the most challenging operations of our careers.

Three hours later, the coast of northern Florida broke through the midday haze, and the Jacksonville Approach controller's confident tone rang through my headset. "Caravan Eight-Charlie-Fox, you're cleared direct Saint Marys. Descend and maintain six thousand."

I turned to Hunter. "You didn't file for Saint Marys, did you? We have to clear customs."

He shook me off. "No, I'm smarter than that. I filed for JAX."

I keyed up. "Approach, Eight-Charlie-Fox. We're international and need to clear customs."

Still with more confidence in his voice than I had in mine, the controller said, "Roger, sir. We've been told Customs and Immigration will meet you on deck at Saint Marys."

I smiled behind my microphone and gave Hunter a wink. "It's nice to have friends at the top."

He motioned toward the radio. "Are you going to read back the clearance or brag about who you know?"

I pressed the button on the yoke, "Eight-Charlie-Fox is direct Saint Marys and leaving twelve thousand for six."

Fifteen minutes later, our home airport came into view, and Hunter took the controls back from the magic robots behind the panel. Although I'd been the radio operator for the entire flight, he keyed up and said, "Approach, Eight-Charlie-Fox has Saint Marys in sight. We'll cancel I-F-R and continue visually. Thanks for the help."

The voice of a new controller filled our ears. "Caravan Eight-Charlie-Fox, the cancelation is received. Squawk VFR, and frequency change is approved. Good day."

With the nose of the Caravan pointed directly across Bonaventure Plantation toward the airport, it was time to run the before-landing checklist, and Hunter pulled the blue sheet from the pouch beside his left foot.

I pointed toward the laminate sheet. "That's the water landing checklist, dummy."

He pointed out the window. "Take a look at your dock, dummy."

Tied to the downstream side of the floating dock at Bonaventure was a sleek, forty-foot, gunmetal-gray boat with the blue striping of the U.S. Customs and Border Protection and the insignia of Homeland Security.

I wore the dummy label and apologized to my partner.

He kissed the surface of the North River as gently as it can be done and laid the plane-turned-boat against the upstream side of the dock.

I climbed down the ladder and hopped to the dock while Hunter ran the shutdown checklist.

"Good afternoon, gentlemen," I said. "It's awfully nice of you to come all the way up here just to welcome us home."

A uniformed, armed officer chuckled. "Mr. Clark Johnson arranged for us to come play welcoming party for you. If you don't have anything to declare, we'll stamp your passports and be on our way."

The rest of the passengers descended the ladders and presented their passports one by one to receive the purple-ink blessing. Without another word, the customs agents climbed back into their boat and roared away. It took less than thirty seconds for them to disappear around the first of a few thousand curves in the North River.

The house felt desolate as we lugged our gear inside and headed for the kitchen. We checked our phones as we devoured sandwiches at the farm-style kitchen table. While the rest of us sorted through useless email, Mongo smiled and stared out the window.

I couldn't resist smiling with him. "They'll be here in a couple of days, big man. Don't you worry. You know how good Penny is on the boat."

He stuffed his phone back into his pocket. "Yeah, I know. I was just thinking how nice it is to have somebody who actually checks in occasionally instead of running off without telling anybody."

"I'm sure it is," I said. "You know, Irina and I had a little talk about you."

He lowered his chin. "Oh, really?"

"She asked me if I thought you were hanging out with Tatiana just to get to her."

"And what did you tell her?"

I slid the platter of sandwiches toward him. "I told her you were a lousy scoundrel and all-around scallywag."

"Scallywag, huh? Is that what you told her?"

"Something like that. She was just checking your references, and I think the job is yours if you want it."

It was rare to see a man of Mongo's size blush, but blush he did, and that sent Hunter into a rousing rendition of "Mongo and Irina sitting in a tree, k-i-s-s-i-n-g. First comes love, then comes—"

Before Hunter could finish, Mongo hooked the stretcher of my partner's chair with his foot and sent him sprawling backward across the kitchen floor.

Hunter wasn't fazed. "Then comes Mongo pushing a baby carriage."

I looked up to see Disco standing in the doorway to the back gallery shaking his head. I shrugged, and he said, "Professionalism. That's the thing I like most about this team of ours . . . professionalism."

That scored a big laugh, but no one offered Hunter a hand getting up from the floor. None of us wanted to be Mongo's next victim.

"Come join us before Mongo eats us out of house and home," I said.

The giant pointed toward Hunter still reclaiming his footing. "Keep it up, and you'll be on the floor with your little buddy."

I raised both hands in surrender, and he nailed me with a wadded-up paper napkin.

Disco took a seat and pulled a sandwich from the tray. "Clark wanted me to tell you to spend the next couple of days training up and shedding the pounds you packed on while playing hooky from work."

Singer came to life for the first time in hours. "I guess that means he doesn't have to shed the weight now that he's permanently assigned to the rear detachment."

Disco threw up a hand. "Hey, don't shoot the messenger. I'm just passing the word. But I do have a few concerns. All of you guys are operators, and I'm just a flyboy. If you're taking me with you, I'm definitely going to need some schooling."

"Don't worry," I said. "You'll be amazed what you can learn in three days. Besides, you proved you're more than a high-speed aluminum-tube driver in Montana. We've all got you to thank for saving our bacon up there."

The next several minutes were spent laying out what happened for Brown. When our stories came to an end, he said, "You guys are a mess, but it sure sounds like you pull it together when it's go time."

Hunter wiped the mustard from his chin. "Yep. We're a pack of twelve-year-old boys 'til the bullets start flying, then it's game on, baby."

* * *

The next two days and nights were spent doing exactly what Clark had ordered. I even found an empty building at the abandoned paper plant we used to practice Lights Out, Night Ops. If the Canadian job came down to a gunfight—or two—we'd need the confidence to shoot, move, and win inside the subterranean bunker the Chinese called home. We trained with blanks inside the abandoned building. Shooting live rounds that could penetrate the exterior walls or fly right through a window would not be a good way to win friends in the neighborhood.

After several thousand rounds of ammo, both live and blanks, Disco was moving like an operator instead of a pilot, and the five of us had lost a combined forty pounds. Al Brown played the role of opposing force as we assaulted the building over and over again. His lifetime of experience and well-trained eyes gave him the ability to find tiny flaws in our technique and work them out. When fractions of a second could mean the difference between life and death, the ability to shoot, move, and communicate as a team by second nature was crucial.

By the time the clock struck noon on our third day back in the real world, the whole team was ready for a break, and it came in the form of a sailboat full of beautiful women.

Chapter 15
Building a Mystery

"You smell like a goat!"

Those weren't the first words I hoped to hear from my favorite sailor, but that's what I got.

"We've been training, and it's hot."

"Yeah," she said. "I can see that. Now, go get a shower and feed me."

Unlike the greeting my bride thumped me with, Tatiana leapt into Mongo's arms as if she'd been shot from a cannon, and Irina wasn't far behind.

As a yardstick for tolerance of smelling like a goat, Tina Ramirez leaned in, giving Hunter a tentative "I love you, but don't get that on me" hug.

Skipper spun her baseball cap backward and danced from the boat and into Disco's empty arms. He returned the hug as if he had no other choice. He stammered. "I . . . uh . . . I mean . . ."

Skipper laughed. "Relax, Disco. You looked lonely while everyone else except Chase was getting a hug, but you smell like a goat, too, so that's as far as this is going."

Demonstrating he was finally making himself at home on the team, Disco leaned toward Skipper, gave a sniff, and recoiled.

"Speaking of goats, how long has it been since *you've* had a shower?"

The analyst's mouth fell agape in disbelief. "Oh, I see how it is. I try to be nice to you, and you throw haymakers. See if you get any more hugs from me, flyboy."

Penny climbed back aboard *Aegis* and returned with an over-stuffed sack of laundry and a garbage bag. Tossing the two bags to the dock, she surveilled the area. "Where's Singer?"

I motioned toward the pasture. "He's checking on your beloved horses. He'll be back as soon as he realizes you're home."

She leaned against the helm station and pressed the horn button, sending one prolonged blast across the marsh.

"That wasn't necessary," I said. "He's a sniper. I doubt you snuck a thirty-ton boat with a sixty-five-foot mast onto the dock without him noticing."

Showers were taken, laundry was started, and Singer showed up. An hour later, we were gathered around a massive table at one of our favorite seafood spots in Saint Marys. I don't know what day of the week it was. Trivial matters such as that have rarely concerned me, but I knew it was a low-country-boil day by the heavy brown paper that had been rolled across every table on the patio, and that made it one of my favorite days.

An apron-clad waiter poured a steaming mound of shrimp, new potatoes, corn, and sausage onto the table and passed out silverware and napkins. "Is there anything else I can bring you?"

"More napkins and another round of sweet tea would be great, but there's no hurry," I said.

He gave me the thumbs-up and headed for the kitchen with his empty pot dangling from one hand.

"What have you been training on?" Penny asked between mouthfuls of the Southern delicacy.

Disco pulled a corn cob from between his teeth and held up a finger. "I'll take this one. We've been training on how to turn an old A-Ten driver into a gunfighter."

Skipper said, "That sounds like some valuable training. Is it working?"

He peeled another shrimp and popped it into his mouth. "Oh, yeah. It's working all right, but I've still got a long way to go. Plus, it's tough keeping up with you young guys. It's almost like you're trying to kill an old man."

Singer picked something from between his two front teeth. "Trust me, if this team was trying to kill you, you'd be long dead, and you would've never seen us coming."

Disco pointed to the dwindling pile of goodness. "That's reassuring. I think I'll continue thinking about shrimp instead of being a target."

Penny looked up and wiped her mouth. "So, you've been shooting?" I nodded, and she frowned. "I guess it's that kind of mission, then, huh?"

Remembering I'd vowed to never lie to her, I said, "It's possible it will turn combative, but we plan to execute the mission without sending any lead into the air."

She swallowed hard and turned away. When she looked back my way, determination replaced concern on her perfect face. "Are you going to be wearing mics like you did during the Montana job?"

I motioned toward Skipper, and she licked her fingers. "We don't know if comms will work from inside the mountain. We may be able to place a pair of repeaters on the way in that will give us satellite comms as long as the Chinese aren't jamming in the tunnel."

I could see the wheels turning in Penny's head as she tried to picture what was to come.

"I want to do it again," she said.

"You want to do what again?" I asked.

"I want to listen in if you're going to use the repeaters."

I glanced to Skipper, and she gave me a solid nod.

I said, "Then, listen you shall."

Al Brown came up for air from the feast in front of us. "I'll join you on the listening party. I'm no good on the ground anymore, but that ops center of yours is impressive. I'm looking forward to standing watch up there."

"It sounds like the ops center is going to be a full house," Skipper said. "I'll be there, of course, but adding Penny, Al, and Clark is going to make it tight quarters."

Al said, "Except for the penetration, we can rotate shifts. When you guys go hot, it's probably a good idea for all of us to be on deck."

"I agree," I said. "If we can bear the load, we'll carry video transmitters so you'll have a live feed. All of that is contingent on how much gear we'll need to penetrate the mountain and whether the Chinese have that place wired with a spiderweb of jamming equipment. We won't know until we get on the ground."

Skipper closed one eye and stared at the ceiling, and I followed her line of sight to the fan twirling above her head. "Maybe, but maybe not," she said. "There's a chance we might . . . Well, not we. *I* might be able to find out how hard they're jamming before any of you boys stick your heads inside that mountain. Don't ask questions yet. I'm still working it out in my head. I'll get back with you as soon as I piece it together."

I tossed a peeled shrimp at her. "That's why you're the best analyst on Earth."

She caught it and threw it back. "And don't you forget it, mister."

I caught it between my teeth and devoured the morsel.

Noticing Mongo's absence from the conversation, I gave him a checking glance. "Everything all right down there, big man?"

He looked down at Tatiana. "Go ahead. Show him," he said.

She grabbed a boiled shrimp in each hand, held them up for everyone to see, and drove her thumbs beneath the shells, peeling both crustaceans simultaneously. She handed one to her mother and one to Mongo.

The demonstration set the whole team in motion trying to recreate Tatiana's feat, but everyone except Penny failed miserably.

When we'd whittled the gourmet mound down to a pile of shrimp shells and soggy napkins, Penny said, "When are you leaving?"

The questions seemed to catch everyone's attention, suddenly making it my turn to demonstrate a little leadership. "We need two more days in the shoot house, a day to load out, and a travel day. What day is today?"

An echo of "Tuesday" reverberated back at me.

"If Clark is ready, we'll leave on Saturday morning." I paused and almost asked if everyone was okay with my timetable, but I caught myself before boring a hole through the faith my team had in me.

"Can I watch?" Penny asked.

"Watch what? The shoot house training?" She nodded, and I said, "Sure, you can watch. We'll make room for you behind the moving firing line, and as long as you don't get in the way, you can watch the drills."

"What about me?" came a small voice from the far end of the table. "I have never seen anyone shoot a real gun."

Mongo's eyes widened into saucers, and he immediately turned to Irina and Tatiana. "I don't know if that's such a good idea."

Irina spoke in Russian—too low for me to hear. Mongo leaned in and listened intently before turning toward me with a face full of unspoken questions.

I slid a collection of folded bills beneath my tea glass. "I've got an idea. Let's have some fun this afternoon. We have almost any kind of small-arms weaponry you can think of and plenty of ammunition. We can all get in some light-hearted target practice."

Tatiana turned sharply to her mother as if begging for a permission slip, and the Russian smiled.

We made a stop by the armory and picked a nice selection of firearms for our afternoon on the range.

Tatiana watched me lay a pair of AR-15s in the back of the van. "Those are assault rifles, no?"

I took a knee beside her and motioned toward the guns. "Rifles don't assault people. They are completely harmless machines, just like cars or airplanes. They have no ability to hurt anyone until a person with evil intent puts one in his hands. There's no history of one of those weapons jumping up and hurting anyone. AR means Armalite Rifle. That's the manufacturer who first produced them. People who don't understand the difference between an evil person and a harmless machine came up with the concept of an 'assault rifle.'"

She seemed to consider my explanation before pointing toward a third rifle. "And that is an AK Forty-Seven, yes?"

"Yes, that's right. That's the standard service rifle for the Russian Army."

"I know," she said. "And AK means *Avtomat Kalashnikova 1947*."

That was not a question.

She stared at the wood and metal weapon whose twin had been carried by countless ancestors of hers. "Maybe you will let me hold this rifle, yes?"

"That's up to your mother, but as far as I'm concerned, you may hold and shoot as many of them as you'd like."

Her face lit up with excitement, and she danced away as if I'd just given her an annual pass to Disney World.

When we made it to the range on the northeast corner of the Bonaventure property, Mongo and Singer had our canopy set up in no time, providing much-needed shade from the coastal Georgia summertime sun.

I sat on the rear bumper of the van. "Anyone who wants to shoot is welcome to do so, but we must do it safely." I pointed downrange. "We will only shoot in that direction, and only after we fully understand the function of the weapon we intend to fire. We'll wear eye and ear protection anytime anyone is firing. Any questions?"

None came, so I motioned to my favorite giant. "Mongo, Irina and Tatiana are yours. Skipper, you're on your own unless you want some instruction. In that case, anybody can jump in with you. Tina, you and Hunter are together. I'll shoot with Penny un-less she'd rather shoot with someone else."

I watched Mongo pull the AK-47 from the truck along with a can of 7.62x39 ammo. He pulled a pair of loaded magazines from the can and handed them to Irina. Without hesitation, she tucked one into her left waistband and slid the second magazine into the rifle. She spun on a heel, cycled the bolt, and thumbed the selector switch. A few seconds later, with a bevy of automatic fire, she'd cut the heart out of a paper target fifty yards away as if she were a Spetsnaz commando.

The demonstration caught everyone's attention, and suddenly, Irina Volkovna turned from a demure, nervous defector into a mystery we couldn't ignore.

I turned with laser focus toward my analyst, and she mouthed, "I'm on it." With no further direction, Skipper stepped behind Irina and reached for the empty magazine.

The Russian narrowed her eyes and pulled the magazine from the rifle's mag well. She slung the weapon across her shoulder with the sling and held the empty magazine in her palm. With the precision of a homicide detective, she rolled her right thumb across the base of the magazine, leaving a perfect fingerprint. "This is what you wanted, no?"

Chapter 16
Who's That Lady?

As he tended to do, Mongo took Irina's demonstration in stride. "Not bad, but let's try it again. And this time, let's see if you can manage the rising tendency a little better."

Irina cocked her head and furrowed her brow, so Mongo repeated the instructions in Russian. "*Neplokho, no davayte poprobuyem yeshche raz, i na etot raz posmotrim, smozhete li vy nemnogo luchshe spravit'sya s voskhodyashchey tendentsiyey.*"

Irina smiled. "I am small woman, and you are big strong man. I cannot stop gun from having, uh . . . *otdacha.*"

"The word is *recoil*," he said, and continued in Russian. "Now, shoulder the weapon again, and put a little more weight on your front foot."

She repositioned, leaned forward, and looked up at her American teacher.

"Good. When you press the trigger this time, I want you to roll your shoulder forward and draw your support arm downward as hard as you can as if you're trying to pull the muzzle to the ground."

She shrugged. "I will try this, but will not work."

She pulled a second magazine from her belt and inserted it into the rifle with the confidence and practiced ease of a Russian infantryman. Mongo gave her left foot a tap with the toe of his boot, and she allowed her front foot to slide forward another six inches.

He engulfed her comparatively tiny left hand with his and gripped the forearm like a vise, then he pressed his right hand against the back of her shoulder. "Press the trigger, and follow my hands."

She depressed the trigger, and the rifle roared its staccato as the rounds left the muzzle at the rate of six hundred per minute, emptying the magazine in three seconds. During the full-auto fire, Irina did just as Mongo guided, and the full metal jacket bullets tore through the paper target, leaving a shot group of less than half the size of her first set.

Mongo backed away. "Reload and do it again."

She dropped the empty magazine and seated another thirty-round mag in the well. When the third magazine was empty, Irina Volkovna had sent thirty rounds through the target in a shot group so tight it could've been covered by even her non-Mongo-sized hand.

"Where did you learn to shoot like that?"

She dropped the empty mag and handed the rifle to Mongo. "You taught me, and you are excellent teacher."

"No, I taught you how to tighten your shot group, but somebody else taught you to shoot."

She looked toward Bonaventure and then back at Mongo. "Skipper will find nothing. I was never soldier, but my father taught me to fight for day when Americans fall from sky."

Mongo froze, obviously shocked by her confession.

She could no longer hold the stoic, icy expression Russian women are so good at, and the sharp, flawless features of her face softened as the corners of her lips turned upward. "This is only joke."

Mongo's shoulders relaxed, and he let out the breath he'd been holding captive in his chest. "That was cruel, and you'll pay for that one. But where did you really learn to shoot like that?"

"It was Papa who taught me and brother. He did not tell us why, but it was important to him."

My phone vibrated, yanking me from my voyeuristic trance at the Mongo and Irina show. I snatched it from my pocket and stuck it to my ear without checking the caller ID. "Yeah."

Skipper said, "She doesn't exist outside the Agency's classified fingerprint network."

"That's what I expected. Thanks."

"Thanks? All you have to say is thanks? We've got a Russian national crawling around inside our team, and you're not concerned that there's no record of her being alive anywhere except in some basement in Foggy Bottom?"

"I'm cautious, but not concerned . . . yet. Please tell me you didn't leave any trail when you went traipsing around in the CIA's back pocket."

"Really, Chase?"

I sighed. "I'm sorry. I should've known better. Thank you for your discretion. Can you set up a—"

"Again, you should've known. The trackers are already set up, and just like Irina, I don't exist."

"You deserve a raise."

She laughed. "You say that a lot, but it never seems to happen."

"I'll get the HR office on it."

The click was the only reply I expected or received.

Our collective surprise waned as the afternoon continued. Mongo continued to play instructor and safety officer for Irina and Tatiana. He pulled the smallest pistol we'd included in the collection and sat on the grass with our favorite ballerina standing wide-eyed in front of him.

"This is a twenty-two caliber pistol, and these are the rounds it fires." He dropped the cartridge into her waiting hand, and she examined it carefully. "Why is it so small?"

He motioned toward her legs. How high can you jump with those small legs of yours?"

She placed the pistol cartridge back in Mongo's hand and giggled. After a deep knee bend, she sprang into the air and easily cleared Mongo's head. She landed behind him as gently as a feather kissing the ground. "I have the strongest legs in all of Bolshoi second company."

He grinned and held up the round. "That's exactly my point. Just because something is small doesn't mean it's not capable of great things—like you jumping over my head. I'll bet you couldn't do that if I were standing up, though."

"Probably not," she admitted. "But it might be fun to try."

"We'll have to give it a try sometime, but for now, let's load the magazine."

He handed her an empty magazine and a few rounds of ammunition. "Hold the mag in your left hand and the bullets in your right. Now, press each one down into the mag and slide it to the rear. It'll get harder with every round you add."

She copied the motion he demonstrated and soon had the magazine filled to capacity.

"Good," he said. "Now, this is the slide. Pull it to the rear, and press up with your thumb on that little button. That's the slide release. Pressing up on it will lock the slide to the rear."

She did as her teacher said, and the lesson continued until she understood the mechanical function of the weapon.

He demonstrated the proper grip and explained sight alignment. "Once you have equal height and light through the sights, you'll slowly and steadily squeeze the trigger until the weapon fires. The most important thing to remember is that you never point a gun at anything you aren't willing to kill. You must treat every weapon as if it is loaded until you've checked for yourself and know that it's empty."

Her first shot hit the backstop, but not the target. "I missed!"

"That doesn't matter," he said. "How did it feel?"

"Kinda no big deal. It was just a loud noise."

"That's why we start shooting with the twenty-two. We'll move up to something bigger after you get the hang of it."

The two continued their dance as teacher and student until she could keep all of her shots on the paper target.

"Why can't I hit the center?"

"You will," Mongo said. "It just takes practice."

"Can you hit the center?"

He gave a slow nod. "Yeah, I can hit the center, but I've fired millions of shots in my life. By the time you've fired as much as me, you'll be a much better shot than I am."

She smirked. "Maybe, but you'll never be a better dancer than me."

By the time we called the range cold, we'd fired several thousand rounds, and everyone was ready for dinner. To my surprise and great delight, I found a magnificent gift waiting for me in the kitchen. Before I made it there from the back gallery, my nose discovered a heavenly delight wafting on the steamy afternoon air. I threw open the screen door to find Maebelle standing in front of the Viking stove with a pot lid in one hand and a wooden spoon in the other.

"Ah! My prayers have been answered. You're finally back from Miami to stay. I'll never be hungry again!"

She replaced the lid on the pot and laid the spoon on its rest. After an apron wipe of her hands, she threw her arms around me. "Oh, you dreamer, you. As much as I miss cooking for all of you crazies at Bonaventure, I'm afraid South Beach would crumble without me."

I returned the hug and snuck a peek at the stove.

Detecting my snooping, she grabbed the wooden spoon and gave my knuckles a little tough love. "Get away from there. You'll see soon enough. How many am I feeding?"

"Eleven if you brought Clark and if my math is still working."

She motioned toward the library. "I didn't *want* to bring him, but you know how clingy he gets."

I gave her a wink. "He used to be clingy with me, but you stole him away."

"It wasn't me," she said. "It was my biscuits and gravy. What can I say? Men—even men like Clark—can't resist my gravy."

Clark materialized in the door to the hallway. "What's up, College Boy? I heard you whipping the team into shape out there on the range."

"Actually, we were just having some fun today. We'll be back in the shoot house tomorrow for some fine-tuning, and we'll be ready to fly on Saturday."

My handler gave his watch a glance. "I've been working on an ingress plan. It's not easy sneaking a team of heavily armed troublemakers into a sovereign country, you know."

I grabbed his shoulder and led him down the hallway. "Let's talk in the library so we don't disturb the master at work in the kitchen."

Clark pulled the door closed behind us, and we fell into my favorite pair of wingbacks.

"I hate to admit it," I said, "but I've not given that part of the operation any thought at all. I guess I assumed you and Skipper would work it out."

He said, "I've got a plan, but it's not a great one, and it's definitely not a speedy entrance."

"I'm intrigued. Let's hear it."

He stared out the window and chuckled. "Look at that. A pair of squirrels are fighting over a single pecan, and there are hundreds of them lying everywhere."

"Maybe it's a really good pecan."

"Or maybe squirrels are idiots and not smart enough to see what's right under their noses." He chewed on his bottom lip for a moment and motioned toward the door with his chin. "Get Brown in here."

I pulled open the door that masqueraded as a bookcase and slipped down the stairs. A thumbprint and an eight-digit code opened the heavy fireproof door into the basement armory. Hunter, Singer, and Brown stood over a worktable cleaning the afternoon's armament.

"Hey, Brown. Clark wants to talk with you upstairs."

He tossed a cleaning rag onto a pile of other discarded rags and patches. "I'm sorry I won't be able to help you finish up, guys. I've been called to the principal's office."

Hunter said, "We'll save some for you. Just hurry back."

Al followed me back up the hidden staircase to the library. "Some secret agent I am. I didn't even realize there was a door on this side of the vault."

"Don't beat yourself up. I helped design the house, and I still don't know everything it can do."

Al settled into an office chair as I reclaimed my wingback, and Clark wasted no time.

"How did you get your team into Canada when you hit the Chinese the first time?"

Brown laughed out loud. "So, that's what this is about. Trust me, guys, you do not want to get in there the way we did it. We split up and hiked in through the Blackfeet Indian Reservation on the eastern edge of Glacier National Park."

Clark frowned. "You humped your gear in?"

"Oh, no, that was another fiasco. We painted up an Idaho Air National Guard C-One-Thirty in Canadian Air Force colors and airdropped our gear, including the ATVs, into the mountains. It would've worked out okay, but our mental heavyweight flight crew clipped some huge Canadian trees. The Hercules's starboard engines turned into giant salad shooters and chopped up those evergreens like onions in a Cuisinart. Needless to say, the crew had to ditch the airplane. What a mess that turned into. To be honest, I think that might be part of the reason the Chinese were able to negotiate such a sweetheart deal with the prime minister."

Clark sucked air through his teeth. "I hate that I missed that carnival, but I'm not sure my plan is any better. I've been charting a nape of the Earth flight out of Eielson Air Force Base through the Yukon and British Columbia to the high Canadian Rockies near a place called Cline River."

Brown let out a low whistle. "That's a long flight in anything with propellers. It's got to be fifteen hundred miles one way. I don't know if a Hercules can pull that off."

Clark said, "You're right, but short of having Scotty beam us down, it looks like the only plausible scenario."

I pointed out the window. "What about all those pecans the squirrels are ignoring while they're fighting over their favorite?"

Clark closed one eye and lowered his chin. "What the hell are you talking about, College Boy?"

"I'm talking about all the pecans that get shipped into Vancouver every day."

Brown furrowed his brow. "Pecans in Vancouver?"

"Yeah, but they don't look like pecans. They look like shipping containers."

Clark slapped his thigh at the same instant Maebelle rang the dinner bell. "I knew all that college learning would pay off sooner or later. You're a genius."

Brown stared back and forth between me and Clark. "I don't know what just happened, but I'd love for someone to explain it to me."

Clark said, "The sound from out in the hallway was the warning that you're about to eat the best meal you've had this decade, and Chase just figured out how to put five commandos and a half ton of toys in the Canadian Rockies."

Chapter 17
Cavemen in Combat Boots

Describing one of Maebelle's dinner spreads is like trying to explain the work of Michelangelo to a blind man. The combinations of flavors created an unrivaled experience for every mouth she fed both in El Juez, her restaurant on South Beach, and at the Bonaventure dinner table.

Al Brown slid back his chair from the table and sighed. "Well, Clark, you were wrong about Maebelle's cooking. You told me it was going to be the best meal I'd had in this decade. But it's likely the best meal I've had in half a century. That was magnificent."

Maebelle offered a slight appreciative bow of her head. "Thank you, Mr. Brown. That's sweet of you to say, and I'm pleased you enjoyed what I threw together."

"Threw together?" he belted. "Nobody *throws together* a meal like that."

Maebelle blushed. "Great meals, like great loves, are never planned. They just happen, and you have to have tried them all over the world to know exactly how delicious either can be right here at home."

He raised his tea glass. "Well said and brilliant. You've certainly found your calling in the kitchen, but if that's an original quote, maybe you're a philosopher as well."

"Thank you for the compliments, Mr. Brown, but you've only had the savory portion so far. Just wait until you taste my dessert."

Brown rubbed his stomach. "Oh, I couldn't eat another bite. I'm absolutely—"

Maebelle pressed her fingers to her lips. "Hush, now. You've not even seen my cobbler yet." She rose from her seat beside Clark and pulled a cloth from a glass baking pan, revealing the most beautiful peach cobbler any of us had ever seen. "I made it with fresh peaches from right here on Bonaventure. I planted the trees myself. Okay, that's not entirely true. I pestered my grandfather while he was planting them over a quarter century ago. Little did I know then that I would one day bake cobblers and pies literally from the fruits of Grandfather's labor. That's what makes this dessert so special."

Brown slid his chair back to the table and replaced his napkin on his lap. "Since you put it like that, only a fool would pass up your cobbler."

She filled bowls with heaping spoonfuls of the delectable treasure. "The peaches aren't the only thing tying this dessert to Bonaventure. Sprinkled on top of the whole thing are candied pecans from the trees you can see right through that door." With the bowls filled, she threw up her hands. "I almost forgot the ice cream."

She pulled a stainless-steel bowl from the freezer and slid it onto the buffet beside the cobbler bowls. "Who wants homemade peach vanilla ice cream? I know that's a peach overload, but there's just a hint of peach and maybe a little taste of brandy in the mix."

Hands went up in a unanimous plea. Seconds later, the only sounds rising from the table were satisfied sighs and spoons striking glass bowls.

Clark swallowed the last of his dessert and threw his arm around Maebelle. "My dear, you've outdone yourself again. And if you keep this up, I'm going to weigh four hundred pounds."

Maebelle gave him a poke to the stomach. "You're well on your way, my darling."

I stood from my seat and lifted my empty bowl. "I want you to sit down and relax, Maebelle. I'll clean up the kitchen."

Irina landed a firm palm on the table, securing everyone's attention. "No! Tatiana and I will clean dishes. The men will have cigars and vodka. It is least I can do."

I eyed my team, and most of them shrugged. "I think I'll replace the vodka with a little Tennessee sipping whiskey, but the cigars certainly sound like a great plan."

With a little more insistence, Irina shooed us from the kitchen.

Clark stood and tossed his napkin over his demolished bowl. "To the gazebo, gentlemen. The smoking lamp is lit. Chase, you bring the stogies. I've got the rest."

I pulled a box of Cuban Cohibas from the humidor in the library and strolled across the lawn. I studied the men sitting in the Adirondack chairs and felt an overwhelming sense of pride at having that collection of warriors as practical family. With the exception of Al Brown, I'd fought, bled, and made enemies bleed with each of those men, and I couldn't imagine my life without them.

I passed out the Cubans while Clark poured the Jack Daniel's Single Barrel.

With plumes of white smoke rising through the rafters of the gazebo, Brown touched the base of the centerpiece of the gazebo with his boot. "This is one fine gazebo, Chase, but what's the story of this cannon?"

I let my eyes caress every inch of the massive, once-feared weapon of war, and I could almost smell the smoke and cinder and feel the concussion within my chest from the roar of the beast back in its heyday on the high seas. "Thanks, Al. The gazebo was built for only one purpose—to house this gun. I pulled that thing from the mud and muck right out there in the Cumberland Sound." I pointed across the marsh toward the placid body of water between the town of Saint Marys, Georgia, and Cumberland Island. "The cannon was most likely cast by the French and fitted aboard one of their frigates in the late seventeen or early eighteen hundreds. The British made great sport of kicking the Frogs' butts on the water and commandeering their ships into the king's service."

Hunter raised a glass. "Here's to butt-kicking and big guns."

A rowdy roar of cheers rose with our cigar smoke.

"Anyway," I said, "it was precisely one such ship that burned and sank in the sound during the early days of the War of Eighteen Twelve. I went to the trouble of finding, excavating, and hauling the cannon from the bottom with a little—okay, a lot of—help from Captain Stinnett of the Research Vessel *Lori Danielle*. The gun was a gift for my great uncle and Maebelle's grandfather, Judge Bernard Henry Huntsinger. The Judge—that's what everybody called him—bequeathed Bonaventure Plantation to me upon his death, essentially dividing his estate between his beloved granddaughter and his only other living heir. Maebelle inherited the financial holdings, and Bonaventure became my home."

Brown raised his glass. "Here's to Fulton blood running through the history of this place. And may it never run over any ground less worthy."

I raised my glass to meet his. "Thank you, Al, but this place fell to me through my mother's bloodline, the Huntsingers, not the Fultons."

He chuckled. "Either way, my toast remains unchanged."

We drank and felt the lengthening shadows fall over the plantation and over each of us.

Clark stomped on the sturdy floorboards of the gazebo. "You've kept us waiting long enough, College Boy. Let's hear this plan of yours to get us and our play-pretties into Alberta without the Canucks knowing we're there."

I took a long draw from my cigar and let the smoke drift from my lips like a morning fog rising from the water. "I don't have all the details worked out, but in my head, I'm calling it the Trojan Container. I think we can build a Land Sea container with all the comforts of home for five and a half men."

Clark recoiled. "Five and a half?"

I motioned toward Mongo. "Yeah, he's at least one and a half. Disco, Hunter, Singer, and I make up the remaining four. I've never actually seen one of these things, but I've read about them. We can power and ventilate the container while we're on the freighter."

Clark leaned forward, suddenly intrigued. "A freighter, huh? I thought you had a truck in mind."

"We'll need a truck once we land in Vancouver, but a border crossing is too risky with a tractor trailer full of commandos and a ton of bullets and bang-bangs. We can ride the ship from Washington into Vancouver, leaving us inside the container for no more than a day. With a truck driver and little financial love for the customs officer, we can be in western Alberta in less than twenty-four hours after the crane lifts us off that boat."

"That's a lot of logistics and even more moving parts," Clark said. "But if anybody can pull it off, it's us . . . and Skipper."

I glanced toward the house. "Speaking of Skipper, she should be in on the conversation. We can't set up any of this without her."

As if walking through time itself, Skipper appeared ten feet from the gazebo. "I *am* in on it."

I jumped. "You scared the crap out of me. How long have you been standing there?"

"Just a few seconds," she said, "but I was listening in. One of the coolest parts of the new ops center is the audio and video network laced all over this place, from the dock to the horse barn and even the hangar at the airport. I can see and hear everything right from the comfort of my favorite office chair."

"That's a little creepy," I said, "but in this case, I'm glad you were listening in. How much did you hear?"

"All of it. I've got the whole system remoted through my phone and to this little earpiece."

"You're going to make a pretty good spy someday, you know that?"

She shrugged. "I don't know about someday, but I think I'm doing okay right now."

"You certainly are. So, what do you think of my plan?"

"I think it's a lot of work. It's certainly doable, and I like it. There are boats in and out of Vancouver every day, so that part is simple. It's getting that container through Canadian customs that's going to be a challenge."

"I thought of that as well," I said. "If we use a forty-foot high-cube Conex for the shell, we can pack legitimate cargo in half of the container with the hidden half being our home sweet home for a couple of days. That eliminates the need to bribe anyone, but we have to make sure we get on the priority customs schedule. We won't have enough air, food, and water for more than a few days."

"That's easy. I can take care of that, no problem," Skipper said. "But what about the, uh, you know . . . Your waste?"

Laughter came from everyone except Disco, who obviously had the same question.

Hunter raised a finger. "I'll take this one. We're knuckle-dragging cavemen in combat boots. You just get us on that boat and onto a truck. We can deal with a little action on the poop deck, if you know what I mean."

She drew a circle in the air to encompass all of us. "You are disgusting. All of you. And I'm done with this whole grown-up Boy Scout meeting. You guys can continue pulling each other's fingers and laughing at the results. I've got work to do." She pointed at me. "And you still owe me a raise."

Before I could respond, she was gone, and we were, once again, the no-girls-allowed club.

Al motioned toward the house with the butt of his cigar. "She's good. Where did you find her?"

I watched the best analyst I knew dance through the back door of the house and vanish inside. "Essentially, she's my little sister, and that'll have to do for now."

Our Cubans burned down to our flesh, and the whiskey bottle ran dry just in time for me to issue the orders for the next day.

"Let's get back in the shoot house at seven thirty tomorrow. I'd like to get some work done before it gets too hot in there. If we can get six more hours of training done—"

Before I could finish, Skipper came bounding down the back steps and across the yard. "Uh, guys . . . How soon can you be ready to go?"

I said, "We need another half day in the shoot house and—"

"There's no time for that," she said. "We've got to get to work on that container. I found a freighter scheduled to leave San Francisco for Vancouver in twelve days. That gives us ten or eleven days to build the box, get it loaded, and move it three thousand miles across the country."

I looked over my team until my eyes fell on Disco, our retired A-10 pilot and the only one of us without knuckle-dragging scars. "You don't have to go if you don't feel comfortable."

"If I felt comfortable about sneaking into a sovereign allied country in a shipping container so we can start a gunfight with the Chinese at a secret underground bunker in the Canadian Rockies, there would be a lot wrong with me. We could train for the rest of the year, and I wouldn't be comfortable, but I'm in."

Al Brown sat in amazed wonder. "You guys are insane. And I'd like to have a thousand more just like you."

Chapter 18
We Need Help

I lay awake most of the night, desperately trying to find, gather, and place the far-flung pieces of the puzzle that had fallen into my lap. As I wrestled with the complexity of the task, my first assignment out of The Ranch poured through my mind.

A pair of mysterious guys had shown up with a sealed envelope containing a photograph of a bucktoothed Russian named Suslik. They told me to find and kill him. I simply had to show up at Homestead Air Force Base and climb aboard a helicopter. Everything about the mission was planned down to the letter . . . by someone else. I followed the orders I was given, found the Russian, and then chopped him into fish food with the propeller of an outboard motor on a borrowed dinghy in Havana Harbor. That part of the mission wasn't particularly challenging, but what followed changed my life forever. Anya Burinkova, the beautiful Russian SVR assassin, literally sliced her way into my life, and what followed was just as unbelievable as a James Bond adventure.

I'd come a million miles and grown from an ambitious boy into a battle-hardened man responsible for the lives of a team unlike any other fighting force on the planet. I bore that responsibility on shoulders that refused to fall, but alone in the darkness of night when the sun hid itself from my world, I sometimes wondered how it would end. Would a young man's blade or a sniper's sting blind me to the coming of another sunrise? Regardless of the end, be it horrible in some distant corner of the globe, or silent and peaceful on the ground where my family toiled and prayed and lived and died, it would come. And I would face it and endure it knowing I hadn't crumbled beneath the weight of the life for which I'd been chosen.

Abandoning my body's cries for sleep and surrendering to my mind's demands to churn and burn, I crept from my bed, leaving Penny breathing the rhythmic sounds of perfect sleep, and I headed for the coffee pot.

To my surprise, the smell of the brew wafted from the kitchen and found my nose halfway down the massive staircase. I could do nothing other than smile as I watched Clark pouring two cups on the counter beside the stove.

He lifted one cup, leaving the other behind. "I'll meet you on the back gallery, College Boy."

Bonaventure's back gallery, as it is called in the coastal low country of the American South, was as close to hallowed ground as I'd ever walk. Penny and I had been married on the steps of that grand old porch. Clark and I had drank and laughed and planned there. Anya had held a tiny, plastic American flag between her fingers at a belated celebration of the Fourth of July in the corner of the gallery and had become an American by choice in that moment. My great uncle, the Judge, had taught Constitutional Law to countless clerks and bright-eyed barristers-to-be from an aged rocking chair. And that morning, in the hours before the world awoke, my friend, brother-at-arms, and handler and I would do it again.

"How did you know?" I asked as I stepped onto the oak planks of new decking that still looked like the old boards overlooking the North River.

Without looking up, Clark sipped his steaming black coffee. "Sleep isn't for men like us in times like these."

I nestled into an oak rocker and laid my feet on the rail. "Men like us. That's an interesting thought. How many are there?"

He inspected the surface of his source of caffeine. "I don't know, but not nearly enough. I fear we're a dying breed. Too many want what we've earned but aren't willing to sacrifice what we have."

"You may be right, but I pray you're not."

"Me, too," he whispered. "Me, too."

I listened to the crickets in the trees and the cry of a distant owl from somewhere within the abandoned paper plant. "We need help on this one, my friend."

"Yep, we sure do. None of us has the skill to build that box, and we don't have a truck or a driver to get it to California, even if we could build it."

"Earl could do it," I said as I stared out over the dock with the Mark V patrol boat bobbing silently. "She built the fuel tanks and cooling shrouds for that thing. We've got the tools, and she's got the skills."

Clark rolled his wrist to read the face of his watch. "What time does the old girl crawl out of bed?"

"I don't know, but we could be laying alongside the dock in Saint Augustine when she does."

"What good will it do having her up here if we don't have a Conex for her to work on?"

"I think I've got that part figured out. They have at least two dozen empty containers over at the Navy base. I'm sure Hunter can score one by the time we get back with Earl."

He stood from his rocker and drained the remains of his coffee. "Let's go, then. We're wasting daylight."

I laughed. "Daylight is still two hours away."

The Mark V patrol boat's twin diesels took their first breath of the warm air of the humid, coastal summer morning and turned that breath and a swallow of fuel into pure raw power. I eased the throttles forward and motored away from the dock, hoping to leave everyone sleeping at Bonaventure.

Once around the third winding turn in the river, I hit the lights and eased the throttles from idle to all ahead one half. The bow came up, temporarily blinding us to everything out front, but the flawless design of the boat's hull soon had us solidly on plane with our vision restored and our speed climbing through thirty knots. As the snakelike river gave way to the open water of Cumberland Sound, I pushed our speed through fifty knots and settled into a smooth, comfortable ride provided by the pneumatic shock absorbers supporting each seat aboard the Mark V. The ocean offered widely spaced swells of a foot or less off the east coast of Florida as we roared southward toward Saint Augustine and Earl at the End.

Earline—Earl to her friends—was a character right out of Alice in Wonderland. She was the best diesel mechanic on the East Coast, but that was just the tip of the iceberg. She'd been a mechanic with Air America, the CIA's private air force during Vietnam and beyond, and she'd adopted me as her personal plaything the first time I met her. At something barely over five feet tall and two hundred pounds, she not only looked unique but also managed to make everyone in her path fall in love with her.

The fifty-five-mile journey from the Saint Marys inlet to the Saint Augustine Pass took only forty-five minutes at the comfortable cruising speed of sixty-five knots. The country's oldest city was still asleep when we motored beneath the Bridge of Lions, the ornate drawbridge across the Matanzas River connecting the Plaza de la Constitución to the island of Saint Augustine Beach. Just south of the bridge lay the Municipal Marina, where I'd once made my home—albeit somewhat temporary—aboard *Aegis*.

The marina had changed since I'd last seen it, and the fuel dock was empty and offered just enough space to lay the eighty-two feet of the Mark V alongside. I made the maneuver at idle power to avoid waking the boaters whose hangovers would not appreciate the growl of nearly five thousand horsepower beneath our decks.

Earl earned her moniker of "Earl at the End" by consuming forty-five feet of the dock all the way at the end of the first pier. When I originally met her, she lived aboard a rotting, decrepit trawler that likely floated only because it was tied to the dock. Since then, she'd upgraded after my team and I had recovered a fortune in gold bars hidden by her late husband, Boomer, during his days as an Air America pilot. Hundreds of pounds of gold bars can change a person's life, but other than upgrading her floating abode, Earl at the End would never change a thing.

"Is that you, Baby Boy? What are you doing way down here this early in the morning?"

I smiled up from the dock. "Good morning, you sexy thing. What are *you* doing up so early?"

"What do you mean, early? The sun's almost up, Stud Muffin. And bless my soul, you brought that fine-ass Clark with you. This may be too much for an old girl's heart to stand. Get yourselves up here, and give Mama a hug . . . a nice long grinding one, if you know what I mean."

We climbed the boarding ladder to the deck of the cruiser and took turns smothering our favorite mechanic. She poured coffee that tasted like kerosene and then nestled into a cushion on the bridge. "Seriously, now, what are you boys doing down here? I get the feeling this ain't no social call."

"You know us too well," I said. "We need help, Earl, and you're the only person who can do what we need."

She waved her stained mug at the two of us. "If either one of you would get rid of them women of yours, I'd show you what a real woman can do for you, but I'm sure that ain't happened yet ... has it?"

"I'm afraid not, and I'm certain I'd never be man enough for you, Old Girl. What we need is a metal fabricator. Are you up for the task?"

She peered around me toward the Mark V. "You better not have gone and messed up them tanks on that thing."

I said, "No, the tanks are fine. This project is a little bigger than fuel tanks. We need to turn a high-cube shipping container into a temporary home for five grown men, but we need it to look like any other Conex from the outside."

Her eyes lit up beneath the crown of spiked gray hair protruding from the top of her head. She set her coffee cup on the console, leaned forward, and rubbed her hands together with anticipation. "When? Where? And how long?"

Clark and I shared a look of relief and satisfaction. "Now, Bonaventure, and one week. Can you do it?"

She laughed from her toes up, and it sounded more like the Wicked Witch of the West than the laugh of a career diesel mechanic. "Can I do it? What kind of question is that? Let me get my hat and a clean pair of drawers. I'll be ready to go in five minutes."

Clark whispered, "A clean pair of drawers?"

"Yeah. Don't you know every metal fabricator needs a clean pair of drawers occasionally?"

He shook his head. "I guess you should wake up Hunter."

"Way ahead of you. I sent him a text when we left Bonaventure." I pulled my phone from my pocket and held it up for him to see. "He's already scored a Conex and a trailer. He's working on finding something to pull it with. Do you have any suggestions?"

"What about Kenny LePine? Surely he's got a truck that can pull it."

"Great idea," I said. "I'll give him a call."

Kenny LePine was a Cajun and the premier earth-moving contractor in Camden County, Georgia. His command of the English language was questionable, but there was no one better when it came to scraping the ground.

I dialed his number, and the scourge of South Louisiana answered. "Mornin'. Dis be Kenny, me, and who dis be callin' me, you?"

"Good morning, Kenny. It's Chase Fulton. You cleaned up after the fire and dug the new foundation for me at Bonaventure Plantation. Remember?"

"I don' be nebber forgettin' nuttin' when it come to you, Missah Chase. How y'all been doin', you? How tings be out at dat fine place of your'n?"

Uncertain what he'd said, I replied, "I'm doing great, Kenny, but I need a favor."

"Day ain't nuttin' you could aks me, you, dat ol' Kenny wouldn't be doin', no. Dus' name it, and I be gettin' her done fo' you be knowin' it, me. You hears me, huh?"

"I don't know what you just said, but I need somebody to haul a Conex container from the Navy base to my workshop at Bonaventure. Do you have somebody you could send over to take care of that this morning?"

"Ha! You sho be da funny one, you. I knows you be knowin' zackly what ol' Kenny be sayin', me. And you ain't be no need to worry ne'er 'gen 'bout no haulin', you. I be der dus' myself, me. An' let me guess, it be Missah Hunter who be getting dis here big ol' box from dat dere Navy base, no?"

I tried not to laugh, but listening to Kenny's Cajun jargon was like trying to pet a porcupine. No matter which way I rubbed, I got stuck.

"Okay, Kenny, I'm going to pretend like you said you'd take care of it. Hunter is over at the main motor pool on Kings Bay. Do you have a pass to get on base?"

"You is one funny dude, you, Missah Chase. I be gettin' on dat dere base, no prob'm. You just wait 'n see, you. I be dere fo' dat ol' rooster crow, don' you be knowin'."

With that, the line went dead, and I turned to Clark with bewilderment dripping from my face.

Clark said, "What did he say? Can he do it?"

I shrugged. "I have no idea what he said, but it sounded positive. I guess we'll see when we get home."

Earl had more than a million dollars in the bank, but nothing about her told such a tale. She emerged from the interior of her boat with a plastic Walmart bag and an Igloo cooler. "I'm ready to go, but you boys'll have to carry my luggage for me. I have to get my welding helmet."

I looked around her and into the boat. "Of course we'll carry your luggage. Where is it?"

She handed the plastic bag to Clark and the cooler to me. "It's right here, you crazy thing. Go on. I'll get my helmet and meet you by your boat."

We chuckled at Earl's idea of luggage, but we followed her instruction nonetheless. Two minutes later, Clark and I lifted her across the gunwale of the Mark V, and she waddled to the helm station as if claiming her throne.

She started the diesels and turned to us with impatience in her eyes. "Well, are you going to cast off or just stand there and stare at me? I know I'm a fine specimen of a woman, but you boys need to pull it together. Now, throw off them lines."

We followed orders, and Earl tore away from the dock as if running from a fire. When we reached the open ocean, she pressed the throttles to their stops and stared over her shoulder at our wake. She adjusted the throttles individually, and the look on her face said something was wrong. She motioned toward the deck plates covering the engine room. "Open them plates up, boys. Something don't feel right."

Still plowing across the Atlantic at full speed, she abandoned the helm and lay down on the deck with her head and shoulders leaning toward the engines. After her inspection, she crawled back to her feet and motioned for us to close the plates. We did, and she said, "How long's it been since you ran this thing wide open?"

"I don't know," I said. "This is the first time we've had it out in several months."

"Several months? This is a high-performance lady, and she gets lonely. You've got to take her out dancing every now and then."

When we pulled into the Bonaventure dock half an hour after sunrise, Kenny LePine was climbing down from his Kenworth tractor with a well-worn, high-cube Conex container resting on the trailer behind.

Chapter 19

If You Build It, We Will Go

We secured the Mark V and headed for the workshop. To my horror, Kenny threw up a hand and started talking—or whatever he does when sounds come out of his mouth.

I grabbed Earl's arm. "I have to warn you. That's Kenny LePine. He's completely insane and doesn't speak anything resembling English, but just do your best to listen for the parts you can understand."

"Hey! Der you be, you. Who you got der wich you dis time? Is dis here be da box you been wantin', you?"

Suddenly, I was even more terrified since I'd understood almost everything he said. "Hey, Kenny. It's good to see you. This is Earl. She's going to do some work on the Conex for us."

He shot a concerned look down at his right hand and yanked a rag from his back pocket. With vigor like I'd never seen from him, he wiped his hand with the rag until the first layer of skin had to have fallen off. With wide eyes and a grin the size of New Orleans, he yanked the cap from his head with his left hand and stuck the well-rubbed right hand toward my mechanic. "Hello der, Miss Earl. I don' be knowin' nobody bein' a girl and dem be name Earl, me. How you do? An' don' be shamed to not be takin' my grubby hand, no. Ain't no fine woman like you don' need be touchin' no grungy, grimy hand like mine, no."

Earl smiled as if Robert Redford were flirting with her, and she slapped Kenny's hand away. "I ain't no hand-shakin' kine woman, no, not me. I be da huggin' kine, and you be dus' da kina man I do love huggin' on da most, me."

Sometimes, when you find just the right spot behind a dog's ear, scratching it will make him thump his foot against the ground and roll his eyes back in his head. That's exactly the response Kenny had to Earl's hug, and I thought I'd been transported into some sort of Cajun Twilight Zone. Who knew Earl from the End was bilingual?

When Earl finally pulled away, Kenny took a knee in front of her, and I thought he was on the verge of pulling out an engagement ring. Thankfully, though, he wiped his brow with the rag and let out a long sigh. "Whoo-eee, it done been a long time since ol' Kenny been hugged like dat, me. You sho be one fine huggin' kina woman, you."

The two talked, flirted, and apparently formed some sort of connection of souls. It was as if nothing else in the world existed while their incomprehensible gibberish persisted. I was frightened to break it up, so Clark and I joined Hunter in the workshop inspecting what would become our home away from home in the new future.

Hunter motioned toward Earl and Kenny. "It looks like you'll have to spray those two with a water hose to get them apart. What's that about?"

"I don't know," I said, "but I don't want to get any of it on me. It's weird enough already. I think I'll just let them keep doing whatever it is they're doing."

"As much as I want to, I just can't look away," Hunter said. "It's like they've got me in some kind of trance."

I stepped in front of him to block his line of sight. "Come on, little voyeur. We've got work to do. How did you talk the Navy out of the Conex?"

"What Conex? This thing has been sitting in the motor pool for over two years. A contractor was supposed to pick it up, but he never showed up. It's not on anybody's books, so the Navy's glad to have it out of their motor pool."

Clark slapped the side of the enormous metal box. "I like your style, Hunter."

"Thanks, but that's not all. I've got a delivery of plate steel and some stainless on the way. It should be here any minute."

"What about the trailer?" I asked.

Hunter kicked a tire. "We'll have to give it back. I'm not sure who owns it, but we can keep it long enough to do what we need. I don't think they'll miss it."

We climbed the back of the trailer and crawled inside the Conex. Even though the sun had only been up for minutes, it was already steamy inside the oversized metal coffin.

"What are we going to do about the heat?" Hunter asked.

"I'm not sure yet, but we'll definitely have to come up with something. Hopefully our little love-sick mechanic out there will have some ideas."

We checked the container for weak spots or signs of water intrusion but found none.

"Hunter, it looks like you stole a fine Conex."

He gasped as if appalled. "I prefer *appropriated* over stole. It makes me sound more sophisticated . . . and less criminal."

I chuckled. "That's exactly the word that comes to mind every time I think of you . . . sophisticated."

Earl finally made her appearance. She stood inside the workshop, hopping up and down, attempting to peer into the container. "I'll have to build a set of steps or find a ladder."

I turned to see one of the worst sights my poor eyes had ever beheld. Cajun Kenny LePine bent over, picked up all two hundred pounds of Earl at the End, and hefted her into the Conex. "Don' you be worryin' 'bout needin' no ladder, you. Dus' long as you gots ol' Kenny roun'."

Earl scampered to her feet and actually blushed. "I may have to keep you around, Kenny."

He laughed loud enough to be heard back on the bayou. "Good luck gettin' rids of me, you."

Earl walked the length of the container, kicking the sides every few feet and peering up at the ceiling as she went. "It looks like a good one to me. What is it you want done to it?"

"We want you to build us living quarters in the front with some kind of ventilation so we won't roast. We also need to move about fifteen hundred pounds of gear, including weapons, ammo, explosives, and provisions."

"How long are you planning to live in this thing?" she asked.

"Hopefully, no more than two days, but I'd like to build it so we could survive at least a week if our plan falls apart."

She let out a low whistle. "What's the climate?"

"Pacific Northwest," I said.

She touched a finger to the corner of her mouth. "Hmm, now what could a team of common folks like you be doing in the Pacific Northwest with that kind of load inside a Trojan Horse?"

"Just a little vacation," I said.

"Yeah, right."

"Can you do it?" I asked.

"Of course I can do it, but I need some supplies. A bunch of plate steel, at least a little stainless, some solar panels, maybe even an ultra-quiet generator, and some ventilation fans. Are you thinking about hiding behind half a cargo load or something like that?"

I smiled almost as wide as Kenny. "Now you're catching on. Hunter has the steel on the way, and it looks like your secret admirer back there has just volunteered to be your apprentice."

She shot a glance across her shoulder. "Oh, I'm gonna make that hottie a lot more than my apprentice."

"You're shameless, Earl."

"If you only knew, Baby Boy . . . if you only knew."

I shook my head. "Trust me. I don't want to know."

She slapped at my arm. "Don't you get all high and mighty now. You know you paraded them girls all around me. First it was that Russian floozy and then that long-legged, crazy-haired thing you went and married. Now it's your turn to be jealous."

"Yep, you got me. Jealousy is exactly what it is. Now, get to work."

"I've got one more question. Are you taking that mountain of a man with you?"

"Mongo? Yes, he's definitely going."

"That monster needs a lot more food, air, and space than you skinny ones, but I think I've got a picture of how I can get it done. Now, get out of here and let me work."

"If you need anything, just tell Kenny."

She looked back and gave LePine a little wink. "Oh, that man knows what I need without me saying a word."

I shuddered. "That's it! I'm out of here. We'll send food and water."

Kenny ignored the three of us as we hopped from the container and headed for the house. Before we were out of earshot, I could've sworn I heard Earl and Kenny singing about having fun on the bayou.

The delivery of steel arrived just as we climbed the stairs into the house, but I didn't have the stomach to accompany the delivery driver to the workshop. Whatever was happening out there was more than I needed running around in my head.

* * *

Twelve hours later, after I'd sent five gallons of Gatorade and two pizzas to the workshop, Earl and Kenny came through the kitchen door, sweat-soaked and dripping.

"You two look like you've had quite a day out there. Are you okay?" I asked.

Kenny said, "Yeah, we be doin' dus' . . ."

I held up a hand. "How about letting Earl tell us?"

Earl said, "Be nice to him, Chase. He's been working hard all day."

"Oh, I know what he's been working," I said.

"Anyway," she said, "we got a lot done for the first day. I'm not ready for you to see it yet, but by this time tomorrow, I think you'll be pleased."

"Thanks, Earl. I knew you'd work a miracle."

"Miracles don't come cheap, Baby Boy, but you'll get my bill."

"You know I've never shied away from your bill. Whatever it is, I'll be happy to pay it."

She looked around the kitchen as if searching for a lost child.

I followed her eyes. "What are you looking for?"

"What did you with my luggage?"

"I put it in the guest room at the end of the hall where you usually sleep."

She shot a glance at Kenny and almost blushed. "Yeah, I think I'll stay somewhere else this time, but we'll be back in the morning before it gets hot."

I grabbed her cooler and Walmart bag from the bedroom. "Something tells me it's going to be hot wherever you two go. Try not to hurt him, please. He's the best excavation contractor around, and the people of this little town need him healthy."

Kenny grabbed the bag and cooler, and the pair vanished before I could launch any more zingers.

Penny looked up from the table. "Well, that was weird. What's going on there?"

"Trust me. You don't want to know, and I don't want to have to tell you."

She stared out the door and cocked her head. "Are they . . . ?"

"Stop asking questions you don't really want me to answer. I'm going to get a shower and hit the sack. I didn't get much sleep last night. Are you coming?"

She quivered a little as she stood from the table. "Yeah, I'm coming, but I'm not sure I'll be able to sleep. I don't think I'll ever get that horrifying mental picture out of my head. Why do you do these things to me? I thought you loved me."

"Love is a many-splintered thing, my dear. Just let it happen."

She rolled her eyes. "Many-splintered? Really?"

"Absolutely. And apparently sweaty, too."

Chapter 20
Home Sweet Home

Still afraid of what I might see or hear, I made plenty of noise when I walked into the workshop. Sparks flew, hammers pounded, and the oversized fan Kenny delivered and set up turned the low-country oven into an almost bearable sauna.

"Hey, Kenny! I know you're wrapped up with Cinderella over there, but I'd love to put a few hundred bucks in your pocket if you could pull yourself away for a little project I'm working on."

He turned and wiped the sweat pouring from his face. "I can do dat. What you be needin' did, you?"

"Come with me, and I'll show you."

I led him from the shop and hopped into the microbus. As we drove to the former paper plant, I handed him a bottle of water. "I really appreciate you working on the box with Earl. I'm sure she can use the help."

"Dat der sho be some mo kina woman, she. I do guarantee dat right der."

"She sure is," I said. "But I thought you had a family already."

He bowed his head. "I did, me, but she done gone home to dat great reward, she. Ol' Kenny, me, been livin' all by myselfs for too many long times, me."

"I'm sorry to hear that. Who knows? Maybe you and Earl—"

He slugged my shoulder. "Yeah, dat's what me be thinkin', too, but don't talk no bad ju-ju on it for mes, now, you hears me, you?"

"I wouldn't dream of it, Kenny. Come on, let me show you what I need."

We climbed from the van, and Kenny followed me into the abandoned warehouse. "We've been doing some weapons training in here, but we've only been able to use blanks because I'm afraid a stray round might escape and hit somebody or one of the horses outside. Penny would kill me dead if that happened. I'd like to bring in a load of railroad crossties and build some interior walls that can stop a nine millimeter. Is that something you and your guys can do?"

He paced the space, counting in a whisper as he walked. When he'd surveyed the space, he turned to study the ceiling. "How high you be wantin' dese here timber walls?"

"I hadn't really thought about that, but I think we should go at least twelve feet high, don't you?"

"Me do. It'll take four or maybe tree mens two days, maybe one and some. Fo' you, Chase, ain't no charge for da labors, no, but somebody's gotta buy dem timbers, yeah."

I shook my head. "As much as I appreciate the offer, I know how it is when you've got men to pay and bills to meet. If you've got a source for the timbers, buy whatever you think we'll need, and I'll pay your men directly if you won't take my money. You're a businessman, and you can't stay in business giving away free labor."

"You's a good mans, you. I knows dus' where to get a mighty whole big truckload of dem crossties at a fine price for a man like you is. My mens be here in da mornin', yeah."

"Sounds good to me. Thanks, Kenny. I'll take you back to the shop if you want a ride."

He stared around the vast open space of the building for a long moment. "My brudders be workin' here long time go, dem, when dis place be makin' papers. All dis be yours now?"

I nodded. "It's all mine. I inherited the whole property from the Judge. He was my great uncle on my mother's side. He gave this part of the plantation to the paper company on a lifetime lease. As long as they were providing jobs for the people around here, they could keep the land. When they shut down, it reverted back to the Judge."

Kenny squinted and locked eyes with me. "And you be some kind of gubment man, you. Ain't dat right?"

"Yeah, something like that."

He gave me a wink. "Who you gon be sneakin' up on in dat der box me and Miss Earline be buildin'?"

It was my turn to give him a wink. "Just some folks who don't need to see us coming, dem."

"Ha!" he roared. "I do guarantee day be some Cajun in you, and you don't even know it, you. Whoo-eee!"

I dropped him off back at the shop to find Earl lying on the floor in front of the fan.

I yelled, "Are you all right?"

She looked up and grinned. "I am now that you brought my man back, but I need to talk to you about something."

"Sure. What is it?"

She motioned toward the container. "You're going to roast in that thing no matter how much air we blow through it. Whatever you're doing sounds important enough that you and your boys need to get to it without melting into greasy spots on the floor. I've got an idea how to air-condition it, but it's going to take a couple generators. I can do it, but it won't be cheap. It'll be at least fifteen grand, maybe a little more."

"Do it. If you need the money up front, I'll pay you now."

She sat up and poured a bottle of water down her throat. "Yeah, that'd be best. Cash always talks better than credit, and I'd rather use your cash than mine. If you've got twenty grand, I can get everything I need today if Kenny's got a big enough truck."

Before I could answer, Kenny said, "You know Kenny be havin' e'reting you be needin', lil' mamma. Dus' say to ol' Kenny, dus' say, dis is what I need, and ol' Kenny be puttin' it on you, das fo' sho.'"

I said, "I'm not sure what he said, but it sounded like he's got a truck."

I pulled twenty-five thousand from the safe and delivered it back to the shop. Earl dropped the stacks of bills into a brown paper bag. "If everything goes the way I expect, you'll have your new home sweet home by this time tomorrow."

"I'd hug you, but you're filthy, and I'm afraid Kenny would stab me."

She grinned through the sweat and grime on her face. "He is one sweet man."

I turned to see Kenny with his phone pressed to his ear, and an idea flashed through my head. I waited for him to hang up, and he said, "Dem timbers be here right now, maybe few minutes. I got you da best price day is on timbers. I gots dem new ones cause dem ol' ones day be sellin' off is all cracked up and twisted up, and some of dem still got dem iron spikes in 'em. Don't be no good for shootin' at, no."

"That's great. Thanks. I've got one more job for you if you're interested. I need to get this Conex to San Francisco when you and Earl finish it. Is that something you can do?"

"You know I be doin' whatever you be needin' did, me. Alls you gots to say is where and when, and it be did fo you knows it."

"Again, I'm not sure what you said, but it sounds like a yes from here. Do you have all the licenses and permits to haul this thing across the country?"

"Yes, sir. We is da real ting. We don't be no half-ass nobody doin' nothin'. It be all legal and fine. I guarantee dat, I do."

Afraid he might start talking again if I said anything else, I shot him a thumbs-up and climbed back into the microbus.

Back at the house, I found Clark and Al on the back gallery. "I solved two of our problems already this morning."

Clark looked up. "Let's hear it."

"The first one is the shoot house. You know how we've been training with blanks in there. I came up with an idea to let us use live rounds. Kenny is going to have a couple of his men—tree, maybe two of dem—build us some interior walls out of new railroad crossties. They're on their way now."

"That's a great idea," Clark said. "What's number two?"

"It turns out that Kenny has all the license and permits as well as the equipment to haul our Conex to San Francisco. He says he'll be happy to do it. Or, at least that's what I think he said."

Brown held up a finger. "That guy's a Cajun, right?"

"Oh, yeah. He's straight out of the bayou."

"That means he probably speaks French. Do you trust him?"

I planted myself in the third rocking chair. "Sure, I trust him. He's a good man."

Brown put on a satisfied smirk. "A truck driver who speaks French sure would come in handy moving a Conex from Vancouver to Alberta."

* * *

Bonaventure Plantation turned into a beehive of activity that afternoon. Front-end loaders and forklifts buzzed nonstop at the paper plant as Kenny's men stacked and anchored hundreds of black creosoted crossties into a maze of corridors and open rooms. The cutting, hammering, and welding continued in the shop. Apparently, Kenny provided a couple of extra welders to give Earl a break. For once, she got to supervise the operation while somebody else did the work. By the time the day was over, I'd spent somewhere close to a hundred thousand dollars in labor and materials.

Over the dinner table spread with another of Maebelle's feasts, I said, "It's a shame we've spent all this money and hard work to abandon that Conex in the Canadian Rockies."

Kenny had invited himself to dinner and shuddered when I mentioned leaving the container behind. "No way. Das too much monies and works to be leavin' in dem mountains up dere. You gots to get dat ting hauled back down here, you."

"That brings up another question, Kenny. Do you speak French? I mean the kind of French somebody in Canada can understand. I know you think you speak English, but I have my doubts."

Kenny laughed. *"Je parle un français parfait et je serais heureux d'aider de toutes les manières possibles."*

Everyone at the table sat in amazement at Kenny's apparent flawless French.

When the meal ended with German chocolate cake that melted in our mouths, I stood and motioned toward the library. "Kenny, if you don't mind, come with us. We need to discuss a deal."

Kenny followed Clark, Al, Hunter, and me down the hallway, and we settled into the library.

"Here's what I need," I began. "You've already agreed to take the Conex to the port of San Francisco for us. After that, I need you to meet us at the Port of Vancouver, where you'll pick up the container again and haul it to Western Alberta in the Canadian Rockies. Are you interested?"

Kenny stared toward the closed door and leaned forward. "If Miss Earline can comes wit me, ol' Kenny'll do it for a dollar a mile, me, but if me gots to do it all by myselfs, it's gonna be two of dem dollars e'ry mile along dat road, yes, sir."

I scanned my teammates for any sign of disagreement, but none came. I stuck my hand in Kenny's. "Deal. But you have to talk to Earl about coming along."

We shook, and Kenny was the first man out the door.

I said, "It looks like our plan is coming together, gentlemen."

"It does," Al said, "but the cast of characters is getting stranger every minute. By the time this thing becomes a full-blown operation, we'll have a troop of clowns and a herd of camels along for the ride."

Chapter 21
Subterranean Field Trip

For the first night since leaving The Bahamas, merciful sleep surrendered herself to me, and I fell into a beautiful cloud of slumber my body desperately needed. Although quality over quantity has always been my mantra, I would've killed for two more hours of silence beneath my sheets. Skipper ended my coma at ten minutes after five a.m.

The pounding on my door was bad enough, but the yelling put the cherry on top of my awakening.

"Chase! Get up! Get up!"

I threw back the covers and stretched, lost in the confusion of a man who'd slept for years. "Stop yelling. What is it?"

Skipper opened the door and stepped inside.

Penny's sleep had reached the same terminus as mine, but she was less hospitable than me. "What's going on, and what are you doing in our bedroom?"

Skipper ignored my wife. "I did it, Chase. I got you a tour of the Cheyenne Mountain Complex, but you have to go now!"

Perhaps it would've been possible to deliver better news than that, but nothing came to mind. I was instantly awake and on my feet. "Get Hunter, Mongo, and Singer. I'll be ready in five minutes."

"They're already on their way to the airport, but you forgot Disco."

"He's the new guy. I'm not even expected to know his name yet, am I?"

Skipper said, "Since he's our driver, it might be nice to remember, but I can make up some nametags if you need them."

Mostly dressed after a quick shower, I kissed Penny and bounded down the stairs in precisely the five minutes I'd predicted. Skipper stood by the kitchen door with her laptop satchel strung across her back and an overnight bag in one hand.

"Are you coming with us?" I asked.

She rolled her eyes. "Duh, of course I'm coming. Nobody passes up a chance to see inside NORAD's secret mountain."

* * *

The rising sun cast brilliant streaks of orange against the black night sky as it gave way to blue. I watched Disco pull the Citation from the hangar as my heart pounded inside my chest like a schoolboy before a field trip. "I don't know how you pulled this off, but it's going to be hard to top this one."

Skipper shrugged. "Ah, no big deal. It's only the third most high-security facility in the world."

"Third?" I asked. "What are the other two?"

She grinned. "I'll let you know when I score us a season pass for them."

Disco drove the tug back into the hangar while I started the preflight inspection. Everything on the Citation was in perfect condition, just as Cotton Jackson, our A&P mechanic and Earl's brother, insisted. With Cotton on the job, nothing remained damaged, missing, or irregular for long. The problem that particular morning wasn't something being mechanically wrong with the airplane, it was a problem of weight and range. The six of us, including Mongo, put our combined weight at just over twelve hundred fifty pounds. That wasn't an issue for the Citation as long as we didn't top off the tanks with jet fuel.

When Disco maneuvered himself across the center console and into the captain's seat, I sat in the co-pilot's perch calculating fuel burn down to the ounce.

"Can we make it?" Disco asked as he pulled the checklist binder from its pouch.

"There's no way. We'll have to stop for fuel. It's twelve hundred thirty miles to Colorado Springs, and the winds aloft are on our nose the whole way."

He sighed. "All right. Plan a stop in Little Rock or Texarkana. That should fall right along our route."

I programmed the route into the flight management system, and Disco taxied us to the runway. We made the takeoff out of Saint Marys, and the Citation climbed like a homesick angel. We were level at thirty-eight thousand feet in minutes and on our way to see something none of us ever dreamed we'd see.

The fuel stop was a quick-turn, and we were back aboard with coffee in hand.

Hunter grabbed my elbow as I started up the stairs. "Do you think I could get some right-seat time?"

I stepped from the stairs and waved into the cabin. "It's all yours. Just don't break anything."

I settled into the main cabin instead of the cockpit and relished the comfort of the captain's chair. "These seats are nice."

"You should spend more time back here with us," Singer said. "I expect a movie and a nice breakfast any minute now."

When we touched down at Colorado Springs, a trio of blue SUVs pulled onto the ramp. As we descended the stairs, the U.S. Air Force markings came clearly into view.

"I'm starting to feel right at home," Disco said. "It's been a while since I've stepped off an airplane and into one of those."

A young man in dress blues, wearing the stripes of a technical sergeant, reached for my hand. "Are you Mr. Fulton?"

"That's right, but please call me Chase."

"Welcome to Colorado, sir. We'll have you at the mountain in just a few minutes."

We climbed into the waiting SUVs and made ourselves comfortable. Twenty-five minutes later, we pulled up in front of an unassuming, squatty building that was unmistakably property of the Air Force.

The driver said, "Please wait here."

I turned to Disco. "Have you ever been here?"

He knocked his Air Force Academy ring against the armrest. "I've been to Colorado Springs, but never this place."

The tech sergeant returned and opened our doors. "If you'll follow me, I'll take you to Colonel P'Pool."

We followed him into a side door and down a long corridor leading to a checkpoint where a young woman in a camouflage uniform, beret, and gun belt said, "Good morning. I'm Senior Airman Sandoval. If you will please deposit your cell phones, watches, and any other device capable of recording in this bin, I'll secure it for you until you return."

We followed her instructions and unpacked our pockets.

Airman Sandoval handed out laminated passes. "Please clip these to your shirt somewhere above your belt so they are visible at all times. Do you have any questions before I turn you over to Colonel P'Pool?"

I had about a billion questions, but they'd have to wait.

"Please wait here," Sandoval said, and disappeared through a pneumatic door. Almost before the door closed behind her, she was back, but two steps in trail of a fit, uniformed man in his forties with a pair of silver eagles resting on his shoulders.

"Good morning, gentlemen . . . and ma'am. I'm Colonel Bret P'Pool. Welcome to NORAD, the North American Aerospace Defense Command at Cheyenne Mountain. Raise your hand if you've been here before, and I won't bore you with the introduction."

Laughing at his own joke, Colonel P'Pool said, "That's what I thought. Let's go spelunking."

The colonel led us to a bus, and we climbed aboard. Seconds later, we drove into a rather common-looking tunnel and into the side of the mountain.

P'Pool started his tour. "This is the North American Aerospace Defense Command, known until March of nineteen eighty-one as the North American Air Defense Command. We're a combined organization of the United States and Canada. Our reason for existence is to provide aerospace warning, air sovereignty, and protection for Northern America. The NORAD commander is always an American four-star general while the deputy commander is a Canadian three-star or a civilian equivalent. We can't have the Canucks outranking us in our own mountain, now, can we?"

Nervous laughter followed, and the colonel pulled off his hat, throwing it onto the dash of the small bus. He scanned our faces in the mirror, took a long breath, and stopped the vehicle a few hundred feet into the tunnel. "Okay, folks. The charade is over. Tell me what's going on."

I checked Hunter and Skipper before either could speak up. "Colonel, we're just here for a tour of your facility. That's all."

"There are no tours of this facility. There never have been, and there never will be."

I slid to the edge of my seat. "I realize you've been put in an uncomfortable situation, but—"

Skipper cleared her throat. "Excuse me, Chase, but I have the secretary of defense on the phone for Lieutenant Colonel P'Pool."

The full-bird colonel's eyes cut through her as he yanked the phone from her hand and demanded, "Who is this?"

Of course, none of us could hear the voice on the other end of the phone, but the look on Colonel P'Pool's face made it clear Skipper hadn't been stretching the truth.

The colonel said, "Yes, sir. Of course, sir. I'm sorry for . . . Yes, sir. Thank you, sir."

P'Pool gently placed the phone back in Skipper's waiting palm and licked his lips. "What do you want to know?"

Skipper smirked. "I guess you won't be demoted back down to lieutenant colonel after all."

P'Pool ignored the poke, and I said, "We want to know the vulnerabilities of a small facility built using this one as a guide."

"North or south of here?" he asked.

The question intrigued me, so I said, "Let's start with the one north of here."

He sucked air through his teeth. "We all hoped that one didn't really exist, but I suppose you being here means that was a wasted hope on our part."

"It exists, Colonel, and we need to know how to get inside, confront its occupants, and get out."

The uniformed man beneath the eagles, who'd spent his life in service to his country—much of it undoubtedly inside Cheyenne Mountain—let his chin fall to his chest and his eyes close in solemn realization of the sickening truth. When he'd endured the painful tide of reality, he cleared his throat. "Okay. I don't know who or what you are, but I have some guesses. I'm smart enough to know you'll neither confirm nor deny my attempts at guessing, so I'll assume I'm correct and that you're here to learn what needs to be done to erase that burdensome little hole in the ground from the face of the Earth."

I gave him a nod. "You're exactly right, Colonel. We'll neither confirm nor deny any of that."

It wasn't exactly a chuckle, but rather a sound born somewhere deep in the man's chest. "In that case, here's the tour you came to see."

He accelerated through the tunnel that looked more like a gopher hole than a highly classified government facility. The walls were rough and covered with mesh resembling chain-link fencing with anchoring bolts scattered every dozen feet.

Colonel P'Pool flipped on a remotely operated floodlight, similar to those found on police cars, and shined it onto the walls. You'll notice the high-tensile-strength mesh. We're occupying space that humans were never meant to see, and we must respect nature's dislike of intruders. We get rockslides and falling debris on a regular basis inside the mountain. Holes in the Earth are inherently unstable, and this one is no exception. I suspect whoever built the cave in question likely didn't have the infrastructure support we had when we built this facility at the height of the Cold War in nineteen fifty-seven."

I followed the beam of light and marveled at the enormity of the project. "It must've been like building the Panama Canal underground."

The colonel nodded. "I've never heard it put in those terms, but I would have to agree. You'll notice the bolts protruding from the rock."

We looked with amazement as he trained the light on the massive head of one of the bolts. "Those are anchors, and some of them are thirty feet long. This mountain held itself together based on pressure from the density of the stone within, but when we removed enough granite to open up a five-acre cavity beneath two thousand feet of mountain, needless to say, we hauled an enormous amount of stability out of here with every dump truck load of rock. Something had to be done to compensate for that lost stability. That's where the anchor bolts come in. They simulate the supporting strength the granite possessed before we blasted it into gravel and carried it into the light for the first time since creation."

Clark asked, "What would happen without the bolts, and how quickly would it happen?"

The colonel doused the light. "You'd have to ask the engineers for the timeline, but in layman's terms, it would all come tumbling down the second an earthquake . . . or thermonuclear detonation occurred."

Clark put on that evil grin of his. "So, without the anchor bolts, the vulnerability to cave-in goes way up, right?"

"Yes, definitely, but not right away. It could take weeks or maybe months for a catastrophic cave-in to occur in the absence of a seismic event."

Hunter caught on and let out a chuckle. "Seismic events are one of our specialties."

P'Pool grinned. "I thought they might be."

We continued our slow drive through the tunnel until the colonel said, "Here's the next necessity of any intra-mountain facility."

We all leaned forward to see what he was about to reveal. With a sharp turn of the wheel, we made a ninety-degree turn to the right.

"Think of a cave system like the barrel of a rifle. The longer and straighter it is, the more time the explosion of powder has to build up energy to force the bullet out of the muzzle. Which one of you is the sniper?"

Singer said, "Today, Colonel, we're just tourists."

"Ah, that must mean you're the long gunner. Well, imagine having the finest rifle ever made and bending the barrel at a right angle. All of a sudden, all that energy has to change directions, and the force is immediately decreased exponentially."

A resounding "Ah" of understanding filled the van, and the colonel said, "We have three of these ninety-degree turns in the access tunnel, but that's not all. We're coming up on one of the most impressive features of the whole system."

He had our full attention, and he pulled to a stop just outside a set of massive doors. "The whole bunker is built to deflect a thirty-megaton nuclear explosion as close as two kilometers. This is the first set of twenty-five-ton blast doors, but it isn't the only set. You'll see several of these as your tour continues."

"Why do you leave them open?" I asked.

"That's a good question," he said. "There's actually no reason to close them unless we detect a missile launch. As I'm sure you're aware, we have the technology to detect such a blast from anywhere in the world. By the time the weapon comes within five thousand miles of Colorado, we'll secure the mountain and continue business as usual."

"Fascinating," I said. "But aren't you afraid of contaminants in the air in here?"

"Sure, we're concerned. That's why we have a network of blast valves with specially designed filters to capture airborne chemical, biological, radiological, and nuclear contaminants."

"It sounds like you thought of everything," I said.

"Oh, no, not me. I wasn't even born when they started building this place. It was a two-country team of brilliant scientists and strategists who developed the plans for this place."

I frowned. "Two countries?"

The colonel met my eyes in the mirror. "I wondered if you'd ever get around to asking about that. This was a joint venture between the U.S. and—this one's gonna sting a little—the Canadians."

My heart sank into my stomach. "The Canadians? Are they still involved in the bunker operation?"

"Now you're asking meaningful questions, Mr. Fulton. The answer is yes. They are still involved. In fact, the vice commander of the facility is a Canadian civilian appointed by the prime minister. How does that make your gut feel?"

"It's not my gut I'm concerned with, Colonel. It's my ass I'm worried about."

"And rightly so. I can probably limit the knowledge of your visit to the facility to those of us wearing American flags on our uniforms, but I can't swear the Canadians won't get wind of it. There's no such thing as security . . . only perceived security."

I said, "We know that all too well, I'm afraid."

We continued through the blast doors and around another sharp turn. The tunnel opened into a vast open space that resembled an amphitheater, and a collective sigh of amazement left our mouths.

The colonel suddenly took on a look of enormous pride. "That's exactly the reaction I had the first time I saw this place. Although you can't see all of them from here, there are fifteen three-story buildings inside the bunker. If I were taking a guess, I would surmise the facility you plan to visit has fewer than three internal structures, and none of them will be multi-story."

He paused as if waiting for confirmation, but my team and I sat in stunned disbelief at the sheer magnitude of the bunker.

Our tour guide continued. "Now that we've sufficiently awed you with the overall facility, let me see if I can do the same with some of the details."

We pulled near one of the nondescript structures and stepped from the van.

The colonel pulled a heavy rubber skirt away from the base of the building. "Shine a light under there."

Like good Boy Scouts, we drew our flashlights, and soon their beams penetrated the darkness beneath the building.

I couldn't believe my eyes. "Those look like massive springs."

"That's exactly what they are. That is part of why this facility will continue to operate after a nearby nuclear blast. All the structures inside the mountain rest on these enormous springs. They act as shock absorbers to prevent the buildings from crumbling as the Earth moves around them."

Hunter looked up. "Would you expect a single-story structure in a much smaller version of this bunker to be similarly built?"

The colonel shook his head. "No, there would be no real reason to take such precautions if such a facility existed. Our neighbors to the north don't represent much of a target for a nuclear warhead, so that bunker—if such a bunker exists—wouldn't need the same protections as ours. Their only real goal would be cover and concealment."

Hunter's eyes said he was compiling volumes of mental notes.

Mongo had been noticeably quiet throughout the tour, but his curiosity finally surfaced. "What about water? Wouldn't an outside water source represent an enormous vulnerability to contamination?"

P'Pool said, "Indeed it would if we had an outside water source. Fortunately, the mountain took care of that for us. There are subterranean springs that feed five reservoirs inside the bunker. We produce far more water than we need. In fact, we have to send some of it out of the mountain as a flood-control measure."

Singer smiled. "It's almost like God Himself knew just what you needed inside a mountain."

Colonel P'Pool finally smiled. "You might say that." Checking his watch, our tour guide suddenly looked concerned. "There's going to be a hundred people roaming around in here in less than fifteen minutes. If there's any hope of keeping your little subterranean field trip a secret, it would be a good idea for us to find our way back to the sunlight."

Chapter 22
Here in the Real World

Colonel P'Pool returned us to the care of Senior Airman Sandoval and ordered, "Give me the visitor log."

Sandoval handed the hefty log to the colonel. "Here you are, sir. I've not logged anyone in today, sir."

P'Pool met my eyes and then shot a look toward the front door. I heard his unspoken command loud and clear. My team and I slipped through the door just as our guide asked Sandoval, "Why would you? We haven't had any guests today."

Expecting to find the nameless tech sergeant and his convoy of blue SUVs out front, I pulled on my sunglasses and scanned the small parking area. I turned to Disco. "Where's our ride?"

Our chief pilot threw up his hands. "How should I know?"

"Come on, Lieutenant Colonel Disco. You're our man in blue."

He shoved a finger toward Hunter. "He's retired Air Force, too."

I said, "Yeah, but he didn't really retire. He *got* retired."

Hunter huffed. "I got shot up, blowed up, and tore up is what I got. That medically retired staff sergeant check I get every month wouldn't start a decent fire."

Clark called a halt to our merriment. "All right. Cut it out. We're obviously on our own, so pick a car that looks easy to steal."

Hunter pointed toward an old Ford F-100 pickup. "That'll do."

I'm not ashamed to admit I believed Hunter might've been seconds away from stealing a truck, but thankfully, a nondescript van with an overweight, sweaty civilian behind the wheel pulled to a stop only a few feet away.

The driver rolled down the window. "Are you the guys needin' a ride to the airport?"

"That would be us," I said, and we piled into the far-less-plush mode of transportation than we'd enjoyed upon our arrival.

At the airport general aviation terminal, I slipped the driver a folded bill, and fifteen minutes later, I was having a cocktail in the first-class cabin of the Citation with Disco and Hunter occupying the cheap seats up front.

Skipper sat across from me with her laptop humming like a sewing machine.

I hooked a finger across her screen and leaned in. "Hey. What did you think of the mountain?"

Without looking up, she growled. "Not now. I'm making notes."

I turned to my right to face Clark. "How about you? Are you taking notes, too?"

He tapped at his temple with the tip of his index finger. "No need. This thing's a steel trap. I never forget anything."

"Whatever, Trapper Johnson. Let's hear it."

He gave his cocktail a swirl. "What we just saw probably bears little resemblance to what we'll see in Canada. The Chi-coms do everything as fast and as cheap as they can, so it's going to be sloppy."

"What about the anchor bolts?"

His crooked grin claimed the lower half of his face. "Great minds think alike, Grasshopper. If they have them, they're going to be barely adequate, but my bet is that they have some kind of internal structures—most likely local tree trunk—wedged into the tunnel and workspace."

I considered his prediction and grimaced. "I don't know. Timbers would make it tough to get a vehicle in and out."

"I don't think it's big enough for a vehicle," he said, "but I like your thinking. You're going to blow it, aren't you?"

"Oh, I'm definitely blowing it. We'll set the charges on the ingress and pull the trigger on the egress. That's the easy part. But I'd love to know the layout before we go charging in under night-vision gear."

Clark swallowed a sip. "I don't think there's any way to make that happen. I doubt it's complex, though. It's likely straight in and straight out."

"So, you don't think they'll have ninety-degree turns and blast doors?"

He shrugged. "Why would they? Nobody's going to bomb Canada."

"How about the springs for building foundations?"

"I don't know . . . maybe. But if I were a betting man, I'd say it's a simple cavern system with ventilation routed through the overhead and blowers to circulate fresh air. It's not like they're going to hunker down in there after an EMP. It's just a high-tech listening post with a satellite uplink. I doubt they even have running water in there."

"I'm not buying it," I said. "I think it's more than that. I think it's probably a command-and-control bunker in the event of an all-out nuclear war. If we nuke the crap out of China, I think they can retaliate from right there in Alberta."

"What makes you think that?"

I shrugged. "It's just a gut feeling. They could've built a remote site to monitor the satellite overhead without putting any personnel inside the mountain. I think it's more than meets the eye."

Clark stared out the window. "I hope you're wrong, College Boy, but if you're not, this mission is a lot bigger than a grab-and-go-and-blow."

"My theory goes deeper than that," I said. "I think they were already building the tunnel system and bunker when Brown and his team hit the freestanding sight. That's why they put up such a fight and had plenty of men to do it."

He sighed. "We'll know soon enough."

* * *

The familiar landscape of the Georgia low country came into view outside the cabin window, and everyone pulled their seatbelts into place. The Citation rolled onto the final approach leg and kept turning. I leaned to the window to watch our ground track. Soon, we were back on course and presumably aligned with the runway. When the wheels touched down, they did so a little more aggressively than they should have, and the world was still moving past my window a little too fast.

The look on Clark's face told me he hadn't missed the show. "We came in a little hot. That's not like Disco."

The taxi from the runway back to the hangar was relatively normal with a little too much braking when we came to a stop.

Hunter opened the cockpit door with embarrassment all over his face. "Sorry. That was all me. It's nothing like the Caravan."

Clark and I chuckled, and I said, "At least you didn't take out the fence at the end of the runway. I had my doubts when you hit the ground at two hundred knots."

"It wasn't two hundred knots, but I was a little hot. I'll do better next time."

I laughed. "I guess too fast is better than too slow. When we get back from Canada, we'll get you some time in the simulators down at FlightSafety in Vero Beach or Daytona."

We deplaned, and the fuel truck arrived to top us off. Mike, the lineman, sauntered from the truck.

"Hey, Mike," I said. "Are you all right? You look like somebody just stole your lollipop."

He looked up at the Citation. "I reckon this'll be the last time I ever get to squirt gas in that thing . . . or any other, for that matter."

"What are you talking about?"

He spat between his boots. "Ain't you heard?"

"Heard what?"

He dragged his heel across the concrete. "We're done. There ain't gonna be no more general aviation airport here. We're locking the gates and turnin' over the keys to some new corporation. Some big-shot company out of Virginia or someplace bought the whole thing—lock, stock, and barrel."

I spun to face Clark. "Did you hear that? I thought we talked about this. I thought we were going to negotiate a deal with the city. Now look what's happened." I spread my arms as if to point out all the flying machines we owned. "What are we supposed to do with all of this? Where are we going to put four airplanes and a helicopter, not to mention all the—"

He took a step toward me and checked over his shoulder. "Calm down, Chase."

"No, I think I have the right to be a little upset. We talked about this, and you said—"

He held up both hands in surrender. "Yes, you're right. We did talk about this, and I told you I'd handle it. And that's exactly what I did. The Virginia corporation who's buying the whole place—lock, stock, and barrel? Look around, Chase. We're that corporation."

I blinked in a wasted effort to try and understand what he was saying. "What? What do you mean, *we're* that corporation?"

He turned to the lineman. "Mike, don't worry. Your job is still here if you want it. We can't run this place without somebody like you who knows every nook and cranny."

Mike's demeanor flashed from dejected to relieved in a second. "All I've done since I graduated high school thirty years ago was mow grass, replace busted lightbulbs, and refuel airplanes right here on the city's airport. I never thought I'd need to do nothin' else. Are you sayin' I can keep doin' them things and still get paid?"

Clark gave me a glance and turned back to Mike. "How many years did you say you've been doing this job?"

"It'll be thirty-one years come September. I took three months off and just messed around when I graduated school, but then I come to work here and ain't never left."

Clark said, "I don't know anything about the city's retirement plan, but you're probably eligible. You can put in your paperwork and start drawing your pension. Then you can come work for us, and we'll match whatever the city is paying you now."

Mike glared down at the palm of his right hand, then wiped the sweat and grime on his navy-blue shirt. With his palm as clean as sweat and a dirty shirt could get it, he stuck his hand in Clark's. "You've sure enough got yourself a deal. Oh, and I can do a lot of other stuff around here other than just mowin' and fuelin'."

"We're sure you can, Mike. Don't worry. We'll take care of you. When you finish topping off the Citation, give the personnel office a call and find out what you need to do to retire. We've got some out-of-town work to do for two or three weeks, but when we get back, we'll work it all out for you to come work for us. How's that sound?"

"Sounds about as great as it could be from where I'm standin'. And I can't thank you enough. I'll not let you down, and you can take that to the bank."

Clark shook his hand free from Mike's and led the way into the hangar. "I've been trying to find the right time to tell you. I wanted it to be a surprise, but not like this."

I bowed my head. "I'm sorry I got loud out there. I was wrong, and I should've trusted you."

He gave me a playful elbow shot to the ribs. "Don't be sorry, College Boy . . . Be better."

* * *

We found Cajun Kenny LePine and Earl on the back gallery at Bonaventure as the shadows that were cast by the setting sun danced like haunting spirits over the marsh.

I said, "It must be nice to sit around on somebody else's gallery and pretend you've got nothing to do."

Kenny started to speak in his Cajun patois I'd never understand, but Earl laid her stubby hand on his arm. "I've got this one, baby."

She shot a look down the steps at me. "There ain't no pretending here, Stud Muffin. Your box is built, your timbers are stacked, and when you get back from wherever you're going, you just might have a new boathouse where you can keep that patrol boat of yours out of the weather."

"In that case," I said, "you do all the sitting you want while we go check out your handiwork."

Clark and I climbed into the Conex to find the first half of the box looking exactly like the inside of any typical shipping container. Upon closer inspection, a small section of the back wall swung outward, revealing an entrance into the real genius of the build. Beyond the opening, and inside the second half of the container, was a wall of bunks three-high. Simple mesh chairs lined an adjacent wall, and a curtain hung from the opposite corner of the space.

Clark pulled back the curtain. "You'll never believe it. Earl built us a latrine."

I poked my head behind the curtain and couldn't believe my eyes. "What would we do without her?"

A voice came blasting through the swinging opening of the space, and Kenny crawled through. "Dis here done be da doggie doe, fo sho it be. And you ain' gon' bleeve dem eyes o your'n what be comin' nex', you. Dus' listen up wiff dem der ears of you's, do." He paused and cupped his hand behind his ear. "Hear dat?"

"No, Kenny. I don't hear anything."

"Das right. What dat is dat you don' be hearin' be dem genera-tors what don' make no noise hardly. And dat ain't be da rest of it, neither. Dat air you be feelin' whirlin' all up 'round dat head o' your'n . . . Dat don' be no regular air, no it don'. Dat be air-condi-tioned air dus' fo' you and dem boys o' yours to ride in comfort, you."

"I don't know what to say, Kenny. I'm impressed. I can't imag-ine how you did all of this in two and a half days."

He shook his head and pointed toward the doggie door. "Dis here ain't got nuffin' to do wiff ole Kenny 'cept for knowing where to buy dem generators and swamper. All o' dis here be da handi-work o' dat fine lady up der on dat chair-o-rocker. I guarantee dat be da troof, me. I ain't never lied to you, no sir."

The doggie door swung open again, and Earl rolled through the opening. "Hey, it feels like somebody's got the air conditioner working in here."

I threw my arms around her. "You're a miracle worker, Earl. That's all there is to it. You've outdone yourself on this one."

"Aw, I can't take all the credit. Kenny did a lot of the work . . . when he wasn't getting in the way."

I looked around the space and noticed the overhead was shorter than it should've been. I pointed upward. "What's going on here?"

Earl giggled like a teenager. "That's my favorite part. Check this out."

She pulled a handle concealed beside the latrine curtain, and the ceiling lowered on motorized hinges to reveal a compartment big enough for all the toys we needed to take with us.

"That's fantastic!"

She held up a palm. "Don't get too excited. It ain't as big as it looks. The floor in here is raised to make room for the generators, fuel tanks, and cold air swampers. The overhead will carry around a thousand pounds before the motors give out. The rest of your gear will have to be stored in the open space around you, but I built in some tie-downs so you could net everything and keep it from sliding around if things get rough on the ship."

We crawled back out through the opening and climbed down to the workshop floor. "Well, Earl, I guess all that's left is for me to pay you what I owe you. The rest of us have a boat to catch."

Earl slapped my hand and laced her arm through Kenny's. "Stop it, Baby Boy. You don't owe momma nothing. I got to build something even *I* didn't know I could do, and I found this fine man to boot. That's more than enough payment for me. Besides, I still owe you one for finding Boomer's buried treasure."

That caught Kenny's attention, and he mumbled something Earl seemed to understand.

She looked up at him and laughed. "Don't you worry, little dirt dauber. I'll tell you that story soon enough. For now, I've got to hug these boys' necks and wish 'em luck. They've got to go off and leave us here in the real world while they save the rest of it."

Chapter 23

Born to Run

By the time I'd given the whole team a tour of our temporary home, stomachs growled and the dinner bell rang. Like one big happy family, we gathered around Maebelle's table and listened to Singer talk to God.

When the amens rang out, I studied the Southern Baptist sniper. "You talk to God as if He's an old fishing buddy."

One of the deadliest men who'd ever lived put on an aw-shucks grin. "He is my buddy, Chase. He's as much a part of my reality as all of you. Just because I can't shake His hand in this world doesn't keep me from taking him fishing with me every time I go. The difference is, he can feed five thousand with just five loaves of bread and two fish. Not even Maebelle can pull that one off."

Seeing such faith worn like an old favorite shirt gave our sniper the look of a man who knew all the answers to the questions we'd never asked.

"I'm sure glad you're on our team, Singer."

His grin expanded. "Me, too, Chase . . . Me, too."

As knives and forks clanged on the family china, the rumbling bellies gave way to sighs and moans of culinary delight.

Clark said, "Sweetheart, I think you'll get pretty good at this cooking gig if you'll stick with it. You've got some real potential."

She thrust a fork toward him. "And you've got some real potential to be sleeping outside if you don't straighten up."

I'd never seen Clark Johnson back down from any man in any fight anywhere in the world, but in that moment, he shrank in his seat and said, "Yes, ma'am."

As Clark and Hunter cleared the table, Maebelle sliced the cake and plated for everyone without asking who was interested. She placed a chunk of cake in front of everyone and passed the ice cream carton. "I hope you like it. It's called a hummingbird cake, so if you find something crunchy inside, don't worry. It's probably just a beak. They're hard to pick out."

Most of the table's occupants laughed, but Maebelle eyed Kenny as he poked at his cake with his fork. "Don't worry, Kenny. No hummingbirds were harmed in the making of this cake. I was only kidding."

His laughter betrayed his attempt to convince our chef he believed her, and he pushed the dessert plate away a few inches. Like vultures, my team descended on the refused plate and made quick work of the confection.

With every belly, except Kenny's, fully sated, I tapped the handle of my fork on the wooden table. "This is the part of every mission I hate the most, and I suspect everyone at this table shares that hatred."

Penny squeezed her eyelids closed and let her chin fall to her chest. Irina looked around the table, taking in the somber expressions on every face. Tatiana stared at her mother.

I said, "This is the part where we temporarily say good bye. There are men and women who are somehow chosen by some force greater than any of us to run toward the fire instead of away from it. Eight such people just shared a magnificent meal, and will, tomorrow, once again, heed that call to run into those flames."

A few faces looked like they were fighting back tears, and I'm sure mine was among them.

Under the weight of responsibility, I continued. "Hunter, we've fought, trained, laughed, and bled together. Mongo, I've marveled at everything about you for years, and I trust you farther than you can throw me—and that's a long way. Singer, just like you trust God to look over and protect you, you lay high on a perch looking down on all of us and crushing anyone who dares bring us harm. There's no one on the Earth I'd rather have on the perch. Disco, you saved our lives in a canyon in the Bitterroot Mountains by showing all of us you're so much more than a high-speed bus driver. You're a warrior, and your sacrifice and devotion to this team—this family—is second to none."

Our chief pilot gave me an appreciative nod.

"Clark, you've taught all of us to stay in the fight as long as there's blood in our veins, and we've learned well. You bear the scars of a lifetime of selfless, boundless service to our country. Your days in the trenches are over, but your decades of experience with your boots in the mud and bullets in the air all over the world make you an asset in the ops center like no other."

He laid a hand on my arm and gave it a squeeze.

"Al Brown, you left part of your body and gallons of your blood on battlefields like tiny corners of Hell all across the globe. Your wisdom and experience place you at Clark's side, and that, we all know, is a place of unquestioned honor."

He offered an abbreviated salute but didn't speak.

"Skipper, compared to the wizardry you invoke every time you pull on that headset and lay your fingertips on that keyboard, our task of dodging bullets and gunning down the bad guys is a walk in the park. I don't know how you do it, but without you, this team of knuckle-draggers might as well be paperboys. You're the keystone that holds all of our skill sets in place, and I know I speak for all of us when I say we trust you with our lives every time we go outside the wire."

A tiny tear ran down her cheek, but she made no effort to catch it.

"And finally, Penny, you've given your life and love to a man who'll never be worthy of either. But I love you from the depths of my soul, and you are the anchor that ties me to sanity and gives me the strength to take these men into the pits of Hell and bring them back time after time. If there's anything good inside my chest, it's because you put it there, and I'll never take your love and support for granted. Never."

Tina, Maebelle, Irina, and Tatiana—the women who didn't understand and couldn't know where we went and what we endured— laid their heads on the chests and shoulders of the men they respected, loved, and treasured. Whispered sadness and celebration filled the air around the table, and time seemed to stand still.

I held my tongue until the whispers became the sounds of tears and fears of the unknown.

I cleared my throat. "Spend the next few hours with those who'll ache for you while we're away, and celebrate one more night of peace before the demands of who and what we are draw us away from those we love and into the waiting arms of the fight that is ours alone."

No one spoke, and everyone left the table.

Penny and I climbed the stairs and locked the world outside our bedroom door. After we cried and laughed and loved and silently held each other, my beautiful wife pressed her body against mine and drifted into sleep with my arms woven around her. And I lay thinking and dreaming of the ocean.

The sea, in all her beauty, elegance, and grace, will never allow herself to become as the masters' paintings, gracing the walls of the world's temples to diligence and devotion and talent. No, she'll not suffer the fool who looks upon her and turns away in apathy. She will, without fail, and without remorse, pour herself from her bounds with a vengeance borne of the gods and driven by the purest forces of Heaven and Earth until she engulfs the chasm between air and water, unleashing her fury in ultimate and undeniable opposition to her beauty when at rest and at peace. No, she will not be taken for granted, and she will never be as the canvas of the painter, waiting in deepest patience and longing desire for the master's return to once again stroke his brush against her inanimate, flaccid form. She is beauty in its purest elegance, but equal is her anger and destruction when she is ignored and thought commonplace.

Perhaps it wasn't the sea that consumed my thoughts. Perhaps it was my team, my family, my soul that would not be ignored. Perhaps the same force that commands the waves pushes men like us to step beyond the bounds of peaceful existence, and instead of fleeing the scorching flames, run, unafraid, into their furious depths. While others lived in blissful ignorance of the darkness, we were born to become the night and raise our swords so others would never have to stand before the fangs of tyranny and devastation.

Chapter 24
By Dawn's Early Light

It wasn't an alarm clock or loudmouthed rooster that brought us to our feet the next morning. It was us demanding that the sun must rise instead of that orange orb demanding it of my team.

The back-up beeper on Kenny LePine's truck echoed off the northern wall of the house as he maneuvered the converted Conex in line with the armory doors. Hunter crossed his arms, forming an X in front of his face, and the truck's air brakes hissed the rig to a stop.

We formed a bucket brigade, handing weapons, ammunition, explosives, and comms gear from the depths of the vault and into the waiting container. I stowed as much of the gear as the motors of the bin could handle in Earl's hidey-hole above the living space. Next came bag after bag and case after case of personal gear, clothes, and contingency gear we hoped we wouldn't need. Hunter stacked with the efficiency of a loadmaster and soon had everything netted and lashed to the deck.

Kenny pulled the rig to the front of the house and slid down from the cab just as Skipper came bounding down the front steps with an armload of folders, clipboards, oversized envelopes, and a Styrofoam cooler.

"What be all dis stuff, Miss Danseuse?"

Skipper frowned up at the Cajun. "*Danseuse?* What does that mean?"

Kenny grinned, exposing the void where his two false teeth should've been. "Das how da French says skipper, dey do."

She hefted the load of paperwork toward him. "I think I like that."

He caught the conglomeration. "E'rting sound better in da French, it do."

"Whatever you say. Anyway, this is the bill of lading for the load you'll pick up in Albuquerque. The address for the warehouse is on the back of the first folder."

He flipped the folder and read the address.

Skipper motioned toward a collection of sealed envelopes. "Those are your logbooks in case you get inspected at a weigh station. There are three sets, plus a fourth blank log in case the ones I wrote up don't match your timing."

"You did da logbooks already into da future?"

Skipper nodded. "I did, but they may not work out with your trip. Look them over and make sure everything looks the way it should before you let anybody with a badge see them."

Kenny slid the first set of envelopes and folders as well as the cooler onto the floorboard of his truck.

Skipper motioned toward what he had left. "This green folder is the address and aerial photographs of the Livermore Municipal Airport in California. That's where you'll meet the team so they can mount up. I marked the spot for you to park on the aerial photo, and I've arranged for the spot to be roped off before you get there. Just toss the ropes and stanchions aside when you get there. Got it?"

He tapped his temple. "Yes, ma'am. I's locked every word inside dis here vault in my head, me."

Skipper pulled the last remaining envelope to the top of the stack in Kenny's hands. "And finally, this is the packet that'll get you onto Pier 93 in San Francisco. That'll be the pier with the gantry cranes. Your contact's name, number, and photograph are inside the folder. Ask specifically for him in the best English you can muster. He's our man on the inside, and he'll make sure the Conex gets loaded on the right boat in the right spot."

"I gots dat, I guarantee. Don' tell nobody but dis here man, him."

I watched the exchange without interrupting, and Kenny filed everything Skipper had given him into a plastic file box in the truck's cab. When I was confident Skipper's briefing was complete, I stepped up. "All right, Kenny. I'm not questioning your ability. I just want some reassurance you've got everything under control."

He spun on a heel and stuck his hand in mine. "I gots it all, and 'tween me and Miss Earline, we be at dat Liver airplane airport in tree days on da mornin', we."

"Three days?" I scoffed. "You can't make Livermore, California, in three days."

"You right 'bout dat, but das only if'n I's one person in dat truck all by meself, me. But dat ain' how it be, no. Miss Earline gots da license and skill to be drivin' dis ol' truck, too, she do. So dus' tree days, and we see you and da rest of dem boys at dat Liver airport."

I wasn't expecting the curveball of having Earl along for the ride, but having her on board would cut the drive time in half. I gave her arm a tug as she pilfered through the cooler. "I need to talk to you for a minute."

"So, talk, Stud Muffin. I can inventory this cooler Maebelle packed and listen at the same time."

Suddenly hoping I'd get a similar cooler before leaving, I said, "Are you sure you want to drive all the way across the country with Kenny? I don't want you to get pressured into doing something you don't want to do."

She pressed the lid closed on the cooler and climbed down from the truck's cab. "When was the last time you saw me getting talked into anything I didn't want to do? I'm going because I want to go. It's been too many decades since I've had myself a good adventure, and I'm not about to turn one down now."

I pulled the bulbous woman into my arms, and we squeezed each other tightly. "I love you, Old Girl. I'm just trying to look after you. God knows somebody has to."

She shot a look between the cab and the container. "I think that's a pretty good man over there, and if he ain't, thanks to you, I've got myself plenty of money. I can hop out of this truck anywhere between here and Timbuktu and hop a first-class flight back home. I ain't never had no money before you brought me that gold. You changed my life for the better the first day you ambled up to my boat on that dock in Saint Augustine. Ain't neither one of us who could say what we'd turn into back then, could we?"

I smiled. "I couldn't agree more. You keep that man straight, and I'll see you in Livermore in three days. Oh, and make sure he knows it's Livermore and not Liver."

She poked at my side. "He's just messin' with Skipper. That's all. Don't let him fool you. That man is smarter than he'll ever let anybody know."

"Speaking of being smarter than the average bear, how are we supposed to get out of this container if nobody opens the door from the outside?"

She burst into raucous laughter. "I wondered if you were ever going to ask that question. Come with me."

She led me to the back of the container and pointed toward the doors. "See those pins sticking through the latches?"

I examined the latching mechanism. "Yes, I see them."

"On the inside of this right-side door, there's a rubber kick-plate. Have Mongo give it a good sturdy kick, and the pins will force open the latch. It'll make some noise, but it'll get you out of there."

"Thanks. I'd hate to run out of food and water and be stuck inside this thing with a bunch of stinky knuckle-draggers."

"Don't thank me yet," she said. "We ain't done. Come around here." She led me to the left side of the container and waddled beneath the trailer, then pointed upward at a set of recessed hinges. "This here is a trapdoor that can only be opened from the inside. This one is a last-resort, abandon-ship-type thing. It opens with a pair of explosive charges about the size of a shotgun shell. The switch is on the back of the control for the overhead storage. Once it's open, you can't close it back without a welder. Anything you put in the container will fit through that hole—except maybe Mongo, but he'll make his own hole. Anyway, I hope you don't need it, but it's there just in case."

We scampered back out from under the trailer.

"What would I do without you, Earl?"

"I ain't got no idea." She shot a thumb toward Kenny. "But thanks to him, your window of opportunity is closing fast."

I waved a dismissive hand Kenny's way. "Ah, I'm not worried about him."

Earl stepped toward me and whispered, "If you think that skinny Russian of yours was scary with a knife, you ain't seen nothing 'til you've seen a pissed-off Cajun with a switchblade. They'll cut you from neck bone to knee bone and play slip 'n slide on your blood."

"Okay," I said, "maybe I'm a little worried about him."

She snapped her stumpy fingers. "Now you're thinking like the smart man you are. Just don't go and get yourself killed doing whatever it is you're planning to do. I kinda like havin' you around, kid."

"I kinda like being around. Don't worry. Thanks to you and your magic box here, those boys and I will be just fine."

With a long blast from the air horn, the Kenny and Earline Express pulled down the long drive lined by ancient pecan trees and then disappeared into the dawn's early light.

Maebelle fed the rest of us, and Skipper gave the pre-deployment briefing.

"Okay, boys. This is how it goes. Your first stop is Albuquerque. I wish I could say I trusted the guys on the ground out there to load the Conex exactly right, but I don't know any of them, and we can't afford a screw-up right out of the gate."

"What's the cargo we'll take on?"

Skipper rolled her eyes. "How many times have I told you not to interrupt me during a briefing? I'll always take questions at the end, if—and that's a big if—I leave anything out along the way."

I threw up my hands. "Sorry."

In unison, voices echoed, "Don't be sorry. Be better."

Skipper continued. "Before I was so rudely interrupted, I was about to tell you the cargo is pillows. They're light, easy to move, and boring. Boring cargo is always a good thing. Nobody's going to inspect a container full of pillows . . . we hope. The key thing to remember is when you're loading the Conex, make sure you can get from your doggie door to the rear doors of the container. Don't block your road."

She paused and looked around the room, but nobody had the courage to speak. "Good. So, the next stop after you leave New Mexico is Livermore. It's just east of San Francisco—for the geographically challenged. The big runway is seven left and two-five right. It's fifty-two hundred feet, so the Citation won't have any trouble getting in and out. Any questions?"

None came, so she kept talking. "Once you're on the boat, it's a thousand miles to Vancouver. It'll take two and a half to three days to make the run. We'll have two-way comms, but that's still a long time to be cooped up in a big metal box. We've got it worked out for yours to be one of the first containers off the ship. Kenny will be there waiting with his empty trailer and official-looking documents to claim the container and expedite it through customs. If everything goes perfectly, you'll find yourselves in the Canadian Rockies and crawling out of your shoebox about twelve hours after your crane ride off the boat. It's only a little over five hundred miles from Vancouver to Banff, Alberta, but there's no interstate. It's a winding road, so make sure you pack your motion-sickness meds. By the time you get there, I'll have solid coordinates for the tunnel entrance. Okay, I'm done. I'll take questions now."

The team sat, staring at each other, but no one spoke up.

I said, "I don't have a question, but I do have something to say."

Groans came from the team, and Hunter said, "This isn't going to be another one of your philosophical pep talks like last night at dinner, is it?"

"It wasn't going to be, but now that you mention it, perhaps I *will* wax eloquent for a couple of hours."

Everyone stood, and Hunter said, "You can wax all the elephants you want, but I've got to cut my toenails or something."

Mongo nodded toward Hunter. "Yeah, and I've got to help him."

Skipper gathered her paperwork and looked up. "I'll listen to whatever you have to say."

"Thank you," I said. "It's nice to know *somebody* cares. I was just going to say there's a lot of moving parts to this one, and we're going to rely on you to keep all the pieces in place."

Skipper stood. "As Earl would say, don't you worry about a thing, Baby Boy. I've got you."

Chapter 25
Poisonous Mushrooms

The thirteen hundred nautical miles separating Albuquerque, New Mexico, from the Chase D Fulton International Airport in Saint Marys, Georgia, was a hurdle our Citation couldn't leap in a single bound. Okay, that's not really the name of the Saint Marys airport Clark and the Board had just purchased, but my ego and I think the name has a nice ring to it.

I'd never been to the Texarkana Regional Airport, but their cheap jet fuel and sixty-six hundred foot runway called to me like a siren's song. There was one more little irresistible goody that made me start down out of the flight levels on our westbound excursion.

I turned to Hunter in the right seat. "Tune up the ATIS for Texarkana. I've got an idea."

He tuned the radio frequency for the Automated Terminal Information Service, and we listened as the recorded voice of the controller said, "Texarkana Regional Airport ATIS information Echo, time one-six-five-two Zulu. Wind two-three-zero at seven. Visibility four miles in haze. Ceiling four hundred overcast. Expect ILS runway two-two. Advise on initial contact you have Echo."

Hunter noted the information on his kneeboard. "Okay, we've got Echo."

I tapped the multi-function display. "Bring up the ILS two-two approach plate and brief it."

Hunter was a better-than-average instrument pilot, but that would be his first approach in real instrument meteorological conditions in the Citation. He briefed each line of the approach exactly as Clark had taught him and then studied the missed approach procedure in the upper right corner of the plate.

It was time for a pop quiz. I asked, "What's the decision height?"

Without looking back at the chart, he said, "Two hundred AGL and five eighty-four MSL."

"Good. What's the missed approach procedure?"

He confidently said, "Climb straight ahead on the localizer back course to two thousand direct MARIE intersection and hold."

"Are we likely to miss?"

He shook his head. "If the ATIS is correct, no. We'll break out at four hundred AGL, but we fly every approach with the intention of flying the missed approach procedure in case we don't break out and see the airport."

"Well done," I said. "The airplane is yours. Put us on the ground."

"I have the controls," he said.

I reached across my shoulder, opened the cockpit door, and waved for Disco to come up front. He did and knelt between the seats.

I said, "Hunter's going to fly the ILS into Texarkana with a four-hundred-foot ceiling, and I thought you might like to watch."

Disco settled in and rubbed his palms together. "Oh, goody! Are you hand-flying or monitoring the autopilot?"

Hunter sighed. "Chase says I have to fly it by hand."

"I didn't say that," I said. "If you want to prove to us the autopilot can fly the ILS to minimums, knock yourself out, but it'd sure be cool if you did it without the robot behind the panel."

Hunter looked over his shoulder. "See, Disco? I told you he said I had to fly it by hand."

My partner managed the descent from thirty-eight thousand feet like a seasoned airline pilot, but things started falling apart when the controller said, "Citation Zero-Charlie-Fox, you are eight miles from TECCO outer marker. Turn left heading two-five-zero. Descend and maintain two thousand one hundred until established on the localizer. Cleared ILS two-two approach."

Hunter stumbled through the readback as the speed and complexity of the Citation began to overwhelm him.

"Just relax," I said. "Slow the airplane down to a hundred and forty knots, and don't fly through the glideslope."

Beads of sweat formed on his forehead, and his breathing rate increased as his hands flew across the controls. His eyes darted back and forth between the checklist and the instrument panel. He glanced up to take a look out the windscreen but was rewarded with nothing but the inside of a pure white cloud. In near panic, he threw his hand toward the flap handle, and I caught his wrist.

"Slow down and fly the airplane. You've flown a thousand ILSs."

He chewed on his bottom lip as we continued through the zero visibility at a hundred and eighty knots. Through gritted teeth, he said, "Can you help me?"

"Sure. Pull your power back, slow us down, get your flaps set and your gear down."

He took a long deep breath and followed my instructions. Soon, he had the airplane properly configured at the appropriate speed.

The controller said, "Citation Zero-Charlie-Fox contact Texarkana tower on one-two-three point eight-seven-five."

Hunter crushed the push-to-talk button. "Zero-Charlie-Fox off to the tower on twenty-three eighty-seven."

I pointed toward his panel. "The glideslope is alive. Don't fly through it. Get your power back."

The green diamond on the right side of his display soared down the scale, and our student probably threw up a little. The instant he realized he'd flown through the glideslope, he pulled the power back to idle and shoved the nose over in a desperate attempt to capture the glideslope from above—a feat that is dangerous at best and deadly at worst.

I looked over my shoulder toward Disco, and he mouthed, "Let him fly it, but be ready."

Our airspeed increased as Hunter dived for the imaginary electronic line in the sky that would lead us safely to the landing threshold. Just as Disco had instructed, I let Hunter chase the airplane all over the sky for another ninety seconds. There was nothing stable about our approach, so I hoped Hunter would recognize our predicament and call off the approach.

Ten seconds later, my partner said, "We need to go around."

"Indeed, we do," I said. "I have the controls."

With a voice laced with exasperation, he lifted his hands. "You have the controls."

"I have it . . . my airplane."

I gently pulled the nose up and added power to stop our descent rate. "And Tower, Zero-Charlie-Fox would like to go back around and try that again."

With more than a little amusement in his tone, the controller said, "Roger, Zero-Charlie-Fox. We thought that might be the case. Turn right heading three-six-zero and climb and maintain three thousand."

I added power to climb. "Right three sixty and out of fifteen for three thousand, Zero-Charlie-Fox."

The tower controller handed us back off to the radar controller, who vectored us around for another attempt at the approach.

I turned to Hunter. "Don't beat yourself up. Just remember, everything happens at least twice as fast in the jet. You have to stay ahead. Don't ever put your airplane anywhere your brain hasn't already been. Fly the approach in your head while you're briefing it. If you ever get behind this plane, you'll never catch up."

He nodded and wiped his brow.

"Do you want to watch me fly it?" I asked.

He shook his head and frowned as if I'd just asked if he wanted me to cut off his foot. "No. I'm not going to learn anything watching somebody else do it. I have the controls."

"You have the controls. Let's start over and brief the approach."

We went through the same steps again, but on the second attempt, Hunter managed the speed beautifully and flew a nearly perfect approach. As if the aviation gods had granted him a reward for overcoming whatever that first attempted approach was, the main landing gear kissed the runway as soft as a falling feather.

"Much better," I said.

Hunter laughed. "I could've crashed into a mountain, and it would've been better than that first approach."

Disco laid a hand on Hunter's shoulder. "You're too hard on yourself. You proved in Montana that you don't crash into mountains. You prefer your wrecks to happen on the river."

Accepting the abuse, Hunter said, "That's fair. I probably deserved that."

We taxied to the transient line and surrendered our chariot to the linemen.

"How much fuel do you need, sir?"

I gave Hunter's shoulder a shove. "He's talking to you, Chuck Yeager."

Our stop turned into a lunch break, and we filled our bellies with barbecued ribs from a food truck that looked as if it may have been on fire . . . several times.

Hunter licked his fingers clean. "I've got to hand it to you, College Boy. I wasn't sure about the ash-and-soot truck, but these ribs are stupid good."

I looked up only long enough to give him a wink in acknowledgment of his praise, but I was having way too much fun with my rack of ribs to engage him in conversation. Then it hit me, and I froze in mid-bite. "Wait a minute! Did you just call me College Boy?"

Singer and Mongo chuckled, and I waggled a rib bone toward them. "It's obvious I'm going to have to limit your time with Clark. He's rubbing off on you guys, and I don't need that kind of mess smeared all over my team."

Singer, Mongo, and Disco all pointed toward Hunter.

The sniper said, "*He* said it. Not us."

"Yeah, maybe, but you laughed, and that's just as bad. Now, finish your ribs so we can get to New Mexico."

Unfazed, Hunter held up a bone as if it were Bugs Bunny's carrot stick. "I knew I should've taken that left turn at Albuquerque."

Two gallons of iced tea later, we hit the head to wash up and leave as much of the tea as possible behind.

Back in the air, we made the seven-hundred-mile second leg of our journey in just over ninety minutes. Just as Skipper promised, our rental car was waiting, and our reservation at the Grand Southwestern Inn proved to be another of Skipper's excellent choices.

Not only did the Grand Southwestern serve breakfast as a part of our stay, they also laid out a dinner spread that would've impressed even Maebelle. Family style had always been my preference when it came to mealtime, but I wasn't so sure I wanted quite the outpouring of curious questions our hostess had for us.

"Where are you guys from?" asked Tiffany, the sixty-something desk clerk who seemed to do everything from checking in the guests to washing the dishes.

I had my mouth full, so Disco fielded the question. "We're from all over. We were in the service together, so we try to get together when we can."

"Oh, that's nice. What did you do in the service?"

Already in over his head, Disco continued to speak for the team. "Uh, we're uh, pilots."

Tiffany beamed. "Isn't that exciting? I was married to a fighter pilot a lifetime ago, and it was just wonderful . . . until he died from eating poisonous mushrooms."

I was instantly glad Disco had volunteered to become the spokesman for the group. He continued to stutter. "I mean . . . um, I'm sorry . . . I guess."

Tiffany chuckled. "Oh, don't be sorry. I upgraded, and my life got a lot better. I noticed you boys are just staying one night, so where are you headed next?"

By that point, it had become a game for every member of the team to wait in silence as Disco verbally danced with Tiffany. The look on his face said he'd caught on, but there was nothing he could do to climb out of the hole he was digging for himself. "Well, you might say we're adventure travelers."

"Oh, that just sounds like so much fun. But I don't know what it means."

Tiffany still had her hooks in Disco, so he kept talking. "Yeah, well, we're catching a boat in San Francisco to Vancouver to do some hiking in the Canadian Rockies."

Her face was still aglow. "I just love boats. I was married to a boat captain for a few years when I was closer to your age, but he died from eating poisonous mushrooms, too."

I had no clue where Tiffany was going, but she was clearly having a great time dragging Disco along behind her.

Our chief pilot finally laid down his fork. "You lost two husbands to poisonous mushrooms? You can't be serious."

"Oh, I couldn't be more serious. It was a terrible tragedy, but all that came to an end when I met my sweet Harold. He bought this beautiful place and moved us out here to the desert. We had such a marvelous life together."

Disco leaned in. "*Had*? Did you lose Harold, too?"

She crossed herself like a good Catholic girl. "I did. It was so sad. He got beaten to death with a cast-iron skillet."

Disco slapped the table with both hands in disbelief. "How on Earth could something like that happen?"

Tiffany grinned. "It happened because I couldn't get that stubborn old goat to eat the mushrooms."

Chapter 26
Canadian Thunder

Tiffany, Albuquerque's own stand-up dinner comedienne, served us breakfast on the back porch of the inn. Made-to-order omelettes, biscuits, gravy, bacon, and fresh preserves consumed the table, and we ate like refugees.

The hostess pulled up a chair beside Disco and laid her chin on his shoulder. "I'd like to apologize for what I did to you last night at dinner."

Disco shook his head. "That was pretty cruel, and I'll accept your apology, but only because this breakfast is fantastic."

She leaned back abruptly, and her eyes widened as if she'd seen the ghosts of three dead husbands. "Oh, I didn't say I was apologizing. I just said I'd *like* to." She cackled at her own joke and pointed into the courtyard. "Do you see that stubborn old goat losing the fight with that tree limb and handsaw?"

Disco followed her finger. "Yes, I see him."

"Honey, that's Harold, and we've been married for thirty-five wonderful years. Forty-eight years all together, but only about thirty-five of them were wonderful." She slapped our pilot on the back and stood. "You boys enjoy your breakfast, and let me know if I can get you anything else."

* * *

The call I'd been waiting for came just as we loaded our backpacks into the rented SUV.

"Hello, this is Chase."

Earl's raspy tone filled my ear. "Good morning, Stud Muffin."

"Good morning. How are my two favorite truckers?"

"This may be the life for me, Baby Boy. I'm loving every minute of it. We're a little ahead of schedule, but I figured you'd already be here. We'll be at the warehouse in less than an hour."

I checked my watch. "That's perfect timing. I've got a truckful of strapping young men who can't wait to load your truck. We'll be at the warehouse when you pull in."

Forty-five minutes later, our Conex came into sight, and Kenny backed it into the loading dock as if he'd done it a million times. Perhaps he had.

I rang the bell on the dock and waited for somebody to open the overhead door. Just before I reached for the bell a second time, a hunchbacked man who looked far too old to work in a warehouse stumbled through the door.

He fumbled with his wire-rimmed glasses and finally got them situated on his face. "Are you here for the pillows?"

"Yes, sir," I said. "I guess that means we're at the right place."

The old man cupped his hand behind his ear. "What's that?"

I leaned in and spoke louder. "Yes, sir. We're here for the pillows."

As if he'd forgotten where he was, he chewed on the parts of his mouth that used to hold teeth. Finally, he said, "Oh, yeah . . . the pillows." He scooted back into the warehouse, and a few seconds later, the roll-up door began its slow rise. Two dozen pallets loaded with plain brown cardboard boxes stamped with the name "Sleep Specialists" appeared just inside the opening.

Kenny threw open the doors to the Conex. The old man pulled his decrepit body onto the seat of a forklift that looked at least as old as its operator. To my astonishment, the man who could barely walk turned into a forklift wizard. He had eight of the twenty-four pallets loaded before I could stop him. When he finally acknowledged me waving my arms like a maniac, he rolled to a stop right in front of me. "Yeah, what is it? Can't you see I'm busy loading this truck? I'll be with you in few minutes. You're here for the pillows, right?"

I motioned toward the Conex. "Those are my pillows, right?"

"Pillows?" the old man said. "We don't sell pillows. All we sell is cast-iron skillets and poisonous mushrooms."

I stood in stunned disbelief, shaking my head until the old man finished gasping for breath after laughing himself nearly to death. "Relax, sonny. I know who and what you are, and I'll leave plenty of room for you and your boys to get in and out of that container." He leaned toward me and hooked a finger. I leaned closer, and he said, "There's a lot more of us than most people know. I knew Rocket Richter when he was your age. I hear he was fond of you."

Memories of Dr. Robert "Rocket" Richter poured through my mind, and I made no effort to stop them. "He was a fine man, and I miss him every day."

"That he was, sonny. That he was. Now, get out of my way and let me finish loading your pillows while I'm still young."

I stepped aside and watched the man manipulate the machine like a master. Soon, the container was loaded perfectly, leaving barely enough room for Mongo to squeeze past the boxes and into the waiting hidey-hole.

Kenny closed the doors to the container, and I shook the old man's hand. "Thank you. It's nice to know we're not alone out here."

He wiped his brow with a sweat-stained handkerchief. "God-speed to you and your men. Whatever you're doing, do it well and come home safe, you hear?"

"Yes, sir. We have every intention of doing just that. Thanks again."

I followed Kenny and Earl back to the cab of their truck. Kenny said something, but I didn't recognize any of the sounds he made as English words, so I turned to Earl.

She said, "We'll meet you in Livermore in twenty-four hours. That'll give us a full day before your ship sails."

I shook my head. "Is that really what he said?"

Earl shook her head. "Nope. He said eighteen hours, but I ain't never seen Lake Havasu, and I intend to see it between here and there, so I chunked on another six hours. We've been swapping out every five or six hours and letting each other sleep."

"How long can you keep that up?" I asked.

She shrugged. "I don't know, but I reckon we've got to do it for another thirty-six hours or so. Then we'll get a break and take our time getting to Vancouver."

I surveyed the truck and trailer. "I'm still not sure why we can't just drive this thing over the border instead of going to all the trouble of getting on and off a ship."

"You've still got a lot to learn, Baby Boy. They've got scales at the border, and if your truck don't weigh what a truckful of pillows is supposed to weigh, they'll tear it apart from stem to stern. Do you know what would happen if you got caught sneaking across the border with a ton of guns and bullets?"

"I guess you're right, but it feels like we're going the long way around our backside to get to our elbow."

"Just play the game, Stud Muffin. You've got a pretty girl waitin' back in Georgia, and you don't want her to divorce you while you're locked up in a Canadian prison for the rest of your life, now do you?"

"You always have quite the knack at putting things in perspective, Earl. I'll see you tomorrow afternoon at Liver-whatever."

* * *

The flight from Albuquerque to Livermore, California, took only an hour and forty minutes, but based on the view outside the window, it would've been easy to believe we'd be transported a million miles away. Compared to the lush, green landscape of Northern California, the desert of New Mexico was a wasteland. There was no bed-and-breakfast with a sassy hostess or two-hundred-year-old men on forklifts, but the town was not without its charm.

Skipper had us booked at the Vineyard Inn. I didn't see any vineyards, but it was nice enough and gave us a collection of comfortable beds for our last night outside the metallic penthouse Earl created for us.

The team's demeanor took a dramatic change when Kenny and Earl came into sight from the confines of the airport.

Hunter said, "There it is. All that's left to know is whether that thing is our coffin or our time capsule."

As I pondered my partner's words, I waited for an answer to the ringing phone on the third-floor operations center back at Bonaventure. Five rings sounded in my ear before a man said, "Ops center, Brown."

Brown? Who's Brown?

Before my brain was sharp enough to remember Al Brown had become one fourth of the ops center personnel, I said, "Where's Skipper?"

"She's off shift. Do you need her?"

My mind's cloud of confusion finally lifted. "It's Chase. We've rendezvoused with Kenny and Earl, and we're ready to mount up."

Suddenly, Al became Master Sergeant Alvin Brown. "Roger. Stand by for ship status. Say condition of the transport vehicle."

I turned to Hunter. "How's the box look?"

He gave me the thumbs-up, so I said, "Transport vehicle is a go. All personnel are status one."

"Roger," Brown said. "Stand by for Ops One."

Skipper's voice soon filled my ear. "Chase, you have to get these guys out of my ops center. Brown and Clark are trying to turn this place into some kind of war-playing boys' club, and it's killing me."

I tried not to laugh, but I couldn't pull it off. "Put those boys in their place, and let them know they're guests in your kingdom."

"I think I prefer the term *queendom*. Less testosterone and more getting stuff done."

"It's your world," I said. "Run it as you see fit. We're ready to load up in Livermore."

"Yeah, I got that. I'm checking the ship's status. It'll come up any second now."

While I waited, I said, "I know you've got your hands full, but you said you may have a way to get a peek inside the entrance tunnel in Canada. Did anything come of that?"

She sighed. "No, and I tried hard. I just couldn't get it to work out. You're going in blind, I'm afraid. The relay beacons are in your kit if you have room to carry them in. If not, we won't have any comms while you're inside the mountain."

I pictured the mobile satellite relay stations in my head. "They're collapsible, right?"

"Yeah, they're about nine pounds each and fold up to the size of a lunchbox. I know nine pounds is a lot of extra weight, but you'll only have to carry them in. There's no reason to hump them back out. Just abandon them in place."

"We don't have a choice. We need comms with you while we're inside, so we're definitely taking them. Besides, we've got Mongo the human pack mule."

"Okay, I've got the ship status. It's alongside in Frisco right now. It's scheduled to take on thirty-eight containers tonight and sail tomorrow morning. If you can't make it, I can delay it, but it won't be easy."

"That's a day ahead of schedule."

"Yes, it is, but apparently, the seas off the West Coast are uncharacteristically calm, and the port captain approved an early arrival."

"That sounds like a good thing for our little cruise," I said.

She groaned. "Maybe, but there's a low-pressure system off the northeast coast of Russia. That'll create some south wind for you. It depends on how strong that system becomes, but you may get some pretty big swells on the stern by the day after tomorrow."

"In that case, we'll be sure to keep the seasickness bags handy. We'll easily make the port in time to get on the boat. It's only an hour from here, and we're ready to roll."

Skipper's fingers danced across the keyboard in a rhythmic staccato. "Okay, it's done. You're on the loading order. You'll be the last container stacked tonight. I've got you on a S.H.I.T. order."

"That doesn't sound good," I said.

She huffed. "It's not what it sounds like, dummy. It means Stack High in Transit. That means you'll be last on and first off."

"If you say so. Is there anything else before we mount up?"

She shuffled through some paperwork. "Just verify everyone is status one and ready to go."

"We're ready," I said. "We all feel fine, and we're anxious to go to work."

She said, "Okay, then. Let's rock and roll. Give me a comms check before you pull out of the airport. If we have to work on anything, we don't want to do it under the nosey eyes of the steve-dores at the docks."

"Will do. Expect a comms check in ten, and tell Brown and Clark to chill out. You've got this."

"Yeah, right, like that'll work. I may just give them something shiny to play with while Penny and I run the op."

"Now you're thinking," I said.

With the phone shut down and stowed away, I followed my team through the maze of cardboard boxes full of pillows and into the inner sanctum. Before crawling through the doggie door, I shoved a box of pillows through the opening and followed it through. With the door sealed, I sliced open the box and tossed pillows to the team. "It's going to be uncomfortable enough in here, so I figured we should make the most of our cargo."

The space definitely felt smaller with the five of us inside and the door sealed. Hunter fluffed his pillow and climbed on top of the netted cargo. "I hope you boys aren't claustrophobic. I'll be right up here if you need me."

I pulled open the master control panel Earl built into the cor-ner of the space. With the push of a couple of buttons and the flip of a switch, the generators hummed to life beneath our feet, and soon, cool air wafted from the vents at each corner.

I brought the comms to life and keyed the mic. "Ops, Charlie-One, radio check, over."

Al Brown's voice boomed through the speaker. "Charlie-One, Ops has you Lima Charlie. How me?"

I could almost see Skipper shaking her head, so I said, "You know, Brown, it's okay to say loud and clear. That actually has one fewer syllable than Lima Charlie, so it makes more sense."

His silence made it clear that my team had a lot more fun than his.

Skipper either kicked him out of the ops center or took control of the radio. "I've started the clock, boys. Operation Canadian Thunder has officially begun."

"Canadian Thunder?" I said.

Skipper giggled. "Yep. Brown insisted we name the operation, so that's what I've named it. I think it's kind of catchy."

"I'll get Singer to write us a jingle for it while we're at sea. Charlie-One, out."

Chapter 27
Where's the Sun

When we closed ourselves into the chamber, the tiny lights Earl installed around the space seemed to have little meaningful effect at defeating the absence of outside light, but as our eyes adjusted and our initial anxiety of encapsulation waned, the lights proved more than adequate to brighten the room.

Yanking me out of the trance into which I'd fallen ten minutes into the ride from Livermore to San Francisco, Earl's voice filled the container. "Hey, boys. It looks like we've got an hour and a half before we make it to the pier. Traffic is heavier than we expected, but as I'm sure you can feel, we're still moving. Is everybody doing all right back there?"

Every eye scanned the space looking for a microphone, but after thirty seconds of searching, I finally said, "Can you hear me, Earl?"

"Sure, I can hear you, Baby Boy. I just wanted to see how long it would take you bunch of mental heavyweights to figure out you had a hot mic."

"We know now," I said. "And we're all good back here. You've really outdone yourself this time. When all of this is over, I'd love to keep this container."

Kenny's voice filled the air, but the intercom did nothing to make his English any more understandable. "Don' you be worryin' none, you. Ol' Kenny be makin' sho dis here ting be gettin' itself all da way back to Georgia, me."

"Does that mean you're bringing the container back across the border? What about the scales and inspection station?"

Kenny started to talk, but Earl cut him off. "What my man is trying to say is, we won't have any trouble getting this thing back home. The scales and inspections are for getting *into* Canada, not getting out."

I said, "There's no way to know how long we'll be on the ground. What are you two going to do while we're . . . working?"

Earl cackled. "Oh, I'm sure we can find something to do. Besides, you boys are gonna need a ride home, ain't you?"

"Yes, we are, but I was hoping for an Air Canada first-class seat to San Francisco with free cocktails and those little foil pouches of a dozen stale peanuts."

"Sorry, Stud Muffin. A steel box and MREs are the best we can do, but I'll put on my skimpy outfit and play flight attendant on that sexy airplane of yours you left in Livermore."

I shuddered. "I'm afraid that would be more than any of us could handle, Earl, but thanks for the offer."

"Your loss," she said, and the connections clicked off.

Hunter leaned up from his perch. "I guess Earl thought of everything, but I'm not sure I like the idea of open comms."

"Don't worry. We'll be on a cargo ship in two hours with nobody to hear a word we're saying."

"Yeah, but we'll only be on that boat for three days. I don't think that's enough time to get the picture of Earl as a flight attendant out of my head."

Ninety minutes later, the air brakes emitted their strained tone of being set, and our motion ended.

An audible click sounded from hidden speakers. "Dis be it, you hear? I be seein' you 'gen in 'bout four or maybe tree days, me. Ol' Kenny needs to be leavin' you wiff one las' tought fore you be goin'. Do you boys be knowin' what be so amazin' 'bout da bayou?"

A collection of bewildered faces stared back at me as if I was supposed to do something to make it stop.

I said, "Let's have it, Kenny. What's so amazing about the bayou?"

"Not only do it be by-*you* house, but it be by-*my* house, too."

The electronic click told us the comms had been closed, and Singer slapped his forehead. "That guy is worse than Clark. Where do you find these people, Chase?"

"I don't find them. They find me. It's like I'm some kind of freak magnet. I mean, just look around. There's nothing normal about anybody on this team, including you, Singer."

An hour passed, and we hadn't moved. The muffled sounds of men working, trucks repositioning, and cranes lifting containers made their way through the walls of our temporary home, but I was beginning to feel alone. Perhaps it was the uncertainty of our situation, but more likely, it was the fact that my team and I were completely powerless to affect the outcome of the next three days. We were nothing more than passive observers and captive stowaways, and that was not a status I enjoyed.

Other than the hum of the generators and air handlers, the interior of the box was devoid of conversation. Every two minutes, someone would check his watch. My unease of our situation was, apparently, contagious.

Ninety minutes, or perhaps two years later, the metallic clang of the crane's clamping mechanism sounded like thunder as the hooks locked themselves in place at the four upper corners of our container.

I spread my feet and gripped the edge of my bunk. "Here we go, boys! Find something to hold on to."

Hunter sat up on his pile of gear, gripped the cargo net with one hand, and threw his other hand into the air like a rodeo cowboy. "I knew I should've been a professional bull rider."

Mongo rolled his eyes. "If we make it through this ordeal, I'm buying you a hat and a bull just so I can watch. Chase, can I put Hunter's bull in the pasture at Bonaventure?"

"Absolutely. Just as long as you promise that bull will torment the horses as badly as they torment me."

Mongo laughed. "You got it! One horse-hating rodeo bull coming up. I can't wait to see Hop Along Hunter on that thing."

The clamps holding us to Kenny LePine's trailer opened, and we became a dangling victim of the gantry crane's will. The ride lasted only a few seconds before we were placed with a thud on top of a stack of containers that looked a lot like ours, but only from the outside.

Disco surveyed the interior of the space as if the walls might collapse at any minute. "That wasn't so bad. I expected it to be a little more violent."

"That was the easy part," I said. "According to Skipper, we're in for some south wind on the open ocean that'll make for a nauseating ride at best."

The vibration of the cargo ship's engines was slightly out of time with the harmonics of the generators built in beneath our feet, making the interior of the container sound like the inside of a car with one rear window rolled down.

Trying to shake off the annoying sound, I said, "I sure hope that goes away when we set sail."

Disco shook his head. "Me, too. That's annoying. Maybe it'll get better when the ship's engines are up to operating speed."

As the afternoon turned into evening outside our confinement, my stomach let me know it was time for dinner.

I pulled open a box of MREs. "Who wants the pork patty?"

Nobody spoke up.

"Okay, I guess that's mine. How about beef stew?"

Hunter held up a hand, so I landed the plastic pouch in his lap.

"I'm holding out for chicken a la king," Singer said.

I flipped through the options and found his pouch. "Here you go."

Disco and Mongo settled for chicken loaf and meatballs in barbeque sauce.

As I choked down the square colorless lump of pudding labeled "pork patty," I thought I was going blind. Everything in the room slowly grew dimmer. Just as I accepted the fact that it must be a side effect of the dehydrated peaches sticking to the roof of my mouth, Disco said, "Is it just me, or is it getting darker in here?"

Relieved sighs resounded through the box, but I was still concerned about our lights growing dim. "I don't think this is a good thing. I'm not excited about spending the next three days in the dark."

I saved the candy and toilet paper from my MRE for obvious reasons and picked up the mic at the comms station. "Ops Center, Charlie-One."

Apparently it was Penny's shift. "Ops Center, go ahead."

"Do you have comms with Earl?"

Penny said, "I'm sure we can call her. Why? Is something wrong?"

"Maybe. The lights are going dim in here, and that makes me think there may be an electrical issue. Maybe Earl can talk us through troubleshooting it before we're completely in the dark."

I thought I detected a guilty giggle in Penny's voice. "Where's the sun, Charlie-One?"

"The sun?" I asked.

"Yeah, check your watch and tell me where the sun should be."

"What are you talking about?" I demanded.

"Just do it," she said.

I checked my watch. "It's seven-twenty-five. The sun is probably . . ."

I stared up at the dimming lights. "You've got to be kidding me!"

Penny's giggle became full-blown laughter. "Nope. Not kidding. Earl built a timer into the lighting system to emulate natural sunlight. It'll be dark inside the box at the same time it's dark outside, so your bodies and minds will retain the natural rhythm of the rest of us who aren't trapped inside a steel box."

"Unbelievable," I said. "She thought of everything."

"Good night, guys. I won't be on shift when you sail tomorrow morning, but make sure you let us know when you leave the dock."

"Good night, my dear, but let's not say things like trapped inside a steel box, okay?"

Our bunks didn't qualify as luxury sleeping accommodations by any means, but they were better than sleeping on the deck. When the midnight watch came on in the bridge of the cargo ship, they must've shut down one of their engines. The harmonics changed just enough to rock us to sleep like babies.

Before drifting off, Singer asked, "Should one of us stay awake and pull fireguard and security?"

I said, "If we catch on fire, there's nothing we can do about it, and I can't think of any security risks stacked at the top of a load of cargo in San Francisco Bay. Who's going to climb up here and assault a container full of pillows?"

The last trickle of light left us, and sleep took the team. Earl's artificial sunrise gently pulled us from our slumber, and one by one, we rolled from our bunks.

The morning's first words came from Hunter. "So help me, Mongo, if you snore tonight, I'm sticking at least one of my sweaty, stinky socks in your mouth. You're not only built like a buffalo, but you snore like one too."

Mongo said, "Did anyone else hear me snoring?"

We shook our heads, and Disco said, "It must be your guilty conscience keeping you awake, Hunter. We didn't hear a thing."

The vibrations of the ship's full complement of engines came up to speed, and the world beneath us began to move.

I pulled the mic from its clip. "Good morning, Ops Center. It's Charlie-One. We're on the move."

Clark's booming voice bellowed from the speaker. "What do you mean, morning? It's lunchtime already."

"Not out here on the West Coast," I said. "We've just left the dock, and I suspect we'll be sailing beneath the Golden Gate Bridge any minute now."

He said, "Roger. There's a small black screen beside the comms panel. Press and hold the two buttons at the bottom."

I found the screen and pressed the buttons. Soon, the screen filled with a black and white image of the coastline of the Pacific Northwest. I said, "Great. It's a map of the coast. What does that do for us?"

Clark said, "Be patient, College Boy."

A few seconds later, a small triangle appeared in Frisco Bay, and it was slowly moving westward.

"Would you look at that?" I said. "It's like our very own *You Are Here map* at the mall."

"Exactly," Clark said. "Enjoy the cruise. We'll check in at every shift change. Let us know if you need anything."

I yawned and stretched. "We could use some room service. Nothing special, just some eggs and bacon and maybe a pot of coffee or two."

"I'll see what I can do," he said.

A heat source, even as seemingly benign as an electric hotplate could spell disaster for five men confined in a box on a ship at sea. Of the thousands of things that could go wrong, a fire was near the top of the list. Perhaps only sinking would qualify as worse. There was no coffee pot, but there was a two-pound bag of chocolate-covered, roasted, coffee beans. Although no substitute exists for fresh-brewed coffee, the sweet treats weren't bad.

Life in our little petri dish of a circadian rhythm experiment continued for two more nights before our movement slowed to allow the Canadian harbor pilot to come aboard and guide us into the Straight of Juan de Fuca and the Salish Sea. I watched the small display with great interest as we sailed through the San Juan Islands and finally into Burrad Inlet and Vancouver Harbour.

When all motion had ceased, and it, once again, sounded like someone rolled down one window, I clicked the mic. "Ops Center, Charlie-One. We're alongside in Vancouver."

This time, the confident voice of the best analyst alive said, "Good morning, Charlie-One. Expect half an hour before the cranes come to life. I just got off the phone with Kenny and Earl. That guy really needs an interpreter. Anyway, they're waiting in line at the port. You should be one of the first containers off the ship. With a little help from some friends, I've arranged to fast-track you through customs."

"How did you pull that off?" I asked.

"You don't want to know, but it was a judgment call. Clark and I put our heads together and made the call. The upside is that you'll be out of the port and headed east in a couple of hours instead of a couple of weeks."

"That sounds great," I said. "But what if it raises a red flag and we get too much attention?"

"That's the downside," she said. "I want you out of that box as soon as possible."

I grimaced. "I agree, but that's a pretty big gamble, isn't it?"

"It is, but the average clearing time out of the Port of Vancouver is eleven days. Are you prepared to spend eleven more days waiting for customs?"

"I don't love decisions like that being made without at least consulting the people it affects the most. In the future, let me in on the discussions before you and Clark summarily decide our fate in the field."

Her tone softened. "It won't happen again. I'll make sure of it."

The same metallic clamping sounds we'd heard just before being lifted from the trailer and stacked aboard the ship in San Francisco roared through the container.

"It sounds like our number has been called. They're lifting us off the ship right now."

"Perfect," she said. "Check back in when you leave the port."

"Wilco. Charlie-One, out."

The gentle ride we enjoyed through the air in San Francisco was not what we got in Vancouver. Either the crane operator was in a hurry, or he was on his seventh cocktail of the morning. When we cleared the stack, our container spun through several rotations, leaving us grasping for anything we could find that wasn't being thrown across the space. The only thing worse than our flight was the landing. We hit the deck as if we'd been dropped. The concussion of the landing jarred the overhead bin so violently it fell open, depositing our cache of weapons, ammo, and explosives across the deck.

"What was that?" Hunter yelled. "Did he drop us?"

I said, "I don't know, but is everybody all right?"

"I think I broke a nail," Disco said. "But other than that, I'm okay."

Mongo said, "Oh, no! Air Force broke a nail. Call in a mede-vac, quick!"

More clangs and bangs rattled through the container until, finally, we slowly started moving forward. The road was rocky enough to make the ride uncomfortable, so we stood by our bunks and held on, hoping the logging road would turn to asphalt soon.

We rumbled and bounced for two or three more minutes, then the ride felt like the delicate handling we'd come to expect after our ride from Livermore to Frisco. I pulled the mic from the comms panel and reported, "Ops Center, Charlie-One. We're on the move and probably clear of the port."

Skipper's nearly panicked voice resounded. "What? Are you sure?"

I didn't like the fear in her voice. "Yes, we're definitely on the move."

In a tone far outside her character, she said, "Chase, you're not on Kenny's truck. They're still in the port."

Chapter 28
Hijacking, Cajun Style

I stared into the GPS screen and buried the push-to-talk button. "There are no roads on this GPS, but we appear to be moving northeast. We could use some guidance here."

A long moment of silence was punctuated by Skipper's trembling voice. "I'm on it, but I'm short on ideas. How fast does it feel like you're moving?"

"I don't know. Faster than the ship, but that's all I've got. Where's Clark?"

Nothing kills more operators than panic. Bullets are bad, but panic is worse.

I turned to my team. "Do any of you have any ideas?"

Bewildered eyes bored through me, but no one spoke.

Suddenly, Clark's voice came on the line. "Charlie-One, we're showing that you're still in the container yard in Vancouver. Are you sure you're moving?"

"Yeah, I'm real sure we're moving."

"Something's going on," he said. "The tracker shows you sitting still in the port."

"The tracker is wrong! Forget the tracker and listen to me. We're moving, and moving fast. The GPS shows a northeast track, but there's no ground speed displayed and no roads on the map."

"Stand by, Chase. I'm on the line with Kenny."

"Hurry. The longer this goes on, the harder we'll be to find." No reply came, so I turned and took a knee. "This isn't good. Let's hear some ideas."

Every head turned toward the emergency trapdoor in the floor.

Singer said, "It's your call, Chase, but I say we blow the door and take our chances on foot."

I ran a billion scenarios through my head and couldn't come up with a better idea. "We're not taking a vote, but does anyone else have an idea?"

Hunter said, "We could kick open the container doors. That would get some attention if there's anybody behind us on the road. They'd likely flag down the driver and get him stopped."

I added his suggestion to my list and turned to Disco, who looked like he was trying to work out a calculus problem. "What's going on in there, Disco?"

He shrugged. "I don't know. I was just thinking . . . What's the worst that could happen if we just ride it out? We have to stop somewhere, sooner or later. When the driver delivers a truckload of pillows to the wrong place, we wait until the sun goes down and the lights go dark, then we slip out."

I pored over the ideas, knowing it was ultimately my call. "Here's what I'm thinking. We have to prioritize. If the mission is blown, our priority is getting out of the country as covertly as possible. There's no fence. If we get out and hike south, we'll walk across a street and be back in the States. That leaves a cargo container full of pillows, guns, and bullets running around western Canada, and our fingerprints are all over it."

Clark's voice broke through my shroud of indecision. "Kenny's on the move. I've got no idea what he said, but it sounded like he's chasing you and he's got a plan."

I keyed the mic. "That's what we need—a crazy Cajun and Earl at the End chasing us through British Columbia in a tractor trailer."

Clark said, "On our short list of options, I'd say praying Kenny catches us has to be at the top of the list."

"Okay," I said. "We'll let it play out until it falls apart. If we don't come up with a better plan, we're blowing the bailout door and torching the trailer at our first stop."

Clark said, "Roger, Charlie-One."

I left the mic hanging from its cord and ordered, "Kit up. This may not be an accident. The Chinese or some of their buddies in the Canadian government may have figured out what's going on. We may be kidnap victims. If that's the case, we're going to make them understand how terrible we are at being victims."

No one hesitated. We sorted through the pile of weaponry scattered around the space, and soon, everyone was in full battle rattle.

I dumped a box of MREs on the deck. "Get some calories down your throat. We may need them."

My panic was gone, replaced by a plan and a determination to control the outcome of our situation. "Get the comms," I ordered.

Hunter pulled the cargo net from our gear bags and passed out our earpieces and radios.

"Here are the rules of engagement," I said. "We assume all contact is hostile until proven otherwise. Shoot only in direct response to potentially deadly aggression. Suppress aggressors by force, if possible. Kill only if there is no other option. Any questions?"

None came.

"Disco, you're on the radio. Mongo and Hunter, you're on the rear doors. Singer, you're backing up from concealment on the back doors. Got it?"

Everyone nodded. ·

I said, "I'll rig the explosives. If we're forced to surrender the vehicle, we'll burn it to the ground the second everyone is clear. Move out!"

Disco took a knee by the comms panel as the remaining team exited the doggie door into the main body of the container. I pulled the detonation cord and plastic explosive from our kit and wired the trailer to become an inferno at the touch of a button.

When I finished lacing the det cord through the space, I said, "Report."

Hunter replied, "Rear guard in place."

Singer said, "Overwatch in place."

Disco reported, "Comms in place."

I said, "Nice work, guys. I've got enough C-Four rigged up to send this thing to the moon."

I'd learned, in my eight years as an operator, that all warriors knew how to wait. They may not like it, but they know how to do it. Apparently, it's an integral part of life in uniform. I'd never know, but my men were standing watch like the elite soldiers they were, and I was praying Cajun Kenny LePine would pull a miracle out of the bayou—or whatever they call swamps in Canada.

The sound of an air horn blared outside the container, growing louder by the second. Whoever was pulling the chain on that horn wanted the whole world to know he was there. Soon, the echoing horn was accompanied by the sound of a massive diesel engine making all the power it was capable of producing. At that moment, I would've given a million dollars for a window. The show unfolding on the Canadian highway was going to be a scene I didn't want to miss.

The horn continued, and our container swerved violently, fishtailing and sending my team bouncing off the walls and cardboard boxes. I had the doggie door propped open so I could see Disco while I stayed in the main compartment in case my shooters needed backup.

Watching the look on Disco's face, I said, "If we go down back here, I want you to blow the trapdoor, cook off the explosives, and run. Got it?"

He stared at me with steely determination in his eyes. "You taught me to shoot, Chase. You never taught me to run."

The jet-jockey-turned-commando impressed me more every time I turned around.

The swerving, sliding, and horn blowing continued long enough for us to adapt to the motion and remain at our posts. Singer was tossed around the trailer from his position up high, but no matter where he landed, the muzzle of his rifle remained trained on the rear doors.

The swerving and speed turned to deceleration, sending all of us tumbling forward. Everyone reclaimed their position quickly as the truck came to an abrupt stop.

The sounds of shouting in what must've been French filled the air and permeated the walls of the container.

"Does anybody speak French?" I asked.

Mongo said, "A little."

"Of course you do," I said. "Get up here and listen."

He crawled through the boxes and took a knee beside the doggie door while I grabbed his rifle and hustled to take his place at the rear door.

Once I was in place, I said, "Okay, Mongo. Let's hear it."

"It's not good French. I'm not even sure it's real French, but he's saying something like, 'That's my load.'"

"Could it be Cajun French?"

The big man laughed. "I gar-on-tee it be, I do, me."

A wave of relief came over the whole team, and the radio crackled to life. "Charlie-One, Ops Center."

Disco keyed up. "Ops Center, Charlie-Five."

"Uh, Charlie-Five, Earl says they've got you stopped on a four-lane road near someplace called Furry Creek. Can you verify?"

Disco said, "We're definitely stopped, but I don't know where. The GPS shows water immediately to the west, but that's all I can see."

Skipper ordered, "Say condition."

Disco froze, and Singer said, "Tell her we're condition three and still concealed."

He passed the information, and Skipper said, "Roger. Stand by."

Disco looked confused. "Somebody is going to have to explain condition three to me when this is over."

Hunter sighed. "You're making the Air Force look bad again, Disco. We'll have combat one-oh-one class if we survive this."

Commotion outside was followed by slow forward motion, followed by another stop.

Mechanical sounds, thuds, and clangs echoed through the container, then the sound of a truck pulling away filled our ears. I was tempted to cut a hole in the roof and climb on top of the container just so I could see what was happening. My ears made terrible eyes, and my brain turned every sound into a potential catastrophe.

A sudden jolt and shudder rocked the container, sending my brain into overdrive, and my desire to open a door was almost impossible to overcome. More banging and clanging was followed by the feeling of a massive U-turn.

Uncertain what we'd just experienced, the optimist in me wanted to believe Kenny had convinced the driver to turn around and take us back to the port so he could straighten everything out, but the tiny optimistic region of my brain was wrong . . . as usual.

As we picked up speed, I heard Kenny LePine's voice ringing through the container. "How you boys is back der? Der don' be no gettin' way from ol' Kenny dat easy, no. I gots you now, and e'reting be dus fine, I guarantee, me do."

I crawled through the boxes and back through the doggie door. "Kenny, what happened out there?"

"Some udder driver done be made off wit my load, he did, but dat don' fly wit ol' Kenny, no it don'.

"What did you tell him to convince him he had the wrong container?"

"You don' need to be worryin' bout dat, you. What we had us was ourselves a good old-fashioned Cajun hijacking, we."

Chapter 29
Boots on the Ground

With the Cajun hijacking in our wake, we were left with one terrified and confused truck driver headed southwest, back toward the Vancouver port, and five covert operatives relaxing for the first time in two hours.

Hoping the intercom between the truck and trailer was still operational, I cast my eyes toward the ceiling. "Earl, are you there?"

"Yeah, Baby Boy, I'm here. What do you need?"

"When we get someplace where it's unlikely we'll encounter any curious onlookers, it would be quite nice to get a breath of fresh air."

She said, "Based on what I'm seeing out to the east, it won't take us long to get where there ain't nobody, curious or otherwise."

"That's good to hear. There's just one more thing."

"What is it?"

"The other truck driver . . . Is he okay?"

"Yeah, Stud Muffin. He's just fine. But whoever does his laundry is going to know how scared he was when my man pulled him outta that truck."

"I know I said there was only one more thing, but I do need to know if Kenny's all right, too."

"That man is made out of leather and steel. You can't hurt him. Just relax back there and consider us to be Allstate."

"Allstate?"

"Yeah, you know Allstate . . . The good hands people. Take it from me. I sure know ol' Kenny's got some good hands up here."

"Yeah, okay, Earl. That's all I really need to know. I don't think my mind's eye can handle much more. Go ahead and close the intercom."

The click came, and everyone in the box sat shaking their heads.

I asked to no one in particular, "Do you think other teams do stuff like this?"

The answer was a unanimous, "No!"

I pulled the mic from the comms panel and pressed the button. "Ops Center, Charlie-One. Sitrep."

Skipper was back at the helm. "Send the situation report, Charlie-One."

"All personnel safe, and we're Charlie Mike. Do you have some grid coordinates for the tunnel entrance yet?"

"Roger. Understand you're continuing mission. I do have the coordinates, and I've already sent them to Earl and Kenny."

I said, "Send them to me just in case something else goes wrong."

"They're sent," she said. "I sent them to your sat-phone as well as the GPS in the box."

"Thanks, Skipper. Do you have an estimate on our ETA to the site?"

"Two things. First, the reason I thought you were still in the container yard at the port is because, apparently, the tracker I mounted on the upper corner of your container got knocked off somehow."

"I think I know how that happened," I said. "The crane operator at the port was anything but gentle. He threw us around like a ragdoll. The tracker probably got knocked off during our crash onto the trailer."

"That makes sense," she said. "The second thing is this. I have a tracker still in place on Kenny's truck, so I'm tracking you in real time now. It's not very far to the entrance, but there are no good roads to get you there. You're probably looking at five or six hours, thanks to the little field trip you took with the wrong driver."

"Great. Another five hours in this coffin."

She huffed. "The Chinese don't exactly build bunkers in foreign countries in the middle of big cities."

"I know. It's just that we're ready to breathe some fresh air and stretch our legs."

I closed the comms with Skipper and turned to the team. "Skipper says we've got five more hours. Let's get out there, rearrange those boxes, and stage our gear near the back of the container."

Without a groan or grumble, everyone leapt to their feet and headed through the doggie door. The task of restacking boxes and staging gear proved to be far more challenging than I expected. The nearly constant switchbacks in the road left us spending more time bouncing off the walls than positioning gear.

An hour into our task, we slowed, and the sound of gravel crunching beneath oversized tires grew louder until we finally stopped. That tiny optimist in my head wanted to believe we'd reached a spot at which we could step outside, even if only for a few minutes, but the realist in me came to full alert.

My thundering heart was relieved when someone struck the door with something hard.

"It be me, ol' Kenny. Don' you be shootin' when I open dis here door, no."

Sunlight crept through the ever-widening crack as Kenny pulled the door through its arc. The sunlight was blinding, but the fresh breeze on our faces felt like the welcome mat to Heaven. One by one, we hopped from the truck as if we'd been suddenly released from prison.

Earl backed up as we hit the ground. "Whoa! You boys smell like you've been trapped in a box for four days."

I threw out my arms to hug her, but she waddled away like a frightened duck.

We took in the scenery of the rising terrain to the east and the coastal planes to the west.

Singer sighed. "I've been to a lot of places on God's Earth, but never here. It's sort of like Montana but even bigger."

"That's a good way to put it," I said. "I've never been here, either, but there's nothing welcoming about those mountains. We're in for a lot of footsteps up there."

He laughed. "Hey, Disco. What was it you told that crazy innkeeper in Albuquerque? We're adventure travelers?"

"Yeah, that was it," Disco said.

Singer pointed to the jagged peaks, some still capped in snow in the middle of summer. "How's that look for adventure travel?"

Disco studied the mountains. "I'd say that'll do."

I took in the breathtaking scenery. "As much as I don't want to do it, we have to get back inside. We've still got a long afternoon ahead of us."

We mounted up, but no one seemed to be in a hurry.

Kenny closed the doors, leaving us, once again, in the darkened cavern of the container. Just as before, our eyes slowly adapted to the limited light being emitted by the LEDs inside our box.

At various times throughout the afternoon, each of us drifted in and out of sleep, knowing the coming night would be anything but restful.

A few minutes past five, the intercom came alive with Earl's voice. "One of you will have to come up here with us and decide where to drop the container."

Everyone volunteered, but positioning our resupply point had the potential to either keep us alive or kill us, and I didn't feel anyone should make that call other than me.

"Pop the rear door," I said. "I'll come out." I climbed into the cab, forcing Earl from the passenger's seat to the sleeper.

Kenny pointed out the windshield. "Dis here be Saskatchewan River Crossing. It ain't much to it, but da good news is they's a field full of containers dus' like dis one here that don' look like nobody been touchin' for long time, no."

I compared our location to the grid coordinates to the tunnel entrance Skipper provided. "I think you didn't need me at all, Kenny. This is the perfect spot. Put us as close to the back of the lot as possible."

He maneuvered the truck and trailer with the hands of a master and soon had us tucked behind six other containers just like ours.

"You've done a great job, Kenny, and I'll see that you're well compensated, but it's time for you to drop the trailer and get out of here. And it's time for us to put some boots on the ground."

He didn't protest. Instead, he lowered the trailer jack and cranked the handle until the feet were carrying the load that had been borne by the truck's fifth wheel. Thirty seconds later, he, Earl, and the truck were gone.

I opened the rear hatch and looked up into the faces of the four men I'd trust to hit the ground anywhere on the planet and do the impossible. They jumped from the container and immediately began forming a perimeter.

I said, "Relax, guys. I don't think we need to pull perimeter guard. I've got good news and bad news. The good news is, we're just over one click from the tunnel entrance if we take the road."

Hunter said, "Something tells me the bad news is that we're not taking the road."

I pointed up the slope behind me. "Nope, we're taking the road less traveled. Let's go take a look."

Mongo asked, "Are we humping the gear in now?"

"Yes. Gear up and drink up. I'll check in with Skipper."

While the team arranged the gear, strapping everything they could carry to themselves, I pulled the satellite phone from my pocket. It took a couple of minutes for the phone to come to life, but it finally detected enough satellites to do its job. I wondered if it could see the satellite that was the central reason we'd come five thousand miles.

Skipper answered promptly, and I made short work of announcing our condition. "We're on the ground and strapped up. We'll move to contact and report before we hit the tunnel."

"Roger. Godspeed, Chase. Be careful up there."

"We will."

Mongo helped load my gear onto my back, and I took the first step on the ground toward our objective. The jagged landscape made movement slow and meticulous, but we'd trained to operate in the most hostile environments on the planet, so our coverage of the terrain wasn't record-setting, but it was efficient.

When the unassuming entrance to the bunker came into sight, I raised a fist, and the team stopped in their tracks. Unlike the Cheyenne Mountain complex in Colorado, there was no road leading into the tunnel. The mouth was so narrow it would've been impossible for any of us, especially Mongo, to fit through the opening with our gear on our backs.

I motioned for Singer, and he took a knee beside me.

"Tell me what you don't see."

The hawklike eyes of our sniper scoured the landscape, committing every inch to memory. "Are you sure this is the entrance?"

I pulled my map from its pouch and replotted the coordinates Skipper provided. "According to Skipper's coordinates, this is it."

Singer said, "It's either the least-monitored entrance to a high-security area I've ever seen, or they're masters at hiding their surveillance gear."

"The trees overhead make satellite imagery useless. What do you know about seismic monitoring?"

He shook his head. "Seismic mics would be worthless up here. That road is only a hundred yards away. Every car that passed by would set off an alarm."

"Could they filter out the noise from the road?"

"Sure, but they can't filter out the wildlife and the trees swaying and rubbing together in the wind. If they did, that would filter out human movement, as well."

"So do we assume the entrance is unmonitored?"

He scratched his chin. "Maybe they don't care what happens outside the tunnel. Nothing out here is a threat until it comes inside."

I studied the entrance and tried to think like a Chinese counter surveillance officer until I developed a plan. "Let's retreat into the tree line as far as possible and still keep the entrance in sight. We'll set a base camp there and move the rest of our gear forward."

The terrain allowed us to move almost three hundred meters deeper into the forest and still put eyes on the sliver of an entrance. Everyone dropped their packs and pulled their commo gear from inside. Hunter established the satellite uplink and gave me a nod.

I keyed my radio. "Ops Center, Charlie-One."

Clark's voice filled our ears. "Go for Ops."

"We're in position about three hundred meters from the tunnel entrance, but I'm not sure this is the main entrance. Do you have intel on any other possible tunnels?"

"Negative, Charlie-One. We have ventilation shafts and one possible emergency egress tunnel, but no other entrances."

"I don't like it," I said. "Something's not right. The opening is less than three feet wide."

"Three feet?" Clark said. "Are you sure?"

"We've got eyes on it right now, and there's no way we can squeeze Mongo through that opening, let alone a vehicle."

"Stand by." He yelled for Skipper and passed the information.

The unmistakable sound of her fingertips on a keyboard played in my ear.

Soon her voice replaced the sound of keys. "Charlie-One, confirm you are at the grid coordinates I provided."

"Confirmed."

A long moment passed before she said, "Can you upload a picture of the opening?"

Singer keyed up. "I'm on it. Give me ten minutes."

Hunter said, "Mongo, Disco, and I will bring the rest of the gear forward."

I nodded, and the three silently moved back toward the container.

Singer was back in half the time he predicted. "Okay, the picture is sent. For scale, I estimate the height of the opening to be eight feet."

Skipper's keyboard rattled again and then fell silent. "Uh, Charlie-One, this isn't what I'm seeing on the satellite shot. Something's not right."

"I agree, but we've got eyes on, and it's definitely not what your imagery shows."

"Chase, I'm out of ideas. There's a disconnect somewhere. Give me half an . . ."

Singer grabbed my arm and stuck his finger to his lips. "Hush and listen!"

Rumbling and the sound of an engine came from the direction of the tunnel, and Singer sprang to his feet. I followed him toward the opening, staying as low as I could and keeping my eyes pasted to the vertical slit in the rocks. We took up a position behind a fallen tree and stared intently as the last thing we could've expected slowly unfolded before our eyes.

Chapter 30
Open Sesame

"Well, I'll be darned," Singer whispered. "Have you ever seen anything like that?"

"Sure, I have," I said. "That's exactly how every garage door works, except this one is horizontal. Get a picture."

Singer took several shots as the narrow opening widened as if the mountain itself was hinged. When the rock face stopped its horizontal motion, the nose of a low-slung mining vehicle protruded from the mouth of the tunnel.

A pair of Asian men in green camouflage uniforms stepped around the vehicle and walked into the clearing. The men didn't appear menacing, but the AK-47 rifles in their hands told me we'd definitely found Skipper's hole in the mountain.

The two men scanned the area around the opening, aligning the barrels of their rifles with their lines of sight until a dozen small rocks rolled down the mountain above the opening, capturing the men's attention. They turned abruptly to bring their weapons to bear on the source of the tiny avalanche.

What they saw seemed to leave the men uncertain what to do next. In excited chatter, they discussed their options in what I could only assume was Mandarin. I don't know the Chinese word for *mountain lion*, but there was little doubt both men had blurted it out.

A flurry of full-auto rifle fire peppered the hillside around the massive cat until he sprinted up the slope and vanished into the trees.

Instantly, my earpiece came alive. "Charlie-One, Charlie-Two. Confirm gunfire. Say status."

Hunter's voice was laced with both concern for Singer and me, but also with envy that someone had started a gunfight without him. The absence of hearing protection over the ears of either soldier gave me the confidence to answer Hunter without fearing the next round of fire would be sent my way.

I whispered, "Gunfire confirmed, but we're not the targets."

There was no doubt in my mind that Hunter had a thousand questions, but he didn't send them.

The demeanor of the soldiers lightened, and they even laughed before remounting their vehicle and vanishing back into the mountain. I watched Singer's lips as he counted the seconds until the opening in the rock wall closed again.

We made our way back to the base camp to see our three teammates double-timing through the timber to the south with gear piled above their heads. They ran into the camp and hit their knees.

Hunter caught his breath. "Who was doing the shooting, and who was the target?"

I motioned toward the tunnel. "A pair of Chinese soldiers were the shooters. Apparently, we set off a monitoring device of some kind, and they came out to check it out. You're not going to believe this, but the opening is on a track system that opens horizontally, making room for a vehicle."

Hunter screwed up his face. "So, they just came out and started shooting randomly?"

"No. Thanks to a mountain lion about Mongo's size, the soldiers apparently believed he was their culprit. They didn't shoot to kill, but they scared him away and headed back inside. Singer and I watched the whole thing from about forty meters."

I called the ops center and passed the same information. I finished the briefing by saying, "I've got a plan to get us inside. I'll fill you in later tonight if I can gather what I need."

Disco smiled. "This is my favorite part. This is when Chase comes up with something insane and everybody goes along just to see if they can do it."

I held up a finger. "Nope, but you're close. This one isn't insane, but it is going to be a lot of fun. Does anybody know what mountain lions eat?"

Mongo said, "Anything they want."

"Exactly," I said. "Now we just have to find something they want."

I briefed my plan, and Singer said. "No problem. I'll find some bait, but I can't promise it'll be a mountain lion who takes a nibble."

I said, "I don't care what takes a bite as long as it's big enough to scare a pair of Chinese soldiers."

Singer pulled an M4 from his pack and threaded a suppressor onto the muzzle. "Come on, Disco. Let's go hunting."

Our pilot drew his pistol and screwed his suppressor in place, then slid the extended weapon back into its holster with the suppressor protruding out the bottom several inches.

* * *

Darkness fell on our camp thirty minutes after our hunting party departed, leaving Hunter, Mongo, and me scanning the mountainside through our night-vision goggles.

My plan wasn't perfect. In fact, it was potentially deadly for all of us, but playing on the natural instincts of the animals in our environment gave us a slight advantage over our prey. We knew what to look for, but they would be flying blind.

Ninety minutes after leaving camp, Singer and Disco appeared on the opposite side of the tunnel opening, dragging the carcass of a bighorn sheep behind them.

Singer took a knee about five hundred meters beyond the opening and keyed up. "One, this is Three. It's go time. I've got at least one bear and a big cat lurking behind us. Are you ready to move?"

"Affirmative. Make it a run and drop. We'll cover you from above. I've staged your rifle behind the log we used for cover this afternoon. Go to hot mics."

We flipped the switches, opening the channel so we could all hear each other without the need to press the talk switch.

I called the ops center. "Ops, Charlie-One. We're operational. It's showtime."

Disco and Singer picked up the pace as they dragged the sheep across the jagged terrain, each of them holding one of the animal's curled horns in their hand.

Mongo, Hunter, and I climbed the slope and positioned ourselves above the opening just as Disco and Singer dropped the animal twenty feet outside the mouth of the tunnel.

"If this works, it's going to be fun to watch," Singer said as he leapt behind the fallen tree and claimed his rifle. He passed the suppressed M4 to Disco and waited for the curtain to come up on the night's entertainment.

They didn't have to wait long. Within minutes, two black bears and an enormous mountain lion arrived on the scene after following the sheep's scent trail. The bears were clumsy and lumbering, but the big cat was terrifyingly silent with its approach. He seemed to sense the environment around him as he crept ever closer to the free meal waiting in front of the tunnel entrance.

Apparently, sensing there's no such thing as a free lunch, the cat remained behind the bears, waiting for the larger animals to make the mistake of falling into such an obvious trap. The bears continued, undaunted by wisdom and driven by hunger until they arrived on the scene. The larger of the two bears stepped on the sheep's carcass and bounced several times as if trying to wake a sleeping friend. Apparently satisfied the dinner bell had been rung, they dived into the sheep's flesh with forceful determination.

I watched the bears out of the corner of my eye, but the cat had my attention. The look on the animal's face shone as if disgusted by the thought of the bears eating his meal. He let out a roar that nearly stopped my heart. The bears looked up from their buffet and into the face of the charging mountain lion. They turned their backs on the sheep and growled back at the threatening cat. Perhaps either bear alone would fear the cat, but as a pair, their bravery and instinct to protect their meal kept them glued to the ground.

The same rumble Singer and I heard earlier in the day came again, and the opening began its widening motion. The sound of the grinding stone behind the bears left them momentarily paralyzed by indecision. The cat was their greatest threat, but the unknown movement behind them had the potential to be even more deadly. The mountain lion noticed the sliding stone as well but paused only long enough to disregard the commotion. The sheep was too tempting to ignore, so he continued his advance.

Light from within the tunnel pierced the darkness, and a pair of Chinese soldiers emerged with their weapons at the ready. The same instant the soldiers cleared the opening, the mountain lion took to the air in an enormous arcing dive toward the ravenous bears.

An explosion of wildlife ferocity filled the scene in front of the two soldiers as they brought their rifles tight against their shoulders and pointed their muzzles into the melee.

Before either could pull a trigger, a pair of suppressed rifle rounds tore through the soldiers' heads, sending their lifeless bodies crashing to the ground. Though quiet, the hiss and crack of the rifles caught the predators' attention, and they froze momentarily. Being the quicker of the three, the mountain lion clamped his jaws around the ankle of one of the fallen soldiers and galloped into the night, dragging the man's body behind him.

The two bears studied the scene and returned to their bighorn sheep smorgasbord.

I said, "Well, that's not exactly how I wanted this to play out, but part of it worked. Anyone know what to do with these bears?"

"I can put them down," Singer said.

I let our limited options roll around in my head for a few seconds. "We're going in, two by two. Hunter and I will go first. Then I want Mongo and Disco to follow behind. Singer, you cover us. If either bear makes a move for us, put him down with a double-tap. They're amped up, so one shot probably won't do it."

I followed Hunter down the slope toward the opening.

Singer said, "Stay low, and keep your backs to the bears. Maybe they won't see you as a threat in that posture. It'll be hard not to look at them, but trust me. I've got you covered."

Singer was right. Moving toward the opening in a crouch without looking over our shoulders at the ravenous black bears was almost impossible. I suddenly felt like Lot's wife leaving Sodom and Gomorrah, but looking back wouldn't turn me into a pillar of salt. It might turn me into bear food.

The plan worked long enough for Hunter and me to make the opening and take cover behind the dead soldiers' vehicle. "Okay, we're in. Mongo and Disco, you're next."

Disco left Singer's side and joined our giant as they made their way toward the tunnel. Mongo's size made him an imposing figure, even staying as low as possible. I held my rifle trained on the larger bear while Hunter kept his sights on the smaller one.

When Disco was less than ten feet from the opening, the larger bear raised his head and stood on his hind legs, towering over the smaller bear and growling a ferocious thundering sound that left Disco and Mongo with no choice other than turning to see the enormous animal filling the air only feet away. With one powerful lunge, the bear could be on top of my men before anything could be done.

I had no choice. The bear had to die. I prepped the trigger of my rifle with my sights aligned with his skull. Just before I pressed through the trigger break, sending a 5.56 millimeter round through the animal's brain at three thousand feet per second, the bear turned abruptly toward Singer, still covered behind the fallen tree. I followed the bear's line of sight and swung my weapon directly toward our sniper. I pressed the trigger five times in rapid succession and watched in horror as the two-hundred-pound mountain lion landed with a sickening thud on Singer's back.

Ignoring the danger, I sprang from my crouch and sprinted through the opening toward our sniper, who lay motionless beneath the massive cat. I'll never know what the bears did while I was running to Singer's aid, but when I reached the fallen tree, I was relieved to hear the Southern Baptist sniper moan, "Good shooting. Now get this thing off my back."

I planted a boot on the cat's shoulder and rolled its body off of Singer. When I turned back to where the bears should've been, I was amazed to see a second cat dragging what remained of the sheep's carcass toward the road a few hundred meters down the slope and the bears pawing at the body of the second soldier.

Being the least of the animals' concerns, Singer and I jogged into the opening of the tunnel and collapsed against the squatty vehicle.

Disco said, "Can somebody please figure out how to close that door?"

Chapter 31
The Tunnel of Love

"I think I like it staying open," I said. "The last thing we need is a bottleneck if we have to run out of here."

Disco said, "I hate to disagree with you, boss, but I think the last thing we need is for one of those animals to decide this tunnel would be a lovely place to drag a body and enjoy it at his leisure."

"You may have a point. Let's close the door."

Hunter found a remote inside the mining vehicle and held down the button until the stone rolled back into place.

Singer took a long breath. "This place just took on a New Testament–tomb vibe, and I don't like it."

I took a knee, pulled the magazine from my rifle, and reloaded the five rounds I'd spent killing Singer's feline friend. "Ops Center, we're inside, and we're going to place your repeaters every hundred meters or so. We'll do a quick radio check every time we place a new one."

Skipper said, "I can't wait to hear what just happened out there."

"That was the easy part," I said. "The real animals are somewhere inside this mountain."

We advanced through the tunnel in two teams. Hunter and I moved along the left wall while Mongo, Singer, and Disco clung to the right side. The small radio repeaters were about the size of a man's shoe, and we placed one after every one hundred strides. Every radio check grew weaker, but we weren't completely cut off from the outside world yet.

Hunter whispered, "There's a fork in the tunnel up ahead."

"Follow the vehicle tracks. Wherever they came from is where I want to be."

We moved past the fork and placed another repeater just as the sound of echoing voices penetrated the darkness. They were speaking Chinese, I assumed, but they didn't sound agitated.

I whispered, "Mongo, are you getting any of that?"

"It's Mandarin. I only know a little Cantonese. I think it's just casual conversation, though."

"Me, too. Keep moving."

As we moved deeper into the mountain and slowly made a ninety-degree turn to the left, the pitch black of the tunnel gradually gave way to fluorescent light.

Singer pulled rear guard, spending most of his time looking backward in the direction we'd come while the rest of us focused on our objective ahead.

The sniper said, "Contact rear."

We were in an impossible position to defend and remain covert. If an element of guards approached from the rear, a gunfight was inevitable, and we were all out of Discovery Channel tricks.

"How many?" I asked.

"At least four."

"Disco, you're on point. Everyone else is rear guard. Blades only, if possible."

The instant the order left my mouth, I longed to have Anya's stealth and lethality back on the team. She would be able to move silently through the darkness, slitting throats until she was the only creature still breathing, but none of us had that skill set. We could fight and win with our knives, but doing it without raising an alarm was Anya's playground.

I watched our giant pull a Ka-Bar fighting knife with his right hand and a karambit curved blade with a finger hole in his left. He moved in the shadows, emulating the wild cat from outside the opening. His massive body disappeared into an indention in the tunnel wall.

The rest of us moved as silently as possible away from the light so we wouldn't be backlit and impossible to miss. The ninety-degree turn did the trick, leaving us with a solid black background.

I lost track of Mongo as we moved through the darkness. Our night-vision NODs brightened the environment only slightly since no natural light found its way into the tunnel.

Four or five silhouettes materialized in the darkness, and at least three of them held rifles. They were moving in a casual column, obviously not expecting an ambush.

An infrared beam fired from the hand of one of the approaching figures, and though invisible to the naked eye, the beam burned like the sun through our NODs. I squinted to filter the light and pressed myself against the wall.

An inquisitive Chinese voice said, "*Shuí zài nà'er?*"

I held my breath, hoping the figures would continue walking, allowing us the opportunity to get behind them. But they were frozen in place.

As if he were a phantom spirit feeding on the darkness, Mongo stepped silently behind the most distant of the oncoming figures, and with both fighting knives, sliced so violently with a crossing stroke that the figure melted like butter. Before the rest of the figures could react, Mongo buried a blade in the necks of two more men, sending them to the deck just like his first victim. The man with the IR light spun, casting a spotlight on the largest human he'd ever seen. Before he could bring his weapon to bear, Mongo lunged forward and down, then drew both blades upward beneath the man's arms. As the blades buried themselves into the man's flesh, he dropped his light and rifle simultaneously.

Obviously sensing more than seeing the final guard, Mongo leveled both blades in front of his body as if they were Samurai swords and spun with the force of a massive uncoiling spring. The upper blade opened the man's throat to the cool, dark air of the tunnel while the second spilled the contents of his abdomen.

Allowing his momentum to bleed off, Mongo stopped his spin in a crouched position and scanned the environment for any additional threat. He sheathed the knives and lifted the IR light from the ground. "This might come in handy later."

Hunter, Singer, and I stood in wide-eyed wonder at what we just witnessed.

"Uh, Mongo, when did you develop that little set of skills?"

Although I couldn't see his face, his tone said he was smiling. "Anya may have never loved me, but at least she taught me to handle a knife or two."

"Who needs love when you can cut out any heart you want?" Hunter asked.

I gave my partner a gentle shove. "Knock it off. Keep moving."

We turned and continued our trek toward the light source beyond the bend in the tunnel. The voices had ceased, so we continued until we came to an area where the tunnel spread out, leading to an enormous room I'd seen before.

Five three-story buildings stood on columns of enormous springs arranged identically to those inside Cheyenne Mountain in Colorado Springs. My mouth went dry, and my heart sank. I couldn't believe my eyes. By the looks on the faces of my team, they were feeling the same.

I whispered, "Retreat."

Without a word, we retraced our steps back into the darkness and relative safety of the tunnel beyond the turn.

Mongo said, "Follow me. I found an alcove."

We let him lead us through the darkness to an opening in the tunnel that led to the left. We stepped inside and took a knee.

"Did everyone see what I saw?" Heads nodded, and I said, "Ops Center, Charlie-One." I waited for a reply, but none came. I repeated my call, and still, no answer came. "Okay, here's the new plan. We have to get close enough to the entrance to get a call off to the ops center. This is bigger than we imagined. We can't take it down without some help."

Hunter said, "Chase, we can't hang out here in this tunnel doing the hokey pokey all night. We killed two guards, and they're somewhere out there turning into cougar crap. Ginsu Goliath over there turned five more guys into shoestrings in the dark. They're going to catch on, and they're going to lock this place down."

"Are you saying we should retreat and run home to Mommy?"

"No, I'm not saying that at all. I'm saying you've got to make a call here. Obviously, this thing is a whole lot bigger than just some satellite listening weather station or whatever, but what's going to happen if we leave and tell the Pentagon? Is the Air Force going to fly up here and bomb Canada because we said the Chinese built themselves a NORAD at someplace called Sasquatch River Crossing?"

I leaned in. "Listen to me. I'm in way over my head here. Hell, we're *all* in way over everybody's head here. I don't know what to do, and we have a chain of command. I'm making the call to pull back before we have to kill a hundred Chinese computer geeks and probably get killed ourselves. The Board has to know, and we have to tell them. It's how it works. We all know that."

Mongo said, "This is like the time Daddy slapped Momma at the Golden Corral. We don't like it when you two argue."

"We're not arguing," I said. "Hunter was just getting my mind right, and he's correct. We've got a lot of decisions to make, but the first one is to send what we know up the chain. Now, form up on me. I've got point, and Singer is rear guard. We're moving to comms range."

The team fell into position, and I led them toward the opening. We had to dance around five dead bodies and one enormous pool of blood, but comms were restored in three hundred meters.

The team formed a perimeter, and I took a knee. "Ops Center, Charlie-One. Sitrep."

Al Brown's voice filled my ear. "Send it."

"Put Clark on," I demanded.

"He's out of the ops center," he said.

"I don't care if he's on the moon. Put him on the line, now!"

"Stand by."

Seconds felt like lifetimes until Clark's winded voice came through my earpiece. "I'm here, Charlie-One. What've you got?"

"Who's in the room with you?"

"Just Brown, but Skipper's on her way up."

"Kick him out, and let me know the second Skipper closes the door."

Clark didn't argue, and seconds later, he said, "Okay, it's just Skipper and me. What's going on out there?"

"The tunnel is a thousand meters long with one fork at four hundred meters in. I don't know where the fork goes, we followed the vehicle tracks, and they took us to a carbon copy of Cheyenne Mountain."

He almost yelled, "What?"

"They've got their own NORAD up here, Clark, right down to the springs under the buildings. There's no blast doors, but everything in the main cavity is identical to what we saw in Colorado."

"Give me a minute," he said.

I could almost see him sitting in that swivel chair and tapping his temple.

When he came back on the line, he spoke barely above a whisper. "Do you think it's a setup? Is that why you had me send Brown out of the room?"

"I don't want to believe that, but we can't rule it out. I need you to bounce him down the stairs if you have to. We've got to know if he knows what's going on up here."

"I can do that, but we have to send it up the chain."

"I know," I said. "Get the Board on the line, and I'll brief what I know."

"Stand by."

After a long series of tones, a familiar voice said, "Gardner here. Send the intel."

I briefed him and waited for a response. Heavy footsteps rang in my earpiece. There was no question in my mind that Clark was on his way to interrogate Brown. I listened closely for the sound of skulls bouncing off sheetrock, but I never heard a thing.

Finally, Gardner said, "How much C-Four do you have?"

"Enough to close the tunnel or take out maybe two buildings, but not both."

He said, "Wait one," and the line went silent for a moment. When he came back on, Gardner asked, "Chase, can you get back inside the tunnel if we airdropped enough C-Four to level that mountain?"

My eyes explored my team. Everyone was nodding.

"Gardner, there are at least two hundred innocent people inside the bunker. If we bury it under a billion tons of falling rock—"

He cut in. "No, Chase. There are at least two hundred Chinese communist technicians operating possibly the most advanced missile command center on the planet, and they're doing it in the last

258 · CAP DANIELS

place on Earth we'd ever drop a nuclear payload. You're not deal-
ing with civilians up there. You stepped in a nest of vipers with
fangs long enough to turn our country inside out and make it
glow in the dark for a thousand years."

I chewed on his words and swallowed hard. "I'll have the coordinates for the DZ in two hours."

Gardner said, "No, Chase, two EA-6B Prowlers just launched
off one of our carriers off the coast of Seattle. They'll be overhead
in less than an hour. They'll put six hundred pounds of C-Four
and accessories right down your gullet. You just have to show
them where you are."

I grabbed Singer's arm. "Did you see anything resembling a
drop zone when you were out hunting for sheep?"

"There's a clearing on top of the ridge about eight hundred
meters up the slope."

"Show me the way."

We fell in behind Singer and headed for the mouth of the
tunnel.

As we sprinted, I said, "We'll be in position in thirty minutes.
Tell me when the Prowlers are close enough to see the IR strobe."

We hit the slope at a run, but our pace slowed as the terrain
steepened.

Hunter fell in beside me. "Hey, this airdrops-on-target
thing . . . That's exactly what I did in the Air Force. Just give me a
radio and a frequency."

My breath was coming hard as we continued up the slope.
"Hey, Gardner. We've got a combat controller. Give us a frequency."

"Will miracles never cease? They're Prowler Six-One and Six-
Two on three-seven-seven point four."

We made the ridgeline, and Singer was right. It was the perfect DZ. The opening was fifty or sixty meters wide and at least two hundred meters long, running the ridgeline north and south.

Hunter stood in silence in the center of the opening and stared into the heavens. A fingernail-shaped sliver of moon shone on the southern horizon.

Hunter turned to Singer. "Who knows more about wind than a sniper?"

Singer said, "Only the birds."

"Give it to me, Dead-Eye."

Singer pulled his compass from a pocket and spun in a slow circle, ten feet from Hunter. "It's three thirty at twelve to fifteen."

"Twelve to fifteen?" Hunter asked. "Is that the best you can do?"

"All right, hotshot. I feel fourteen knots on my face, but I've killed a sheep, dragged it half a mile, been attacked by a dead mountain lion, and roamed around in the dark inside a mountain for three hours. My face may be out of calibration by a knot or two."

Hunter chuckled. "Twelve to fifteen it is. Now, get off my drop zone and get that IR beacon flashing at the south end."

"Whatever you say, Air Force."

Hunter sprinted to the north end of the clearing and watched the western sky like a hawk. I don't know where he got his call sign, but when Hunter keyed up, he left no question who was in command of the DZ.

"Prowler Six-One flight, Hellfire Six-Niner, mission."

I could hear the pilot's transmissions through the open-channel comms Hunter had failed to disengage.

"Hellfire six-niner, Prowler Six-One flight. Flight of two Prowlers three zero miles southwest, inbound, overhead in five mikes."

"Roger, Prowler. IR strobe marks the southern boundary. DZ is two hundred meters bearing three-five-zero. Wind is from three-three-zero at one-four, over."

"Strobe in sight, Hellfire. Stand by."

The flight of two Navy electronic warfare platforms never designed to drop care packages of C4 into the Canadian Rockies roared overhead.

"Bombs away!"

Every eye turned skyward as the infrared strobes on the nose of each pod flashed as they descended beneath a cargo chute and landed like falling leaves in the dead center of the makeshift drop zone.

Hunter said, "Good show, Prowler. Many thanks."

"I wish we could stick around for the fireworks, Hellfire, but we've got an aircraft carrier to find. Prowler Six-One flight, out."

Chapter 32
Dragons Can Fly

By the time the pods containing our fireworks floated to the ground beneath their parachutes, all five of us were waiting like kids on Christmas morning.

The cigar-shaped pods fell within a hundred feet of each other, so we split into two teams to manage them. Since Mongo almost equaled the strength of two men, he and Singer took control of the pod closer to the slope we'd climbed to our makeshift drop zone. They rolled the pod like a barrel to the edge of the slope and waited for my team to join them.

The five of us stood at the edge of the ridge, looking down the steep slope to the tunnel entrance.

Disco was the first to speak. "This looks impossible."

The rest of my team chuckled, and Mongo threw an arm around our chief pilot. "Disco, we've done so much for so long with so little that we're now qualified to do anything with nothing. The difficult we knock out immediately. The impossible takes us just a bit longer. Grab a pair of parachute lines, and prepare for the ride of your life."

Each of us took a pair of parachute lines in each hand and eased the first pod over the precipice. As the five-hundred-pound pod picked up speed, we hit the ground butt-first, keeping our feet well in front of us for the ride to the bottom. The limited resistance the five of us provided kept the pod from accelerating out of control. As the vertical slope transitioned closer to the horizontal, we dug our heels into the earth, stopping the pod less than a hundred feet from the tunnel entrance.

Repeating the same procedure put our two pods of plastic explosive right where we needed them. Hunter sprinted to the tunnel and returned moments later with the low-slung mining vehicle. By the time he arrived with the hauler, we had the pods open and a rough inventory completed.

As we loaded the vehicle with the green bags of explosive, Disco handled each satchel as if it were a newborn baby.

Hunter yanked a satchel from his hands and swung it wildly over his head, sending it crashing down onto the stack. "See, Disco, you can't hurt this stuff. It's as stable as a rock. It won't go off until we force it to. Just throw it on the cart."

Mongo lifted at least ten of the satchels in his massive arms and laid them on the vehicle. "Man, I'm glad they sent the M-one-eight-three satchels instead of just the M-one-one-two blocks. This would've taken all night."

Disco abandoned his delicate handling and joined the rest of us, who were moving as quickly as possible. "When this is all over, somebody needs to explain this M-one-one-whatever thing to me."

"Keep working," I said. "It's simple. M-one-one-two is a pound and a quarter block wrapped in plastic with a glue strip on the back. These M-one-eight-five satchels are sixteen of those blocks already packaged for detonation. All we have to do is place the satchel charges, wire the detonators, set the timers, and run."

Disco paused to catch his breath. "You make it sound like a walk in the park, but where are we going to run?"

That question stopped my team in their tracks.

"Disco's got a point," Hunter said. "When we cook this thing off, it's going to get a lot of attention."

I'd forgotten we were still on open-channel comms, but Skipper's voice in my earpiece reminded me. "I'm already working that problem. You boys just keep doing what you're doing. I'll have an exfil plan by the time you're ready to run."

"I should've known," I said. "Thanks, Skipper. We're running out of darkness, so we'll need a plan that'll work in the daylight."

"Speaking of daylight," she said, "I've been working on a rough layout of the bunker, and I think I know where that first fork in the tunnel goes."

"Let's hear it," I said.

"If they built their bunker on the concept of the Cheyenne Mountain complex, it can only be one of two things. It's either liquids storage such as fuel and water, or it's the generator complex. Based on the position of the ventilation ports in the mountainside, I think it's the generators."

"Skipper, if you were here, I'd kiss you right on the forehead. You're a genius."

"Duh. Everybody knows I'm a genius."

"Yes, they do, but I need one more lucky guess from you if you've got one left in your bag of tricks. Find me another exit from that bunker."

"I'm way ahead of you. There's another section of mountain that looks a lot like the spot you're on now. It's due east across the ridge. I think that was probably the original entrance, but it was a little too exposed, so they moved the main entrance to where you are now."

"Great work, Skipper. Keep working on getting us a ride out of here."

"I'm on it."

The vehicle was loaded with all the C4 it could carry, so I pulled two satchels from the stack and tossed them to Disco. "Do you remember where our base camp and our container are?"

He pointed to the south. "Sure, I know where they are."

I set two timers for 90 minutes and wired them to the satchel charges. "I want you to build a pile of gear with one of these satchels right in the middle of it. Then I want you to place the second charge inside our container. We can't leave any evidence that could be traced back to us. You got that?"

"Yeah, I got it, but where do I go afterwards?"

"Start the timer by pressing these two buttons simultaneously, then head for the ridgeline where we left the IR beacon. We'll rendezvous there when we're finished inside."

"And you're going to do all that in ninety minutes?" he asked.

"No, I figure it'll take you an hour to get all that done, so that gives us a little extra cushion of time."

He slung the charges over his shoulder and headed for the base camp without another word.

Singer laid a hand on my shoulder and shut off his open-channel comms. "That's big of you, Chase, sending Disco on a milk-run. We're going to get caught in there, aren't we?"

I nodded and flipped my switch. "I don't see any way around it. Let's go to work, guys."

The vehicle carried the load of my team and a quarter ton of explosives without complaint, but it was slow. We made it to the first fork in the tunnel without contact with any hostiles, but the knot in my stomach told me that luxury was almost over.

Hunter managed the vehicle as if he'd been operating it for years, but we had no choice but to abandon it temporarily to examine Skipper's hunch. Like most of her guesses, she nailed that one. The fork led to an excavated room with half a dozen generators, air purifiers, and various other machines I couldn't identify. Unfortunately, though, that's not all the space contained.

Singer whispered, "I've got four on the left and two on the right. What's your count?"

Hunter whispered, "Same."

I gave the order. "Head shots only. We need those uniforms."

The decision to kill the equipment operators left a bad taste in my mouth, but I justified the action, knowing a head shot would be far more enjoyable than entrapment in a collapsed bunker under a billion tons of mountain.

Singer sent three suppressed rounds to the left side of the opening while Hunter downed the fourth target on that side. Mongo and I took out the two targets to the right. We waited, expecting to witness panic from anyone else who may have been working behind a machine, but nothing moved in the space.

I said, "It's time for the Mongo show. You're the breacher, so tell us what to do."

He ripped open one of the satchel charges and tossed it toward Hunter. "Cut this apart and wire six of the M-one-one-two blocks in a daisy chain."

We did as he instructed, leaving C4 residue on our fingers that smelled like motor oil. One by one, Mongo placed the single charges on the underside of each of the pieces of machinery in the room while the rest of us pulled the green coveralls from the fallen guards.

Back at the entrance to the space, we donned the uniforms and then stared at Mongo.

Our beloved giant stood with a Chinese uniform hanging from his hand. "I think I'll wear my own party dress for the ball, thank you."

We backed from the space and returned to our borrowed vehicle.

Mongo said, "We've got two minutes until the lights go out on Broadway."

Retreating to the relative safety of the main tunnel, we turned through the ninety-degree bend just as Mongo's handiwork paid off. The explosion sent a shockwave through the tunnel that left us more than confident we had enough C4 to bring down the mountain.

Instantly, the lights in the buildings and open spaces of the bunker failed, but a few slowly returned to a modest glow that reminded me of Earl's lighting in the box. A few lights in the ceiling of the massive opening began to return to service as the battery backup systems fed them emergency power. Singer made short work of the external lights with the suppressed M4, but there was nothing we could do about the interior lighting.

Hugging the wall as closely as possible, Hunter maneuvered the vehicle around the back sides of the buildings while a few guards scurried about in a combination of panic and confusion. Mongo and I ran alongside the cart while Singer dealt with each guard who stepped in our path. As we ran, we hurled satchel charges beneath the buildings. We were moving too quickly to count, but each of the five buildings got at least seven charges. Even if the guards discovered some of the charges, they'd never be able to disarm them all in time.

At the opposite end of the room, we discovered a scene that left me sickened by the decision I would have to make. Three tunnels led from the space. The center tunnel was slightly smaller than the two outside openings, but vehicle tracks led into each of them. Drawing a mental picture of the layout we'd seen, coupled with Skipper's intel on the only other exit from the mountain, I ordered, "Blow the left and center tunnels. We're taking the right one."

No one hesitated. Mongo tossed me a pair of satchels wired with one-minute timers. He sprinted into the left tunnel, and I ran a hundred strides down the center opening. I spun like a hammer thrower and tossed my satchels as far into the tunnel as possible.

Mongo and I leapt onto the vehicle simultaneously as Hunter pressed the machine as hard as it would go, giving us a snail's pace of maybe ten miles per hour.

I counted the remaining charges and made a judgment call. "It's time to burn a bridge!"

Mongo and I stood on the flatbed of the cart and wrapped the straps of the remaining satchels to the ends of the bolts protruding from the ceiling of the tunnel.

"Abandon ship!" I ordered, and Hunter locked the brakes.

The four of us leapt from the cart and sprinted down the tunnel. Bullets from unsuppressed AK-47s ricocheted off the rock walls, and the hiss and crack of Singer's suppressed M4 answered every volley.

As I ran, I checked over my shoulder with every fifth or sixth stride. Hunter had joined the fight, returning fire in a haphazard barrage of full-auto bursts.

Mongo said, "I hope you were right, Chase. Otherwise, this is going to end badly."

Before I could answer, the sound of lead tearing through muscle filled my ears.

Nothing hurts. I'm still running. It's not me. Who is it?

I turned left to see Singer grabbing his left upper arm, his rifle dangling uselessly on its sling.

"Singer! Can you continue?"

His breath came hard. "Not for long! It's a big hole."

"Dig in and fight!"

Yanking my tourniquet from my belt, I followed Singer to the deck. He drew his pistol with his right hand and sent a volley of nine-millimeter fire back down the tunnel. I wrapped his upper arm, turned the tensioning handle, and set the Velcro strap. He was right. The wound was massive.

We were right in the middle of the worst gunfight I'd ever witnessed, and we had only two riflemen, a one-handed sniper with a pistol, and me playing medic.

Singer yelled, "Magazine!" as he thumbed the release on his Glock, dropping the empty mag to the deck. He held up the pistol with the empty magazine well pointed directly at me.

I shoved the roll of gauze into my mouth and yanked a magazine from my belt. In one swift motion, I jammed the mag into Singer's pistol, and he was back in the fight.

I spit out the gauze and ripped open a packet of blood-clotting powder. I poured the powder into Singer's wound and filled the gaping hole with gauze. I wrapped the biceps in tape with more layers than I could count and then slightly loosened the tourniquet. I had to save the arm, if possible, and leaving the tourniquet in place meant amputation was in my sniper's future.

Finally, I was free to join the fight. Every incoming round sounded like a thousand bullets as it collided with the walls of the tunnel, sending shards of limestone in every direction. Our position in the tunnel was impossible to defend. There was no cover other than the jagged edges of rock protruding from the walls. We were in the open, hiding behind nothing more than a wall of bullets. The only advantage we had was the slight bend in the tunnel that gave us the ability to see every aggressor who dared poke his head around the corner.

Singer, our wounded sniper, lay at the far left of the tunnel with me a foot to his right. Mongo was lying prone three feet away, and Hunter was standing with his rifle pressed to his left shoulder, picking off every pair of eyes he could see as they came around the bend.

I didn't like anything about our position until my partner yelled, "Hey, catcher! I'll bet you can't pick off that runner stealing second."

I looked up to see a baseball-sized grenade floating through the air between Hunter and me. I jumped to my feet, caught the grenade in my right hand, and simultaneously pulled the pin with my left. I'd gunned down more runners sliding into second base than any catcher in the history of University of Georgia baseball. If anybody on Earth knew how to make that throw, it was me.

I launched the grenade with my arm that had once been a deadly cannon on the baseball field, but that day, I prayed my arm still had the snap it wielded when I wore the number 21 on my back.

The world moved in slow motion as I watched the weapon soar through the darkness of the tunnel. The grenade hit the rock floor and bounced like a rubber ball, colliding with the wall, then turning hard right and disappearing behind the bend. The explosion was going to be loud and concussive, but I had no way to know just how loud and painful it would be.

I'll never know which explosion happened first, but in the same millisecond, the grenade and at least one of the satchel charges hanging from the bolts in the ceiling cooked off together, sending a massive shockwave through the tunnel that we hadn't expected. The horrific explosion rendered every member of my team instantly deaf and shell-shocked. Explosion after explosion cooked off farther down the tunnel as we pawed at our ears and scrambled to our feet.

Giving the order to run would've been wasted-and-unnecessary effort. No one would hear me, and no one needed to be told to get out of the mountain.

We were met with a ninety-degree turn a few strides into our sprint, but that's not all we met. A squad of soldiers bearing rifles and headlamps blocked the tunnel ahead. Apparently, they hadn't expected to see four men running for their lives from the opposite direction, so we had the momentary advantage of surprise. We raised our weapons and mowed down the squad in seconds before any of them could get off a single shot. Leaping across the bodies, we continued our full-throttle exit.

The presence of the incoming security force reaffirmed my decision to take the right-hand tunnel. Those men had come from somewhere, and I prayed it was through the only other exterior door to the bunker. A sliver of dim light cut through an opening ahead, and we breathed a sigh of relief.

The slit was barely larger than Mongo's shoulders, but the speed we carried would've made the big man look like the Kool-Aid man bursting through the wall if it hadn't been wide enough for his girth. We flipped up our NODs as the brightening eastern sky came into view.

We started up the mountainside as fast as our feet, lungs, and adrenaline would carry us. Two hundred meters up the slope, the beautiful sound of a huge helicopter thudded through the trees, but the sound was punctuated by the sight of our sniper collapsing and rolling back down the slope.

I looked up, hoping to see the chopper, but the western sky above the ridge was still black. Mongo watched Singer hit the ground, and he sprang into action. In fewer than ten strides, the giant had caught the rolling sniper and thrown him over his shoulder. At our now slower pace, we continued to climb the slope, but even Mongo's strength wasn't enough to overcome Singer's added weight.

Our sprint became a jog, and then finally a winded, exhausted crawl. Fifty meters below the ridgeline, a single explosion echoed through the mountains, and I smiled through my exhaustion.

"That had to be one of Disco's," I yelled, but I doubt if anyone heard me.

As we continued, a figure appeared ahead, clumsily descending the slope. As the figure grew closer, it morphed into Disco, and our team was whole again—if we could only keep Singer alive long enough to find a surgeon.

Without protest, Mongo dumped Singer onto Disco's shoulder, and we continued up the mountainside. The final few meters of the climb felt like miles as a second explosion in the distance filled the air.

"That would be our gear," Disco yelled. "The first one was the worst pillow fight in history."

We reached the edge of the clearing, and the most beautiful sight I'd ever seen came to a hover a hundred feet away. A U.S. Navy MH-53 Sea Dragon touched down with its massive rotors blowing debris in every direction. Six helmet-clad crewmen jumped from the doorway of one of the largest helicopters on Earth and ran directly toward us. Six more figures poured from the chopper and set up a perimeter with rifles at the ready.

How we made those last few steps to the safety of the Sea Dragon is something I'll never know. Maybe the men in helmets carried us, or maybe the hand of God scooped us up and tossed us aboard. Regardless of how it happened, I'll never forget how it felt to watch the beautiful peaks and valleys of the Canadian Rockies glide away beneath us as the fire, smoke, and gas from six hundred pounds of C4 devoured the mountain from deep within its belly.

Epilogue

We landed on the deck of the USS *Ronald Reagan* a hundred miles west of Vancouver Island in the North Pacific. Singer was stable with a pair of IVs in his right arm and his left thumb pressed inside a miniature New Testament. Hunter lay in the webbed seat along the portside bulkhead, and Mongo rested in the oversized nest he'd built in the middle of the cargo space.

I pulled the small Bible from Singer's grip and read the page bearing the stains of our sniper's blood and grit. With a lump in my throat, I read 2 Corinthians, 10:4.

The weapons we fight with are not the weapons of the world. On the contrary, they have divine power to demolish strongholds.

I don't know if we were doing God's work in the summer of 2004, but I knew, without a doubt, the world was a little safer than it had been before we rode into those mountains inside Earl's creation and dealt the Chinese a blow they would never admit receiving. Diplomatic relations with Canada may have taken a hit that day, but those are the problems of necktie-wearing people with clean fingernails. Men like my team preferred life in the down-and-dirty world of doing the things we could never talk about in most circles. I'm sure we owned a necktie or two among us, but we were a little short on clean fingernails.

I doubt it was the first military aircraft to touch down at the Livermore Airport, but I'd put money on it being the first C-2 Greyhound carrying a team of civilian covert operatives launched from the deck of the *Ronald Reagan* to do so. We thanked the Navy flight crew and stepped inside the general aviation terminal to finalize our bill for leaving our Citation on the ramp while we were off playing adventure tourists.

As the young lady behind the desk slid the credit card receipt toward me for my signature, Hunter stepped from the hallway to the pilot's lounge. "Hey, Chase. You've got to check this out."

I signed the receipt and joined my partner in the small lounge. I followed his pointing figure to the television, where a talking head was rambling on about a bizarre mining accident in western Alberta, at which hundreds of miners were trapped and feared killed in the horrific explosion.

I shrugged. "Everybody knows that type of mining is dangerous business."

Abandoning the lounge, we climbed aboard our Citation with its leather seats, air-conditioning, and well-stocked bar for the cross-country flight—this time with the wind at our backs—to rejoin the people we love and the treasured peace of home.

The welcome-home party featured another of Maebelle's feasts and prolonged explanations why we had to destroy Earl's magic box. After lunch, Hunter and Tina sat at the end of the dock with their feet dangling into the North River. Singer discovered he could still play the organ at his beloved church, even with his left arm bound. Disco chose to spend a few days fly-fishing in the Tennessee mountains. And Mongo practiced ballet with Tatiana as Irina giggled every time he fell.

Penny and I sat on the porch swing on the back gallery at Bonaventure, watching the pelicans dive on bait in the edge of the marsh.

She squeezed my hand. "The prescreening for my movie is next weekend, and you promised you'd go."

Before I could answer, Skipper stepped through the door on the gallery and handed me a telephone. "It's some ambassador from somewhere."

Politics were the last thing on my mind, but I pressed the phone to my ear. "Hello, this is Chase."

"Chase, it's John Woodford, the U.S. ambassador to The Bahamas. Do you remember me?"

"Yes, sir. Of course I remember. Thank you again for getting me out of that little situation on the island."

He cleared his throat. "Don't mention it. That's not why I'm calling. I'm sure you've seen the news about your missing Supreme Court justice."

"No, I've not seen any news in a couple of days. I've been out of the country."

"So I hear," he said. "The diplomatic channels are burning up with supposition on some sort of mining accident in Canada."

"I wouldn't know anything about that, Mr. Ambassador."

"Of course you wouldn't, but I'm calling about something even more threatening than communists in Alberta."

He suddenly had my full attention. "Go on."

"You see, Chase, I've just gotten off the phone with our mutual friend, Mr. Gardner, and he gave me tasking authority for you and your team."

I cleared my throat. "Sir, Mr. Gardner doesn't have tasking authority or the authority to delegate such authority. We are an at-will team of operators, as I'm sure you know."

"Not this time, you're not. This time, you're under orders to save the very foundation on which our country was founded."

A chill claimed my spine and reverberated through my soul. "What do you need?"

"It's not me, Chase. It's your country that needs you. The missing Supreme Court justice isn't just missing. He's been kidnapped, and he's only the first of many victims to come if someone doesn't get to his captors in time. And Chase . . . that someone is you."

Author's Note

As always, I wish to express my deepest gratitude for including my work on your reading list. I'm honored to be your personal story-teller. With the creation of each new novel, I fall more deeply in love with the craft of writing, and I treasure the moments I'm for-tunate to spend at the keyboard putting those fascinating voices in my head on paper. As long as you'll keep reading, I'll keep writing. So, without any further delay, here are my thoughts on the novel you've just finished.

First, it's important for me to make it clear that I have no ani-mosity or negative emotions of any kind against the great country of Canada, her citizens, or partnership with our government in matters of national security. During my research for this novel, I found absolutely no evidence that Canadian officials would ever become involved in the fictional situations depicted in this work of fiction. Further, there is no evidence that the communist Chinese government has ever or would ever build a military facility on Canadian soil for any sinister purpose. Likewise, I hold no ani-mosity toward the people of China; however, I have strong dis-trust of the Chinese government and enjoy using that government as the bad guy in many of my stories.

As you already know, I take great pride in using real locations, facilities, and technology in my novels. However, in this book, I took enormous leaps with my literary license and created a network of satellites that likely do not exist. If they do exist, mine was merely a lucky guess. I'm confident the satellites I named, if they exist, do not bear the fictional names I applied to them. I included the satellite network in this story simply because I love the phrase *geosynchronous orbit.*

Concerning Cheyenne Mountain in the Colorado Rockies . . . Of course, the facility exists and is one of the great feats of engineering and constructions in the previous century. I have never seen the facility, nor do I suspect I'll ever be invited for a tour. Handing that sort of information over to an espionage novelist is like giving the jester the key to the kingdom. I conducted extensive research through publicly available sources to paint a relatively accurate picture of the underground, top-secret facility. I have no way to verify the validity or accuracy of the research I performed, so it is best if we consider my descriptions of the bunker to be purely fictional, with a thread of accuracy woven into the web of make believe. Ultimately, I had a lot of fun reading thousands of words on the facility, its construction, and function, and I hope you had at least as much fun reading as I had while researching.

Now, let's talk about the U.S. naval aircraft flown from the deck of the USS *Ronald Reagan* in the North Pacific. The EA-6B Prowler existed and flew for decades of noble service. The last Prowler was retired in 1999, but according to the flight crews I spoke with about the airplane, they'd love to have the old girl back in the inventory. The Prowler was a derivative of the A-6 Intruder famous for countless daring raids during the Vietnam War. If you'd like to see the airplane in action, there's an excellent old movie entitled *Flight of the Intruder* starring Willem Dafoe that you'll likely find interesting.

The helicopter that winged Chase and his team to safety after their mission was the MH-53E Sea Dragon. It is the U.S. Navy's primary aerial mine countermeasures aircraft, but it is capable of far more than AMCM missions. It is inconceivable that such aircraft would take part in a clandestine operation in Canadian airspace, but it was fun inviting them to the party.

Now, it's time for something a little more lighthearted. Cooking with Maebelle is one of my favorite parts of creating this series. She comes up with some of the most unforgettable dishes and never leaves the team hungry. I got to have a little fun with one of my mother's favorite jokes when describing her hummingbird cake. She loves to warn diners at her table that the crunchy parts inside the cake are likely the beaks that are so difficult to pick out of the cake. I love when I can work in little tidbits of real life into these stories, and that scene was one of my favorites in this novel.

I suppose I should mention the legal system in The Bahamas since I had such great sport with the law enforcement professionals on Eleuthera. I know zero . . . zilch . . . nada about their legal system, so please don't have your attorney send me hate mail about police procedure on the islands. The first portion of this novel was written entirely for the purpose of setting up book sixteen in the series, "The Smuggler's Chase." I needed to introduce some characters and lay the groundwork for the team's next mission. Sir Edwin Castlebury and the firm of Castlebury Chambers do not, as far as I know, exist anywhere in The Bahamas. Sir Edwin's character was a study in absurdity for the sake of comedy and entertainment. The scenario I described involving the attorneys and police officers is neither likely nor plausible, and is purely the creation of my imagination.

Finally, I wish to ask a tremendous favor of you. If you enjoyed this or any other of my books, please take the time to leave an honest review on Amazon or Audible in the case of the audiobook. Reviews are critically important for writers, and they serve to both encourage us and give us a window into the minds of our wonderful readers. If you didn't enjoy this story, please pretend James Patterson or Stephen King wrote this piece of garbage and take it out on one of them. They can take it, but I'm delicate and easily wounded.

Thank you again for allowing me and my cast of oddball characters into your life for the fifteenth time. I'm flattered beyond words to have been given the beautiful gift of writing just for you. There's plenty still to come. I plan to write at least thirty novels in The Chase Fulton Novels series and at least fourteen starring Anya Burinkova, everyone's favorite Russian assassin (well, everyone but Penny's), in The Avenging Angel Series. Until next time, watch out for those hummingbird beaks, and I wish you fair winds and following seas.

—Cap

Editor's Note

It was April of 2018 when I wrapped up an edit and realized I had an immediate gap in my schedule. I thought, "Hey, I'll take a few weeks off and maybe line up a trip to somewhere beachy." That sand between my toes was not meant to be. The following day, a new writer reached out to me about editing a story he wasn't sure would be a series or a standalone novel. After a fantastic phone call and a scan of his manuscript, I abandoned all thoughts of a fruity drink inside a tiki hut because I immediately knew this guy was writing best-selling material—that something amazing was already written in the stars for him.

And while I knew something great was going to happen for him based on this original manuscript (maybe you've heard of *The Opening Chase*), the funny thing is, we tore that sucker to shreds, cutting out dozens of passages and rewriting even more. He hated me, and I'm pretty sure I made him cry behind closed doors, but at the end of that literary annihilation, that first novel became his initial and worthy work of art, indicating the brilliance that is Cap Daniels's writing.

Every draft he's sent me since has only proven to me his vehement desire to learn and improve upon his writing, immediately turning those "weaknesses" (of course, that is far too strong of a word) around and creating something even greater than he did the day before. I worry that someday soon he'll produce a draft that lands on my desk and has no need for the scary red pen he pretends to fear so much.

I've enjoyed a front-row seat to an incredible journey that has followed one author's path to the achievement of his dreams. It's beyond inspiring, and because I'm deeply aware of the hard work that goes on behind the scenes, it gives me absolute joy to witness the ringing of the bell after climbing what can often be a greasy, slippery rope to success.

It has been such a privilege to work with Cap and play at least some role in helping to share his incredibly creative, funny, and immersive stories all over the world. He writes with pure genius and spirit and makes my "job" feel like a playground. Not only that, but I love witnessing his constant interaction with his readers. It's absolute proof of his humility and appreciation for you all. Oh, and Cap loves this stuff! After concocting some strange witch's brew, channeling his crazy characters, and getting their best-selling stories down on paper, I have to believe that interacting with his readers is his second-favorite part of the job.

There are clients in my life who are so talented, entertaining, driven, and who write such exciting stories that they never let me forget just why I got into and never want to leave this business. He is one of them. And Cap, as you've said to me, "I never want to do this job without you."

Cheers to a lifetime of doing what you were no doubt put on Earth to do.

Sarah Flores
Proud Editor
Write Down the Line, L.L.C.

About the Author

Cap Daniels

Cap Daniels is a former sailing charter captain, scuba and sailing instructor, pilot, Air Force combat veteran, and civil servant of the U.S. Department of Defense. Raised far from the ocean in rural East Tennessee, his early infatuation with salt water was sparked by the fascinating, and sometimes true, sea stories told by his father, a retired Navy Chief Petty Officer. Those stories of adventure on the high seas sent Cap in search of adventure of his own, which eventually landed him on Florida's Gulf Coast where he spends as much time as possible on, in, and under the waters of the Emerald Coast.

With a headful of larger-than-life characters and their thrilling exploits, Cap pours his love of adventure and passion for the ocean onto the pages of the Chase Fulton Novels and the Avenging Angel - Seven Deadly Sins series.

Visit www.CapDaniels.com to join the mailing list to receive newsletter and release updates.

Connect with Cap Daniels:

Facebook: www.Facebook.com/WriterCapDaniels
Instagram: https://www.instagram.com/authorcapdaniels/
BookBub: https://www.bookbub.com/profile/cap-daniels

Books in This Series

Books in
The Avenging Angel – Seven Deadly Sins Series

Other Books by Cap Daniels